Out
of the
Garden   Colin MacInnes
A Novel

Hart-Davis, MacGibbon
London

Granada Publishing Limited
First published in Great Britain 1974 by Hart-Davis, MacGibbon Ltd
Frogmore, St Albans, Hertfordshire AL2 2NF and
3 Upper James Street, London W1R 4BP

ISBN 0 246 10782 0

Printed in Great Britain by
Northumberland Press Ltd,
Gateshead

For Peter Williams

WILTSHIRE LIBRARY
& MUSEUM SERVICE

Headquarters : Bythesea Road, Trowbridge.

Items should be returned to the library from which they
were borrowed on or before the date stamped above,
unless a renewal has been granted.   LM6.108.1

Sewing the Seed

'You won't know it's heaven till you leave it.'

'The army, sir? It's been a rough and ready paradise, I'd say.'

'Not "sir" any longer, sergeant: you're going back into the brisk civilian world.'

'Then no "sergeant", captain, if you please.'

'Or "captain" either: I'll be following you home and out within the month. So let's both get used to mistering each other. Your health, Mr Adams.'

'Yours, Mr Rattler. Though I wish these bloody wogs would let us have some booze.'

'The world has austere faiths, Mr Adams. Here, until dawn, we have the Muslim sabbath. Tomorrow is the turn of ancient Israel. England will greet you the next day with its grim offering of Christian gloom. However, I have a hip-flask: allow me to top up your non-alcoholic beverage.'

A foolish conglomeration of lavish stars. On and off, electric at dawn and dusk. Excessive festoons of fire, and so promiscuous: so wantonly theatrical!

The RAF type appeared, articulated delays through buck teeth and moustachios, and departed, sweating briskly.

'An extraordinary organization, the air force, Mr Adams. For consider: emerging from obscurity in World War One, it captured the imagination of mankind. Today, after a brief half century of existence, we see it relegated once again, through the development of more potent and accurate missiles, to its original role of aerial cavalry and artillery. The armies of the world, as well as its navies, have fought battles which "altered history". As other than auxiliaries, have air forces fought any such?'

'The Battle of Britain? The Japs in the Pacific?'

'Oh well, yes, there were those ... Here comes Flying Officer Icarus again. No wings, you'll notice, on this sky-blue articled clerk. Though perhaps that's better than roasting noble savages from the safety of thirty thousand feet. Yes, my dear fellow?'

'Ewing tu er further r'gr'tt'ble de-lay, we're off-ring light snecks in apprupriate messes, soh.'

'Officers' baked beans for officers, and other ranks' for others, dear old chap?'

'In apprupriate messes, soh.'

'The Royal Air Force, Wing Commander, can take its baked beans, cans and all, and stuff them up its appropriate arse. All we of the army ask of you—just once, my God, oh just but once—is to get those Imperial Airways crates off mother earth at something approximating to the advertised time.'

'Gud ev'n'ng, soh.'

'You shouldn't take the mickey, Mr Rattler. When you fly out yourself, that admin manipulator could fuck you up.'

'I'll tell you something, ex-sergeant Adams. No one—but no one—fucks up Captain, ex-acting Lt Colonel, Rattler, when his grim little mind's made up. Mark that, and remember it! For you and I, as is agreed, are going to meet again in the civilian world, and work together, as we have done so successfully against the Queen's enemies, both of opposing troops, and among our own. Driver!'

'Sir?'

'Did you, as I instructed, pack a hamper into the truck with the sergeant's baggage?'

''Course, sir.'

'Fetch it for me, then. Mr Adams, this was supposed to be a surprise for your bird's-eye view of Arabia Deserta.

8

However, we'd better broach it now. God! Aircraft! The army's not the same since the decline of troopships.'

'There speaks the officer, reclining on his first-class bunk, the respectful lascar serving him gin-slings. You were ever *on* a troopship, Mr Rattler?'

'Of course.'

'How often did you visit the troop decks in the hold?'

'As infrequently as possible.'

'There you are! The fine old tradition that the officers look after their men first. We never saw one of you down below, and we'd have slung you in the drink if ever we had.'

'Mutinous words: you speak as if with a grievance.'

'In twenty-two years of service, troopships were the only experience I found humiliating. Action's nothing to it: it's a picnic.'

'And the officers abandoned you.'

'They always do, whenever there's a crisis. Look what happens in a prisoner-of-war camp: they just don't want to know you any longer.'

'Have I not, Mr Adams, with these two hands, equipped with weaponry of course, protected your homely person on several critical occasions?'

'As I have yours: but that's battle, the great equalizer. As soon as the guns stop firing, officers head it for their clubs, and send other ranks to the high-grade doss-house.'

'You're still a soldier for forty-eight hours, you know: I think I'll fix you a court-martial.'

'Try it: I could spill so much dirt about you, the judge-advocate would flip his wig.'

'He would never believe you: you have the wrong kind of accent.'

'And what is more, if it comes to a subversive attitude towards the army, or any authority for that matter, you're ten times as bolshie as I am.'

'True; but I have the gift of appearing not to be. In addition to which, if acting Lt Colonel Rattler blots his copy-book, they hush it up; if Sergeant Adams does, they have him away, but quick.'

'Right! But all that's in the past, or nearly so. You can spare more of that gin?'

'The flask's a parting gift. Keep some for your arrival, if you can, at an icy airfield in mid winter where you'll find everything shut tight as an Arab maiden's pussy.'

'Horrible! I've hated this heat, but in two days' time, my civvy bollocks will be frozen off.'

'Your dear wife will have to warm them for you. You think that she'll still love you?'

'Not that I fancy myself all that much, but she will.'

'Why?'

'You know, Mr Rattler, if you said that sort of thing in the sergeants' mess, they'd take a poke at you.'

'Go ahead, if you feel like it, for I would not press charges; though I doubt not Flying Officer Thing would be pleased to do so. Well—why will she still love you?'

'Listen, listen, you fucking conceited aristocratic shit. Listen and learn, because you're one of the few honest men I've met within the service—I mean who's frank about yourself, and the whole system.'

'Flattering: say on.'

'You imagine you're a soldier, Mr Rattler—a regular soldier. What does this mean? You joined the army for kicks, a good regiment and all that, because you'd nothing better to do, and now you're sick of it, you're cutting out. As an officer, you weren't bad at all, cynical but effective —adequate, anyway. But no one ever believed you loved and respected the service as a real soldier does, and has to.'

'All too true, but I can't see what that's got to do with Mrs Evie Adams.'

'What it has to do is this. I joined the army as a boy

soldier at fourteen, out of a bad family, as it's called, and the army became my family. Six years later, I met Evie, two years younger than me, and from what, in my world, is called a good family. They were against us marrying, and so was the army, because I was too young; but when I got her pregnant or, as a matter of fact, she did, they both surrendered, and I was married to her at twenty, she eighteen. We had two sons right off, now fifteen and a year younger, and quite a handful. So far, so ordinary, you may say. But mark this. No one who's not been through it can imagine what the life of a junior soldier's wife is like: with children, with paltry allowances; with him overseas half the time and no married quarters. And don't think she's not had offers to desert me—she's had dozens: some I know of, some I never will. A man who doesn't know that kind of life doesn't know the army, and has no right to make cheap cracks and think a half-empty gin bottle and a chicken bone is going to put things straight again.'

Fingers rattled on the wobbly plastic table, and the gin flask tottered. 'Soldier, recall the Crater! I saved your skin at grave risk to my estimable own.'

'You did your duty.'

'Above, beyond, and you damn well know it.'

'That gives you the right to insult my wife?'

'Insult! My God, oh God! Who's been insulting whom throughout your eloquent soliloquy? Shit, rotten officer, who ran three times back under Muslim fire, and couldn't recommend himself for a medal because his gallant sergeant got stuck where he was.'

'You're going to hold that over me all my life?'

'No, you are, unless you admit we can all be cowards and stop resenting that the only man in the world who knows about it doesn't give a fuck! I hate brave men, anyway: I mean the perpetually brave. Cowardice is human, and *no* man is brave, in my book, until he's explored the deepest recesses of his own terror.'

'You've been a coward too, Captain?'

'If only you knew! Dear man, dear ex-sergeant, dear soldier Adams! I'm a bullshitting poltroon, believe me, but I can cover up like nobody's business.'

'Well now, look, Mr Rattler, there's no need to start weeping about it.'

'It's the gin: don't think this mini-flask is my first today. And as for marital woes, and love, and all that caper—why! Your hard life is an idyll compared with mine.'

'It is? And what about that chick whose scented letters so excite my post corporal? Don't tell me she's your daughter...'

'She is, Adams, and she's my wife, my mother, and my mistress, all rolled into one intolerable eighteen-year-old form.'

'That smells of incest.'

'Now who's being insulting about his fellow soldier's intimate affairs? However: you shall judge of all this when you meet Aspen.'

'Aspen like the tree?'

'Or Cleopatra's cherished serpent: at any rate, it's after that she named herself.'

'She did? Kids like to choose their own names, don't they? Take my own: they won't call themselves what we named them, and the eldest has become Kik, and the younger, Mas.'

'Do I sniff Kenya in all this?'

'No wonder you made Intelligence officer—yes. You remember our first meeting in Mombassa?'

'Lieutenant Rattler, pink from an English depôt, greeted by bronzed and confident Corporal Adams. Oh yes: who could forget that embarrassing encounter?'

'Ever since Kenya days, my eldest has rooted for the

12

Kikuyu, and my younger, for the Masai.'

'The tiller of soil and the herdsman of wild cattle? But surely your loyal progeny should have rooted for their gallant dads.'

'Mas still does: he wants to join the army.'

'Prevent him.'

'I'll try to.'

'And Master Kikuyu?'

'He wants to get into security.'

'Good God! I thought the youth of England was rebellious!'

'Boys get crazy notions.'

'You certainly once did ... But that's all in the past, and it behoves us to consider our sombre futures. Do not forget our pledge: we rendezvous in London within thirty days. You have your plan, I have mine, and I think they could profitably coalesce.'

'These are old soldiers' dreams, Mr Rattler. I bet you: once out in civvy street, you'll forget me and go your way, and I'll have to go mine.'

'By no means—please have faith: I see a great future for us both: and a future in which neither can operate without the other.'

'Time will show. I'll also have to hear what Evie has to say.'

'And I, hearken to dearest Aspen. Oh—ho! Here comes Flying Officer Funk, his whiskers bristling officiously. I believe your antique aerothing is finally to become airborne. So farewell, Mr Adams, to this hospitable Eden of Aden; and hail to our next meeting in the down-swinging metropolis.'

'So long for now, Mr Rattler. We'll meet again if we do.'

Weary, monotonous dawn, a tentative shimmer. The untidy procession meandered into the grey oily whale. Flickering lights, and roars, and one more heave of defiance against old gravity. Ex-sergeant Adams declined to adjust his seat-belt, and soon-to-be-ex-Captain Rattler scowled at the RAF type, heaved his sleepy driver into the side seat, and raced down the singing tar, with one hand holding the flask he'd perhaps forgotten to press upon his past and future comrade.

January 3

'Tea, Dad?'

'No.'

'Drink?'

'What drink?'

'Beer or whisky.'

'Whisky! How come you can afford whisky? He send you some over duty free?'

'You want one?'

'Might as well.'

The location in Kilburn. The accommodation, two rooms, mini-kitchen, outside lavatory, and no bath. The back room the den of Kik and Mas, silent when they frequently slept out, din-ridden by rows and stereo when in. The front was the marital bedroom and, divan dowered by cascades of cushions, the family saloon.

'You're driving out to meet him, Evie?'

'Obviously.'

'In that car of yours? I don't see how you can afford it.'

'Nor do I.'

'You can borrow mine, if you like.'

'I will, if you come out to the airport with me.'

'No thank you.'

'Please yourself.'

'And how's he going to support you now? Not that he

has done properly for the past sixteen years.'

'I think I'll have a drink too, Dad.'

'Is that wise, if you're driving?'

'No, it's not wise. Nor was marrying Soldier wise. Nor was having our two children wise at all. But much to your annoyance, I've not regretted it.'

'I'm not annoyed: I'm just resigned to my own daughter's folly.'

'Let her be the judge of that; and Soldier; and our sons.'

'Layabouts, I'd call them.'

'You would, and you'd probably be right. But Kik and Mas exist, and that's enough for them and me. Another drink?'

'I might, but you'd best not.'

'You're damn right I'd best not; but if I don't, you'll drive me up the wall. Because, you see, the only thing that's left in life for you, Dad, is coming round here and having a good old nag at me.'

'I'm your father, aren't I?'

'That's why I let you come, and as far as I'm concerned you're always welcome, though I can't speak for the boys, or for Soldier when he gets home.'

'So you think your little lot's all I've got to live for!'

'Well—what else?'

'The Party: that's what.'

'The dear old Party doesn't give a bugger for you, Dad. You're a veteran member? You almost fought for the Brigade in Spain? You had your head cut open at Olympia in thirty-something? You've been a tough shop steward until they dropped you? Right every time! And where does all that leave you?'

'Loyal: steadfast: I've never wavered.'

'No, not once you haven't: the Pact, the Purges, every zig-zag of the Line, you've gulped down the damn lot of them. And that's why I respect you, and I'm not kidding:

15

you're as faithful to the Party as I've been to Soldier Adams. And it's an idea you've been faithful to, and me, a man.'

'I should have made that speech.'

'You're an obstinate old bastard, but I love you; all I wish is you could get on with Soldier—just put up with him, is all I ask.'

'Since he joined the British army, in 1949, he's been a counter-revolutionary in colonial wars. I can put up with his signing on as a boy, when he knew no better, but I can't put up with his continuing as a man, and turning you into a practically grass widow.'

'My choice: you coming to the airport?'

'Very well—provided I drive, and it's my car. You ready?'

'We'll give the boys ten minutes more—they said they'd come.'

'Knowing what loyal sons they are, I can tell you they've both forgotten.'

'They *are* loyal sons.'

'To what?'

'To me.'

'Their loyalty consists in truancy from the schools you managed to get them into, doing bugger-all around the house, and poncing on your allotment from HM Forces plus the meagre wages you earn from the non-union office cleaning firm that's been exploiting you.'

'They tell me stories.'

'I'll bet they do.'

'They like to natter with me.'

'Prior to tapping you.'

'They miss their father: that's why they depend so much on me.'

'They'll wish him back in the Crater, once he's been here a week.'

Dad was a steady driver: he hogged the crown of the road and kept well below the speed limit. Winter eve fell on the freezing highways. Father and daughter reached for the lurching bottle.

'Penny for your thoughts, Dad, if they're at all pleasant.'

'There's still time to get rid of him. You're only thirty-four, and it's not too late to wed again.'

*　　*　　*

Kik and Mas disputed who'd drive the scooter.

'You're under age, pimple.'

'You too; and I nicked the vehicle.'

'I look all of sixteen; and you didn't nick it, you borrowed it from your faggoty youth-leader.'

'Go ahead and drive, but you'll find I've removed the lead.'

'Come on, give, mother's boy.'

'It's not me who flogged her missing engagement ring.'

'She said she didn't mind so much when she found out.'

'How could she, when you slobbered all over her kleenexes?'

'Give, boy—the lead.'

'Like fuck I will.'

Kik unscrewed the petrol cap, pushed the scooter over, and headed off to ready for a hitch. Mas righted the bike, and roared close past his elder brother, who flung a rock. Mas slowed down and waited, looking back; his elder brother sloped after, slouched across the pillion, and Mas accelerated before he could be pulled off.

*　　*　　*

Over France, the airborne warriors adjusted to the thought

of home and beauty. Soldier's night companion was a gnarled royal engineer.

'You got a job fixed, sarge?'

'I'm thinking of going into business.'

'On your Tod? Ah—chancy: me, I'm teaming up with my uncle, in his garridge.'

'I'm thinking of cars too: a mini business in a small way.'

'Ah—dicey; and cut-throat competition. Me, after the army, I want a steady life.'

'Yes, whatever they say, the army doesn't make a man ambitious.'

'Despite the struggle for a stripe or two, I'd say that's true; nor greedy for money either, like the civvies.'

'And yet, merit does get recognized better than anywhere else.'

'But there are those who live chasing after medals...'

'Not many ... I think the worst habit the army gives you is to make you idle: chiefly because, three quarters of the time, there's just bugger-all to do.'

'Idle and crafty, as they say of an old soldier.'

'Well, that's what we are now: we must make sure we never die or, for that matter, fade away...'

January 4

The aircraft was delayed into the night. Kik and Mas smoked bush upon the airport roof: senior in gangland gear, junior in sloppy Afro, officials liking the look of neither. They had not made contact with Evie and their Grandad, consuming obscene coffees in the spectral lounge.

'The soldier's return has always been to the shit-house, girl. After each war, since Julius Caesar and beyond.

18

Young, strong and foolish, and they enlist to flags flying, bugles blaring. Time-expired, out they're thrown upon the scrap-heap.'

'As with most jobs, I'd say.'

'Not so: a hired killer's left without a skill.'

'Soldier's an MT sergeant: he can pick any car to pieces and put it together.'

'And can he, his marriage? But I've been into all that, and I'm buggering off. Give your husband this envelope, will you?'

'The car, Dad: how'll we get home?'

'Here's the keys: I'll make it on public transport.'

Two coffee-grounds later, the hot whale disgorged its Jonahs on the icy tarmac. Soldiers and wives and girls grabbed bodies openly: erotic whispers entered deafened ears.

'Soldier!'

'Fuck me! You've put on weight.'

'I will, I have: you missed me?'

'Wanked myself silly for you. Oh, my God, she's crying.'

On the edge of the throng, the heirs to England's glory scanned the scene.

'Mas, they revolt me: elderly orgies should be suppressed by law.'

'He looks nice, though, doesn't he: will you ever make so fine a figure of a man?'

'Not in that fucking bus conductor's gear. Watch out—they've spotted us.'

'Well—Kikuyu: how's the tribe?'

'Rebellious. This acne-ridden child is Mas.'

'Old Mas: the cattle?'

'Blood and milk daily, Dad. How was your flight?'

'And how did you lot get here, for Chrissake?'

'We borrowed a scooter, Mum. We thought you old

19

folk should bill and coo solo, out of consideration for your grey hairs.'

'They're bigger and cheekier, but they haven't changed.'

'We have—you'll see.'

'We'll cut out now, pop: you two will doubtless need a natter.'

The youth group departed as if they owned the airport, and despised it.

'What a family! Only your old Dad's missing.'

'He was here too, and left you this.'

'A summons for desertion? Let's see what the old sod's said. Christ, look at this! He's donating us a tenner!'

'And those papers?'

'Later, later. You got the car out there?'

They pulled off the speedway, over surviving country, to call upon 'the Councillor'.

'Ex-regimental sergeant-major mate of mine who's got himself a boozer. I *must* have some drinks, even before you.'

'He's really a Councillor?'

'Yeah, a political soldier—always has been.'

The Councillor's greeting was austere and unsurprised; booze, and hotted-up pie, were on the house.

'Now, Evie: who's going to tell who first?'

'I'm going to ask first: you been faithful? Whether or not, say "yes".'

'Largely because of lack of opportunity, I have. You, beautiful?'

'The boys are my only love; but I'm not sure I'm theirs, and they're certainly not each other's.'

'They're fifteen and fourteen, at which sort of age I was on my own. Therefore: any trouble from Kik, and he's out on his arse to fend for his sweet self; and I don't care a bugger what he does, or what becomes of him. Mas has a year to go—then likewise.'

'You can treat sons like that, even these days?'

'Boys, yes: it's the only way. They want to be independent? Let them be independent. If they come back, and want anything I've got, then they can have it. Otherwise they're on their own.'

'You haven't asked my opinion.'

'Have they? Will they? They'll only start taking an interest in your opinion when they see that they need you, and they've got to learn to ask.'

'I'm a bit soppy about them still. And they're both still at school, or supposed to be ...'

'Pack in being soppy. And how often *are* they at school? Let them learn a trade after hours, then: *any* trade— legitimate, hustling, whatever they fancy. But now I'm back, I'm not having three *men* inside the house.'

'You've not seen enough of them to care for them.'

'Evie, I care for *boys*: men I care for differently, and they've got to decide which they are.'

'But I want them to get some education.'

'There's only two things these days any young man needs to know: karate, and languages, if he wants to move around. The rest, if they want to, they'll pick up as they go along. England is full of over-educated nits. If that's what they want to be, let them be good little boys, behave themselves at home and study hard, and earn themselves a heap of scholarships: if that's it, I'll encourage them. If they want to be men at their age, I'm all for it, but they've got to do it all by their own sweet selves.'

'And if Mas still wants to be a soldier?'

'Then of course I'll help him; but I won't encourage him.'

'And Kik the security operative?'

'He's been seeing the wrong telly programmes. Where did he get that idea?'

The Councillor bore flagons. 'Take this lot home, lad: I'll put them on the slate.'

'Councillor, you haven't changed.'

'I'm soliciting your vote. We're closing in ten minutes, but you're welcome if you care to step upstairs.'

Bells rang, as they do.

'Soldier, I'm glad you're back.'

'Me too: let's look at your Dad's document':

Minicabs: formation of Company of.

1. The minicab business is a racket. It undercuts legitimate taxis, over-charges, under-services, and is non-unionised.

2. In a modern capitalist society, it is however one of the few businesses that can be started by brains alone. To embark on such an undertaking, the following basic desiderata are required:

(a) a telephone, intelligently manned by night and day. This can be anywhere: a mere bedroom may suffice.

(b) acquaintance with owners of vehicles who, during their partial or permanent off hours, can be telephoned to take on jobs supplied by the Company, on terms to be mutually arranged.

(c) a minimum number of vehicles (two at the very least) for use when no outside contact is available, and for securing the plum jobs.

(d) means of diffusing rapidly and widely the Company's telephone number, so that it becomes known to potential clients.

3. It is suggested that my daughter and son-in-law, if having nothing better in mind, should consider embarking on this enterprise. Its salient characteristic is that there's possibly something to be gained and little, if unsuccessful, to be lost thereby.

4. Though contrary to my principles, I am prepared, on a preliminary basis, to offer my own car and services, until and if the project gets off the ground, or otherwise.

'Well, well, well—your old Dad! What would the Party say?'

'Ask for a cut: you think there's anything in it?'

'Certainly: but first, I'll see what the Captain thinks about it.'

'Which Captain?'

'That's another story. We take up the Councillor's offer of the upstairs room?'

January 10

'Rattler, my heart!'

'Aspen, dearest, most indispensable of creatures! Kiss, kiss, I think, but not in the VIP lounge. You have a vehicle?'

'A Capri, will it do? And where to may I escort you?'

'I don't want the big city yet: a little inn beside the Thames would be a dream.'

'Boneheads, then.'

'A new name: how the Thames valley alters!'

'You haven't much, my sweet ... or have you?'

'In my utter devotion to you—never: we are as one. The Services have marked their scars on me, however: I left my child a fighter—yes; but now I come back to you entrained for battle.'

'Your child has been diligent: my takings, I'll bet, already exceed your own.'

'Oh, would that you were my child! But never mind, a guardian spirit's a comfortable relationship. So, earnings from your escort agencies, my dear: your letters were strangely vague as to their nature.'

'I escort, dear Rattler: selected Lonelyhearts—our agency are not procurers. Save in the sense that clients aspire to savour young ladies of gentle birth and breeding.'

'And ravishing appearances: how exquisite you've grown to be!'

Boneheads offered principally décor: the plates came as an afterthought, the wines to finance the mode. Chill mist cushioned the river beyond air-conditioned glass.

'Now, tell, Rattler: your "resignation" sounded to me suspect.'

'An officer's privilege, my dear. Even in the midst of warfare, generals bewitch politicos by threatening resignations that would ensure any common soldier a firing-squad at dawn.'

'You've had enough?'

'I learned things I wanted to: for instance, that soldiering is licensed killing, which is why many men embark upon it; but I, who have no objection whatever to slaying my fellow men, disliked the mechanized compulsion. However, I'll not be missed: officers, despite their science, are expendable. All revolutionary armies have discovered this: I cite France and Russia as prime instances. The outstanding commander of World War I was a Jewish intellectual wearing pince-nez. The Israeli army, now the most efficient in the world, made officers out of brave and intelligent citizens.'

'Dear England can't do that?'

'Oh, but need you ask! Our army was once run by bone-headed gentry from among whom geniuses occasionally emerged. Today, when what's left of the upper classes are abandoning the career of arms, instead of rapid promotion from the brilliant among the ranks, the army makes spurious gentlemen, who convince neither themselves nor their supposed inferiors.'

'So you've wasted the ten years since you adopted and abandoned me?'

'By no means, dear Aspen. The army being, like all armies, archaic, it teaches you as does nothing else—I bow here to the navy, which doubtless does the same—the historical forces that have created, and still impel, the social fabric of your native land. An army is an essence, a microcosm, of whatever social organisms survive, struggle, and seek eventually to prevail.'

'That leaves me with a question.'

'I shall try to answer it. The Korean war was the last in which the British army fought as did armies as we have hitherto understood them. Since then, it has engaged in what amounts to political warfare overseas. I needn't quote you a list of erstwhile colonial territories where this novel type of warfare has been pursued; but just point out that now, at last, the army is engaged in warfare on British soil.'

'And you didn't like this.'

'You are not yet with me, Aspen: think less of your beauty, and deploy your brain. Political warfare produces political soldiers; officers in particular, and even more so, at the critical ranks of Colonel and Brigadier. I could call a resounding roll among these ranks, in every continent, who've felt the compelling call to politics. In England, they are making themselves manifest somewhat surreptitiously, as yet; but will so openly increasingly, applauded by multitudes who will mistake them for strong men.'

'Am I dim, Rattler? If so, why leave now?'

'Because history teaches me that political officers mistake the shadow for the substance. And I, as you know, am by essence, if anything, a manipulator. I do not at all deny the potential power of these military philosophers: what I do, is their persistence and resilience under trial.'

25

'So what now, then? And how can I help you to your goal?'

'Chiefly by being, as you always so wonderfully have. Also, by aiding me in plans to make some absolutely necessary money.'

'I'm listening carefully to you now.'

'And closely, then. A second son is, as one from a seed as illustrious as yours knows all too well, a highly distinguished pauper. Three things only, he can count on: a name he may use as unscrupulously as he thinks fit; an education at the one institution in our country which was, is and, pray God, always will be, utterly indifferent to anything except instilling into the infant soul his own pre-eminence, and that, following somewhat after, of his ignoble fellows; and then, a web of contacts, both inherited and acquired, whose threads festoon even the most plebeian institutions of our land. Equipped with this three-pronged weapon, it's up to him to make his own lamentable way.'

'So many of them try marriage. It's old-fashioned, Rattler, but why don't you consider little Miss Loot?'

'Because I love only you; yet blood, calculation, and even some feeling for your heart, forbid a measure disastrous to yourself, and not to my own interests as I see them.'

'You speak as if you'd asked, and I'd said yes.'

'I know I do, and what your reply would be: linked to me though you are, you would say no. So let me offer you my devotion, and to you only, always. Incidentally, if *you* want to marry, I'll find you someone more than suitable in less than no time.'

'Rattler, you exceed yourself at moments. Dear little Aspen! She can't make that scene, if she wants to, on her own?'

'But of course: do let me hold your hand.'

'You can pour me some more of this whatever it's intended to be, instead. So now—money: what have you been dreaming up?'

'Ah!'

'Ah?'

'I am going to throw open, to a public as yet unaware of its existence, the ultimate in stately homes.'

'You are?'

'I am.'

'Excuse me, Rattler: but totting up rapidly, I think your family, though it possesses half a dozen mortgaged mansions, so fiddled its genes that none of these dwellings is anywhere near belonging to their most deserving son.'

'Does Great-Great-aunt Clarissa ring a bell?'

'Of the most distant: she's on mummy's side, is it, or daddy's?'

'Strictly speaking, neither: there are cross-polinated illegitimacies, in my family, so intricate that I'd need graph paper to explain them to you. But the gist of it all is that she adores me, and possesses a mid-Victorian ruin.'

'So not a historic ruin.'

'Mid-Victorian *is* now historic. This particular one, or what remains of it, including several acres of derelict parkland, was built by one of my forebears actually *às* a ruin; but since he ran out of cash, or inclination, possibly both, it remained unfinished, so that it's a ruined ruin.'

'To which you intend to invite the paying public.'

'Indeed, Aspen! Where's your imagination? Otranto Towers—the possibilities are infinite! Past the obligatory parking point, visitors will be conducted in creaking goat-carts through arbours of poisonously syrupy foliage towards a hideous pile which they will find infested with bats, reptiles, sepulchral electronic voices and, after additional charge for admission, they will proceed further into laudanum parlours, child brothels, and gambling hell-holes of the most permissively Victorian order. It will be irresistible, apart from being less than an hour's drive from central London.'

'And what if they faint from the excitement?'

'Pakistani doctors, flanked by Caribbean nurses, will be in professional attendance.'

'Rattler: how long have you been in Africa and the Mid East?'

'You know as well as I do; you've been inundated with informative air letters.'

'The sun didn't get at you at all?'

'Oh, my! That *pitying* look you give me even, and specially, when you're wrong! Hearken attentively, if you want to come in with me on this, which I damn well know you will. Clarissa's been trying to market that ruin to anyone, for but anything, and there's been no takers, because the soil's foul—it's sited on a marsh, adventurously selected by my ancestor. Capital will be needed: funk funds are available to me from petrified suckers in Belfast. Planning permissions: my homework in the desert for the past twelve months, and I know how to by-pass and short-circuit them for long enough to get things started. Design will be my baby, and publicity, from now, will be your own.'

'It all sounds too bad to be true.'

'I can see you, Aspen, gowned as a bewitching witch, entertaining favoured guests to a Borgia buffet at fifty guineas a chipped plate.'

'You can?'

'I can.'

'You don't sense paranoia in all this?'

'As in all unusual enterprises—yes.'

'I see. Who else is coming in on it?'

'As principals, no one as yet except for my gallant sergeant.'

'Mr Adams?'

'I see you *have* read my letters. Yes. Let me revert a moment to our military theme. Armies are run by sergeants: they have to be good because they simply can't cover up, as any private soldier can, let alone a general. Thus, though often bovine and pedantic, when it comes to the crunch, they know their stuff as does no other. Astoundingly, many are also honest however guileful, brave however unadventurous, and loyal however obstinately so. The army taught me to rely on them, and even to feel, of which I am a bit ashamed, that I can't quite do without them. So—enter Sergeant Adams.'

'You've known him long?'

'Since Kenya: which, anthropologists now tell us, is the habitat of original man, the surprising Eden of the human race.'

'And there's a Mrs Sergeant Adams?'

'Apparently. Also two junior males, all of whom will need some looking into. And that, yet again, is where you come in, my dear.'

'As what?'

'I intend to have you give them a once over, if you'll be so kind. I take it you'll agree to?'

The lights dimmed in a hint departure would be welcomed.

'What you've just described to me so vividly, my dearest, is spurious and three parts illegal. So you *don't* want me to look this honest, brave, loyal, and so on family over: you want me to help you con them into your own deep water.'

'Precisely: but what else can you do?'

'What else, Rattler? But, as you must know by now, only on my own pityingly unimaginative terms.'

'Shot of another Saturday. This is becoming slave labour.'

'Like shit it is: all you have to do is lie on your bed, which you do all day anyway, and make intelligent arrangements on the phone.'

'You should take the whole shift, junior: this mini caper isn't my bag at all.'

'I don't think it's Dad's either, but he's going to give it a fling. And when he asks you to take a shift, he pays you.'

'Pays me! I could hustle up twice as much on half the time.'

'What doing? Poncing? Flogging bush? Busting meters?'

'I could hit you, Miss Masai.'

'You could try, but those days are over. I don't know if you've noticed, but I'm catching up on you, muscle-wise. By the time I'm full-grown, you'll be a dwarf.'

'But I have the brains, baby; and all you have is your ladylike judo class.'

'Try me.'

'I will, in my own good time. Ah, there she blows. Car service. Yes, madam. To where did you say? Yes—indeed we can. It's a Daimler, madam, driven by a Hong Kong Chinese. Oh, no, completely reliable—and he's practically on your doorstep now. Not at all, *madame*—anything to oblige.'

'I don't think that's very intelligent.'

'Well, all the cars, such as they are, are out, so what am I supposed to do?'

'You could try our Cypriot Turk again.'

'Look, brother, here's the instrument. I can't wait to hear you get no answer, or a sorry I'm busy, from Cypriot

Abdul, Provisional Pat, Little Miss Lib, or any of Councillor Boozer's unreliable volunteers.'

'Dad may get in: you should have told the client you'd call her back.'

'Dad, if he's going to do this thing properly, should rent himself a radio call service.'

'He would, if he had the bread.'

'He's just not made for business, Mas: he should join the Corps of Commissionaires, and salute electric doors.'

'Or a security company, like clever Kik?'

'Don't *sneer* at my modest ambitions, boy. I tell you: I want a life of legalized crime, and that's where I'm going to find it. What else is there for the vital sector of English youth?'

'Grandad could get you into Smithfield: why do you turn that down? The money's startling.'

'For an apprentice? You see me toting bloody carcasses around? You think Grandpa's still got any influence there? It's not a Commie set-up, junior. Meat men are born conservatives: all food people are.'

'Well, you might help Dad without grumbling till you find something worthy of your ambitions.'

'Sarcasm does not befit your acne, Corporal cannon-fodder.'

'They're pimples, and you had twice as many.'

'They're disgusting: you should get yourself a fuck, and stop all that wanking.'

'Or the clap, like you did.'

'I hope you've kept *that* secret, in your cosy confabulations with our Mum, and your arsehole-sucking sessions with Sergeant Dad.'

'I said I would, if you got it fixed.'

'I didn't need you to tell me that. And what's more, here's another top secret for you: I'm cutting out.'

'Living rent-free here doesn't suit you?'

'Living with you doesn't, but that I can endure. No: it's the bed-rattling next door that's getting to be obscene.'

'You mean they're too old for it?'

'Not necessarily: just that they're so noisy about it all. Honest, if anyone recorded what I hear through that wall, they could flog the tape in a Soho sex-shop.'

'Well—there's an idea for you.'

'I've considered it, but it's too revolting, even for me. Ah—there she blows again. You want to take it, since I'm so incompetent?'

'Okay. Car service, madam, good morning. No, not just at present, I'm sorry to say, but I could call you back. Oh, you want Mr Adams personally? Well, now, if you'd hang on just a ...'

'Gimme that!'

'Fuck off!'

'Gimme!'

'No, it's all right, madam, it's a faulty connection. What I could—bugger you!'

'Oh, good *morning*, madam, this *is* Mr Adams, personally: I'm sorry you had that bit of bother with my assistant. No trouble at all—I'll come over myself immediately. Yes, I have noted the address—a very nice one, if I may say so. There's just one small thing, though, madam: as I take it, by your melodious voice, that you're a youthful lady, would you have any objection to a scooter? Yes, I said a scooter—our four-wheeled fleet's all out on the road, just at the moment. Oh, most comfortable, madam, and a young lady looks ravishing astride it: besides, we charge far less. You will? May I congratulate you on your enterprise? We'll be starting a new trend, and you'll find that on a scooter, the traffic problem solves itself, so to speak. I should wrap up, though, against the chill. At once, madam, I'll be right over—so good-bye for now. Give me that lead, Mas.'

32

'Like fuck, I will.'

'Oh, come *on*. I'm showing enterprise, aren't I? Aren't I doing what you *said*?'

'You're supposed to stay on duty for two hours. If Dad rings in and finds you've scarpered, he'll blow his top.'

'Oh no, he won't—he'll admire my initiative. So do be a sweet little brother just for once, now I've set this thing up.'

'Okay, then. Don't fiddle on the fare.'

'Mas—ai! You *are* a dainty giver! See you later.'

*   *   *

'Good morning again, madam. This is Mr Adams on your doorstep, with his scooter parked right outside, and not a traffic warden in sight.'

'Would you mind coming up before we leave?'

'Not at all, madam—I'd be delighted. Shall I sign off the loud-hailer and wait for you to buzz the lock of this forbidding door?'

'Exactly, Mr Adams. The lift's straight ahead, the floor's number four, and I'll be ready for you on your arrival.'

'*Au revoir*, then, *madame*. Ah! Open sesame.'

Elegant, impersonal, builder-architect's north-W1. No pot plants, though a faint smell of cement. The lift was small and slow, but carpeted in beige.

'Here I am, *madame*, entirely at your service.'

'Haven't you shrunk?'

'I *beg* your fucking pardon?'

'I expected someone in their middle thirties.'

'Oh! I see! Yes, yes! You were expecting Mr Adams *nior*. But since you didn't specify, I thought I'd do.'

'You being Mr Adams junior.'

'That's *it*. Senior junior, as it happens.'

'Kikuyu.'

33

'Now, how did you know that?'

'Come on in. Does your conscience allow you to have a drink?'

'If my passenger has no objection. My, oh my! This is a darling pad. So who told you my name?'

'Your father and I share a friend.'

'Ah! Light's dawning on me dimly. Could this be the Captain Rattler I've heard far too much about?'

'Right on.'

'So that makes you Lady Aspen Somebody.'

'Right again.'

'And you really *desire* this scooter, your ladyship?'

'Don't be cheeky. No: I wanted to speak to Mr Adams.'

'Oh, that can be arranged, I'm sure.'

'I don't doubt it. But since I'm lumbered with you, I might chat you up instead.'

'You won't mind my charging you waiting time?'

'Not particularly. Take your feet off that chair, and blow your nose before we begin.'

'My word—you *are* bossy, aren't you?'

'Only to louts. This drink's okay?'

'Look, I don't think I want it. In fact, I don't think I care to stay at all. So if you'll hand over eighty brand new p., I'll bugger off.'

'Please yourself. You can keep the change, of course.

'Someone's going to give you a smack in the kisser, one of these days.'

'It's been often tried. So long for now, Mr Adams, and ask your father to call me.'

'On second thoughts, I'll stick around a while, if that okay with you.'

'Perfectly. Just be your age, though, which is a lovely one, if you learn how to use it.'

'The insults we drivers take from customers, you wouldn't believe! Or perhaps you would. So, now the

What you want to know about the Adams family?'

'Whatever floats through your mind.'

'Ah! Well—a lot does. So let's script the material a bit. You know who Dad is, I take it?'

'Sort of, but you can fill me in.'

'So: let's try to be just—impartial, and all that. If ex-professional soldiers are your dish, then he's okay. Tough, practical, pig-headed—all that sort of thing. Handsome in his way, too, if you care for the type.'

'Go on...'

'Don't harass me, or you'll interrupt the flow. Considered as a father, all I feel I owe him is one of those countless million spermatozoa.'

'Well, that's something.'

'Oh—you bet! And then there's Mum. You know about the Commie background?'

'Vaguely.'

'Born into the Party, but grew a bit disenchanted, as the years rolled by. But she has the basic training. I mean she's one of the few women I've met I'd describe as *educated*—who's worked out some sort of a pattern. For instance: if you mention any topic to her under the sun, she doesn't just *gape* at you: she puts on her marxist considering cap, and has a bit of a think.'

'And you've picked up the habit?'

'Something's rubbed off, I guess ... But I wouldn't describe myself as an intellectual—just intelligent, and interested in oddities. I mean, things don't surprise me.'

'But your mother is an intellectual.'

'Well—yes. I know the word's a smelly one, and such people are usually horrible, but I really think she is: I mean, she can relate *themes*. And in a woman, I think that's unusual.'

'You think women are stupid.'

'No, no, no, you're quite wrong—I don't. But I think

they've been brainwashed into believing they're gorgeous idiots. Mum's never fallen for that crap at all; though what's curious is, she *is* rather gorgeous herself.'

'She is?'

'Oh yes, I do believe she is. You think I'm boasting, or something? Well no, I'm not: she's all of thirty-four, but I really rather fancy her myself. Ruled out, of course, on grounds of incest and all that, but I do find myself clocking her like I do a bird. And I've noticed my mates do, too, despite her age. I mean—she *appeals*. There's no question of it.'

'I think you've spoken very nicely of her. No, I'm not having you on, Kikuyu. I'd like a son to speak like that of me.'

'Now, don't embarrass me, or I'll slip my groove. And I assure you, I can be very critical and nasty if I want to.'

'Oh sure—you've shown me.'

'Yeah. Well now, that leaves little Mas, our darling baby. If I try to wrench myself away from the loathsome thought that we shared Mum's womb and were produced by Dad's whisky-sodden spunk, then I suppose he has his points. For instance, he's rather pretty: a bit too fucking pretty for my taste, in fact, though perhaps not for the faggot and old lady belts, if you see what I mean. He's not altogether stupid, either, though not, I'd say, as brainy as Mum or me. Also, he's affectionate, in a rather soppy sort of way, which I'm not at all: though I can be *kind*, at times, which I think is something different. Perhaps you wouldn't believe this, but about once a year I find myself being really *kind*: it's astounding!'

'Well, you strike me as a very nice family, taken all in all.'

'Yeah, yeah, aren't we just? Now, what about you? Come on! Take a little, give a little. Who *is* this Captain

Rattler, and are you really a ladyship, or is that a bit of front?'

'No, you'll find me in the reference books at the public library. As for Rattler—well now: where to begin? He wants to put your father in the way of a business enterprise he's starting.'

'Look, you are a cheat! You're just not telling me a damn thing!'

'Truly, Kikuyu, with Rattler, you'll have to find out for yourself: I don't think any description I could give would make much sense until you've met him.'

'Oh! Highly mysterious, and all that. Well, if he can hoist Dad out of the mess he's getting himself into just at present, he'll really be doing him a favour.'

'The minicab business isn't prospering?'

'I suppose it could do, given a year or so of slogging. But a thing like that's too rickety to get off the ground without the right resources. I mean, I ask you. As reliable drivers we have Dad and, if he's in the mood for it, old Grandpa. Also one or two ex-military types an army pal of Dad's has resuscitated, though I find their attitude so revolting that I'd rather walk ten miles in the rain than ride with either of them. On top of this trustworthy nucleus, we have attracted every expatriate freak in northwest London; and their vehicles, you just wouldn't believe. Do you know I've had to send a West German tycoon in a delivery van to London Airport?'

'How did he react to that?'

'He had no alternative, poor bugger, or he'd have missed his plane. But he phoned me from the airport to express his disgust and indignation. I had great pleasure telling him I hoped his aircraft would crash in scarifying flames. Which brings me to the customers we have to accept, some of whom are just too much. We've had both sexes of them trying to seduce drivers, wanting to hold hash parties in the rear seat, and of under- and total non-payers, I forbear to speak; particularly of the distinguished Aussie who actually contrived to nick our refugee Iraqui driver's entire vehicle, leaving him stranded and speechless in a lay-by on the M1.'

'My, oh my!'

'No: in my opinion, Dad should flog the goodwill for what he can get, and pack it in; though I suppose they'll still keep ringing us in the small hours till the crack of doom, unless we can get the number altered.'

'You're a pessimist, Kikuyu.'

'No, no, I'm not—you're absolutely wrong. I'm a highly enthusiastic guy about anything conceivable that's not half-arsed. Everyone sneers at me, and waxes sarcastic, but what *I* want to try, one of these fine days, is build up a first-rate security business.'

'You see a future in these axe-handles and transatlantic caps?'

'You bet I do. Violence is on the wax, and so is counter-violence. The thing's mushroomed since I was a kid, and it's only just getting up steam. A few years from now, there will be private armies whizzing all over England, and I want to lead one.'

'Not serve in a public army, like your brother.'

'Good God, no! I mean—just look at me.'

'Yes—I see what you mean. And you're not interested in a bit more education?'

'Oh, of course! But if you mean schools, and colleges, definitely not.'

'No use to you?'

'If I was scientifically minded, probably. As I'm not, they're a waste of time. I've already been saturated with enough middle class nonsense to last me a lifetime, and I don't want to hear those ignorant educated voices any more.'

'It was all nonsense?'

'Ninety per cent of it, and I'm not kidding. Certain facts they couldn't cheat about—I mean, the cube root of nine is three, and the Nile is longer than the Thames, and things of that sort. But their interpretations! It's pure indoctrination.'

'Why didn't you tell them?'

'I did—thousands of times. "Right sir," I'd say. "Wellington was a goodie, and Napoleon was a baddie, and the goodies triumphed, and that was lovely for everyone. But how do you know it was, since you weren't there, apart from your being, to my certain knowledge, an accredited conchie?"'

'He didn't care for that?'

'Didn't seem to get the point at all. I could give you a million instances of the uselessness of teachers. The only person I've learned anything from is Mum, and certain writers of certain non-bullshitting books.'

'She agrees with you about all this?'

'Not exactly. The passage of time has made her a bit defeatist. She realizes English education's shit, but she thinks that, if you know the corrective co-efficients, you can adapt it to give you something.'

'So the wide world will be your university. You like another drink?'

'Yeah. Thanks. I say, you're not forgetting that waiting time, are you? I mean, you're not expecting me to tell you all this for free?'

'Oh dear, no! Don't be so suspicious.'

'But so many clients try it. "Do come in and have a glass of water and a biscuit, and will they be okay instead of the correct fare?"'

'Have no fear: you will be generously, though reasonably, rewarded.'

39

'Well—we'll see. Listen, you don't fancy me at all, do you?'

'A bit, yes, but you must remember I earn thirty guineas a session as a superior escort girl, which makes me rather expensive, even in any hopeful preliminary attempt.'

'No kidding—you knock that much back? That's healthy bread.'

'And when I say "earn" it is earn, too, believe me.'

'They try to paw you, and so on? Make incredible promises the wicked fellows don't intend to keep?'

'That sort of thing: one learns to handle it.'

'I've always wished I could use the word "one" with real conviction. I've tried, but it actually makes me blush.'

'Have a go!'

'Right. What would one think if one suggested one needn't pay one the waiting time if one gave one a fucking great sexy kiss?'

'I don't think that sounds right.'

'You mean the phraseology, or the whole idea?'

'Both, really.'

'Oh come on! Look, I don't want to rape you—you probably know karate, all the chicks do these days, and anyway, it's not my style. But what about a sort of tongue-mingling embrace?'

'Tongues?'

'Yeah—these things.'

'Any minute, Kik, you're going to try to make a grab at me.'

'The thought was passing through my prick...'

'You won't mind a word of warning? It happens so often, I use this.'

The Lady Aspen sprayed her visitor with ether. He collapsed on the beige carpet while she opened a window to admit the whine of northerly W1. She watched him revive: he looked picturesque and undignified.

'Christ! What was that secret weapon?'

'So sorry, dear lad. But one's forced to use it in impending emergencies.'

'You crafty bitch! Still, I admit my intentions weren't honourable at all.'

'Quite okay: it's a sort of compliment, after all. Do finish your drink, or have a little lie down if you need it. The waiting time's still okay ...'

'Is it? Oh, dear! Foiled by chemical warfare—it's the first time it's happened to me.'

'You should carry a smog mask for any further encounters.'

'Or get in myself with the stuff first. Is it a local product?'

'No, Japanese.'

'They think of everything: I admire them enormously.'

'Me too: perhaps I'll take you there some day.'

'"Take" me? Aspen, believe me, if we ever do go, I'll take you.'

'Well spoken. You feel okay now?'

'Sort of. You mind if I phone base?'

'Do go ahead. If you get your Dad, will you make an appointment for me?'

'Sure, why not? Perhaps the generation gap will work in his favour, and he'll have better luck than me. I say, you *have* got a beautiful arse, you know, so you just can't blame me. Oh, hul—*lo*! That you, Dad? Kik. I know you know it is. Mission completed, and I'm returning with funds for the community chest. No, no, she had no objection whatever to the scooter, and as a matter of fact, I'm a guest at her pad this very moment, and as a further matter of fact, she knows you and wants a date. Name of Aspen, friend of your Captain Rattler. Yeah. You can? I'll tell her. Business brisk your end? Good show, as the soldiers say. Farewell. He invites you for booze at 6 p.m.'

'Lovely. And here's a fiver.'

'Oh, you *are* nice. Do you think it would be honest if I only declared two of them to the firm?'

'Not really, but I do think you've earned the bit extra.'

'Nicely put. So what happens now?'

'What happens is you take yourself off, and we meet again later if you're on the premises.'

'I think I will be. In fact, I think I'll cancel a dreadful date to have the joy of swinging open the front door for you. How do you feel about that?'

'Much honoured. Grateful, as well.'

'I'm glad you approve. Good-bye, Aspen.'

'Good-bye, Kikuyu.'

'I'm going to lay you one day, you know.'

'We'll see.'

*　　*　　*

'Dear Aspen?'

'Herself. Where are you?'

'In a freezing call-box with a superb vista of the estate. I've been planning plans with our ingenuous builder.'

'He's getting the idea?'

'His initial surprise has yielded to reckless enthusiasm: he's even making bright suggestions.'

'Any useful ones?'

'Oh yes—indeed. He proposes a waterlogged dungeon in the cellarage, with plastic corpses floating in the penumbra.'

'Brilliant fellow. Is that technically feasible?'

'Apparently: we have a spring, did you know?, whence rippling streams flow in four useful directions.'

'How pretty.'

'My dear, it *does* look pretty. I'd forgotten how exquisite bits of England can still be. And even—perhaps specially—in winter. As I stood this morning gazing at the old pile beneath that spectacular ash outside its crumbling façade, the light was positively paradisical. My heart almost missed a beat.'

'Poor ravished England! How I love her!'

'And what news your end? You've contacted my erstwhile subordinate?'

'It's to be this evening; but I've met his elder son.'

'Indeed? How did that happen?'

'A mix-up: too long for the telephone.'

'Nothing ever is—but still. And how did he impress you?'

'His demeanour suggested good looks, intelligence, and intricate neuroses in the family.'

'Splendid: we must seek to sublimate them appropriately.'

'I don't know about Sergeant Adams, Rattler, but I don't think Mrs Evie sounds a push-over.'

'You derived this impression from intercourse with her son?'

'From conversation, Rattler: yes.'

'I see. Then it's all the more important you should meet the pair of them before I do, to create the appropriate atmosphere of confidence, and arouse their legitimate ambitions for a more glamorous future. Stress also the advantages of our project to the entire family.'

'I'll do my best. You intend to remain modestly in the background for the moment?'

'Until I hear from you, I shall. Give Adams my comradely regards.'

'And Mrs Adams?'

'My respects would, I think, be best at this stage of our endeavours.'

*　　*　　*

'Evie?'

'Speaking. You'll be back by six to see this dame?'

'Of course: but I wonder why he's sending her to us first, and not contacting me direct like he suggested.'

'The thought struck me too, Soldier. Can I make a suggestion without your saying I'm interfering?'

'Of course, and I know what it is: you think you ought to give her a woman-to-woman once-over first; is that it?'

'Well, what about it?'

'I think yes. Suppose I'm unfortunately delayed and turn up at seven, instead of six?'

'It might be best. You know I'm a bit dubious about your Captain, Soldier.'

'Me too, as a matter of fact, but we must hear his proposition. So far this mini-lark is only about breaking even.'

'Right, then: I give her a drink, or a tea, and a chat. That it?'

'Yeah: I'll be interested in your opinion.'

'I think you should be. See you later, then. Masai!'

'Mum?'

'Come on in here. Do you mind a serious conversation?'

'Any time: what's on my old Mum's mind?'

'Cheeky bastard: it's the army. You really certain about following in Dad's footsteps?'

'Who's following—aren't they my own? I admit the influence, but I've thought it over good.'

'Okay, then. What's the army going to teach you?'

'Soldiering.'

'Mas, this is seventy-one: soldiering's just not enough. They *can't* teach you what you could learn as a civilian.'

'They have educational schemes, and trades.'

'I know, I know, and it's not like in Dad's young days: soldiers are specialists now, or some of them. In nineteen thirty-five, when your Dad was born, it was an escape

44

from the means test and the dole. All the same, there are better civilian escape routes now than the army for a working class lad who wants some skills and knowledge.'

'I know all about that, but you won't shake me, Mum.'

'What about trying to make it as an officer?'

'Why didn't Dad? He could have tried.'

'Your Dad's a different generation. The idea, when he joined, was that workers grabbed what they could from Them, but didn't try to *be* Them: you "stuck with the lads", as they used to say. Today, there are civilian sectors with a prosperous working class infiltrating executive positions, so if you must join the army, why not aim at that?'

'Coming from you, Mum, this is a surprise. Aren't officers the class enemy?'

'Well, join the enemy, learn their tricks, and stay true to your own people.'

'Grandad would burst a blood vessel, if he heard this.'

'Grandad's a fine man, but he's stuck in the nineteen thirties. You're not: think about it.'

'In the ranks, in time, I'll make sergeant-major: what do you bet me? As an officer, I'd be stuck till the age of forty at full lieutenant. You know it, and I do: our background's wrong.'

'Not in a technical corps, necessarily.'

'Sure, but I want the infantry: they're *soldiers*.'

'Think of it all the same: higher education's everything, these days. I can't teach you any more, schools certainly won't, but the army could, if you're prepared to overcome a prejudice against officers.'

'It's not against officers: I'm against their class. Put me in a promotion-by-merit army, and I'd aim at field rank with everything I've got. But the army's still class-ridden, and I'd rather aim at top NCO rank than be a tolerated token in the officers' mess.'

'I see you've thought a lot about this.'

'Yes, and chatted up dozens of regulars, too. All of them say the same.'

'Masai: you're sure it's not just prejudice in reverse?'

'I'm positive. No, it's common sense.'

'All right, then: aim at warrant officer, and you can always try to switch if you change your mind.'

'I might do; but I couldn't change back from subaltern to sergeant if I found I'd made that mistake too early.'

'Sure. That's the bell: you let her in?'

'Kik's stationed himself on the front steps: I think he fancies Lady Bountiful.'

'Oh, does he? But does she him? Kik fancies himself too much.'

'Well, I don't admire my brother, as you know, but I don't resent his aiming high, even if he falls flat on his arse trying.'

'He'd pick himself up again, I guess … Well, that's it: you'd better bugger off and let me handle her alone.'

Kikuyu presented the visitor with a flourish. 'Mother, meet Aspen, a prodigious person, the Milady of Marble Arch.'

'Good evening, Miss. Kik, you can make yourself scarce.'

'You'd not like me to stick around and serve the drinks? Do my polished footman performance?'

'Sod off, son, and don't listen at the keyhole.'

'You're not giving me much of a build-up, Mum. Till soon, Aspen. I'll be around when you've got acquainted with the old folks.'

'Kikuyu, you want a sharp belt on the arse? Hop it, and don't slam the door. Well, Miss Aspen—that's the boys.'

'Aspen. Ah, yes: the weaker sex, so they have to act frantically at times.'

'I wasn't brought up to believe men are weaker: Cypriot wine or tea?'

'Tea, please. No, but you believe they are: all women do.'

'Do I? Perhaps so. Is that why your Captain friend is working on my husband's feelings?'

'How can he, when in the long run he's himself so feeble? He's dynamic, though: he has ideas, and carries them energetically through. After all, you don't make acting-colonel in your thirties without something.'

'Name, school and accent, imposed on working class docility.'

'Mrs Evie, it's not quite as simple as *that*.'

'Evie will do. No? Captain Rattler would make colonel in a revolutionary army?'

'Oh, certainly! If he believed in anything, that is. On guts, brains, and orderly room politics, he'd make it.'

'You may be right. So what's he up to now he's de-mobbed?'

'He's going into business, and wants your husband as a partner.'

'What can Adams offer him? He's poor, and knows nothing about trade.'

'Rattler trusts him: and I think nobody else, except me.'

'Like a man trusts his dog.'

'You've got the right to say this before you know Rattler? Wait and see: he *believes* in Sergeant Adams. He feels he can't operate without him.'

'No? What about the money?'

'Rattler will give you both the details. It'll be good, though; but of course, depending on whether the enterprise succeeds.'

'It'll be up to Adams. Personally, I should tell you I'm against it.'

47

'Instinct or reason?'

'Both. No offence, but I don't trust your class. Also, I'd prefer Adams to make it on his own: at anything, almost, but on his own.'

'Rattler could do a lot for Kik and your other son.'

'Such as what, that we and they can't do?'

'Evie: do I have to tell you three quarters of everything is influence and money?'

'That leaves you your own quarter, doesn't it?'

'It leaves a man with one limb instead of four.'

'And what if he can't handle gifts and favours?'

'Then, yes, you're right, he should rely on his own one limb. But your sons are really so independent? Or so corruptible?'

'I'm not really sure. But I am that it's too early for them to dive into the cess-pool to see if they can swim.'

'Okay ... But you'll speak with Rattler? He could see that they got some useful knowledge: *everyone* needs that now.'

'If Adams really wants it, I'll have to agree. My habit is to go wherever he goes, come what may.'

'Not to steer him a bit, sometimes?'

'It's difficult at long-distance in the army; but perhaps it's about time I did so a bit more.'

'You weren't out there stationed with him in all those places?'

'Never. For junior ranks it was impossible; and when he got promotion, neither of us wanted it. He didn't like the thought of me looking over his shoulder when he held a gun, and I didn't care much for married quarters, and the sort of woman they encourage. Also, we thought the boys might get educated better here.'

'So they never were in Kenya, or those exotic, hateful bases.'

'Oh, no. "Kikuyu" and "Masai" were just football teams

48

to them. You might say they were long-distance supporters.'

'And you've had to rear them.'

'Yes: though I've tried not to let them become mother's
boys. Unfortunately, they both are quite a bit. You
mightn't think it of Kik, but in point of fact, he's been
harder for me to wean than Mas.'

'Is it okay if I say I liked him?'

'Most people do, funnily enough, despite his ridiculous
behaviour. They all seem to want to stroke his hair and
wash his socks for him. Did you do that?'

'Not exactly. It was suggested, but I mastered the inclination.'

'That's just as well.'

'Isn't it. You know, Mrs Adams...'

'Is it to be Evie, or isn't it?'

'Evie, I'll push off now: I think Rattler had better meet
you first, with Sergeant Adams. Otherwise, it might look
like I'm swinging my allure at him.'

'That was the idea, wasn't it?'

'No, not exactly. But I think that on business, Rattler
should speak to you and him direct.'

'So do I. Righty-oh. You want Kik to drive you back?'

'I couldn't meet Mas instead, could I?'

'You're not proposing to turn my little boys on, are
you?'

'Oh dear, no. I really am a well adjusted girl, you know.'

'I hope so. Well, if he has no objection. Mas!'

'Yes, Mum?'

'No—not you, Kik. Where's Masai?'

'On duty on the blower.'

'I see. Since he did your stint, you can take a turn at
his. Send him in, will you?'

'But Mum! Aspen's *my* mate, not his.'

'Ask her.'

'Oh, come on—*As*pen!'

'Kik, Kik: be nice, and do what you're asked to.'

'But my cancelled date! All wasted! And I've borrowed the bike from Mas!'

'Renegotiate it. I'm sure to be seeing you ...'

'Well, I dunno ... You certainly like them young, don't you?'

'Kik, will you do what you're told, or would you like me to belt you one?'

'You think you still could, Mum? Okay, okay, hands off—I'm going. Mas! You want to walk a pretty peeress home?'

*　　*　　*

The Ben Disraeli was favourite rendezvous for Mas. Its clients made Aspen feel antique: also deafened, by their cries and musical selections.

'So how did you make out with Kik?'

'I confess he impressed me, in a dreadful sort of way.'

'You know he detests me?'

'He probably doesn't: just suffers from *Brüderhass*.'

'Translation?'

'The Germans, who should know, have invented a word for brotherly dislike. "Brother hatred" it would be in English, but it doesn't sound quite right.'

'You think it doesn't exist?'

'At about your ages, yes: before, there can be love; afterwards, indifference.'

'You think we're both trying to prove something.'

'Stop telling me what I think, and tell me what you do.'

'Kik is a nihilist.'

'So? He's frank about it.'

'I disapprove of nihilists.'

50

'Please don't ever use the word "disapprove" before you're forty, and know no better. Dislike, despise, anything you care for, but not "disapprove".'

'Despise, then.'

'Okay: but why?'

'They're users, not makers.'

'True enough...'

'There are too many of them around.'

'You're not going to say they should get their hair cut and be conscripted?'

'Certainly not: they should be forced into their place and kept there.'

'You *are* a young authoritarian!'

'I believe in authority.'

'Whose?'

'In *authority.*'

'For what?'

'For order of some kind.'

'Heigh-ho—here we go again. And so, for you—the army?'

'Yes.'

'It's always struck me as being organized anarchy.'

'It would, a woman.'

'Don't give me that "would, a woman". Women don't understand armies, so you'd say? Not Mrs Gandhi? Mrs Meier? Hundreds of thousands of girl soldiers and guerillas?'

'All right—you don't.'

'The love of my life has been a soldier. Believe me, I've heard plenty.'

'At second hand.'

'You, too: you've been listening to old soldiers' tales.'

'Soldiers *protect* a country.'

'When it's invaded, yes, and not always then: they're apt to make funny deals with the enemy. When it's not being invaded, they sometimes like to do that for themselves.'

'Oh, yes?'

'Oh yes, indeed. Look around. Take a peep in our own back yard.'

'You mean in Ireland?'

'Where else? You want to go and shoot an Irishman or two? You'll be wanting to shoot the English, next.'

'If they deserve it.'

'Who decides?'

'If layabouts who've nicked some gelignite are trying to overthrow things.'

'You think guerilla troops are layabouts? Who had stricter discipline: Castro or Batista?'

'They were *organized* guerillas: not like the student tearaways who go on demos.'

'I'm sorry to say I rather agree with you there.'

'It's just for the sexual kick, like football crowds. Or because they really want to be fighters, but don't care to accept the rules.'

'Or because youth just likes war, I fear.'

'Well—it does: *you* look around.'

'So okay: you join the dopes, toughs and failed criminals of HM Forces.'

'With rules and rights, such men can be made *soldiers*.'

'I expect. And once in uniform, they're not dangerous?'

'Militarily, yes. Socially, no.'

'I agree with the former, not the latter.'

'Okay—we disagree. You care for another coke?'

'You *are* a darling: your brother didn't offer me a thing.'

'I'll bet he did...'

'Well yes, there was a little incident.'

'He imagines I'm a faggot.'

'Not true, of course.'

'There have been propositions ... it's the bugbear of my age-group. We're thought to be randy, frustrated nits. In fact, we spend half our time fighting off adults of both sexes.'

'It must be a strain ... I seem to remember the same horrible experience.'

'You kept them at bay?'

'Mostly ... it's all very difficult. One gets confused.'

'Who confused you more: the guys or chicks?'

'Men: women I don't count—I mean for women.'

'Oh, so you're a bit sort of les, if you don't mind my asking?'

'Not really, but I don't feel that sort of thing counts.'

'Well, I do, let me tell you.'

'Oh, sure: it's different with men.'

'And don't take the mickey.'

'As a matter of fact, I'm not. Look—none of my business, and all that. But if you *must* be a soldier, why not get some sort of education first?'

'That means being an officer.'

'Well, what's so *wrong* with that? You working class boys are so resolutely defeatist.'

'I'll tell you, between ourselves ... Despite parental naggings, I *have* been considering it.'

'Consider it, then: Captain Rattler could help you there a lot.'

'Why should he?'

'He respects your father.'

'He's not a faggot, is he?'

'Rattler? Dear me, no. Doubtless, of course, there have been episodes ... there usually are. But on that score, you need have no fear.'

'Who said I had?'

'You're certainly aggressive enough to be a soldier. Mind if I shoot off now?'

'You'd like me to walk you back to your front door?'

'If you'd care to—yes, indeed.'

'Well, I wouldn't mind. No, no, I'll pay for these.'

'Oh, you are gallant, Mas! Thank you.'

'Well, you're a handsome woman.'

*   *   *

'Rattler—what a sweet surprise! I imagined you shivering in the Towers.'

'My antennae told me I should come up at once to London. You've seen my sergeant?'

'No: his wife and both sons, though. I've just left one on the doorstep.'

'I say: he *is* a persistent lad.'

'No, it's the other one: Masai.'

'The boys are infatuated, I see. But what about Evie Adams?'

'She's a tough nut: I did my best, but you'll have to speak to her.'

'And her sergeant: don't tell me you chickened out from seeing *him*?'

'As a matter of fact—yes.'

'Aspen! This isn't like you.'

'Rattler! Nor like you either. You're usually so brilliant and dogged at doing your own dirty work.'

'Now, now ... Well, let's think: revise our plan, like Marlborough at Blenheim. All right. I'll tackle Evie, but you *must* have a go at Adams: the female element's essential.'

'Dear old boy: do you really have to drag this nice, odd, family into your machinations?'

'Aspen, I *do*. I can't, but just *can't*, do *any*thing without Adams.'

'Okay—no hysteria: don't explode on me.'

'I have my hysterical side, I own: all thoroughbreds are noted for it.'

'And all nihilists.'

'I'm a *positive* nihilist, Aspen. It was the great lesson of my erstwhile academy. What is, isn't: what was, is no longer relevant. Hence: accelerating activity about nothing solves all the problems of the future.'

'Oh. So what do we do?'

'We organize our sabbath tactically. A meal for the entire family, I think: prior to which I'll arrange private interviews of you with him, and her with me.'

'Is it to be luncheon, dear? And here?'

'Dinner: at midday I must see my greedy, petrified Belfast Prod.'

'He's disgorging to your satisfaction?'

'Not lavishly enough: I fear I must arrange for a mercenary group to incinerate another of his warehouses.'

'You *do* think of everything.'

'I'm fated to. Aspen, hold my hands. I can count utterly on you?'

'Eternally, unfortunately, I suppose.'

January 17

Rattler attended catholic mass at a neo-Gothic off the Edgware road; he felt the need of heightened venom for his interview, in the public lounge of Aspen's block, with Mr McCorquodale, from Belfast.

'My dear fellow, what a pleasure! A drink is called for —cognac for the cockles, I propose. You had a satisfactory flight?'

'I came overnight by train and boat.'

'Sea kindly?'

'Look, Rattler: you've had that ten, and I haven't even seen a piece of paper.'

'Mister *McCorquodale*—oh, sir! It was, you know, a peculiar ten thousand. You really want documentary evidence of transfer? Of the funny little country that it comes from, and that equivocal emissary with his bulging bag?'

'I want proof you got and owe it.'

'You have my word.'

'Your word.'

'*Word*, McCorquodale! This whole transaction's built on faith. As soon as I have the remaining forty that you promised, you have a half share in the Towers, with every legal document your heart desires. And pray—dinna forget! I have put all of myself into Otranto on the strength of *your* word alone.'

'It's hard raising funds in the six counties, Mr Rattler.'

'It'll be harder keeping them there, believe me. Any further incidents?'

'My insurance claims are nearing the quarter million.'

'So you see! No personal difficulties, I hope.'

'I've been sniped at: they say I'm on a list.'

'Whose?'

'Nobody knows: or tells. I think it's a group of free-lance psychopaths.'

'Amateurs—they're sure to miss. You're staying in Belfast?'

'I just can't leave, because I just can't sell: where are the buyers? All I can do is channel out some funny money: and that means using characters like you.'

'"Using?" Well, well—needs must. But don't get panicky: I'm out to make cash for us both, and will do. Surely Aspen convinced you thoroughly of that.'

'She's a convincing young woman, and frankly, if she hadn't spoken up for you, I wouldn't have considered anything so fancy.'

'Fancy? Otranto Towers? My dear fellow, the new-wave stately home is in its infancy: you'll see.'

'I'm going to. What have you done there yet?'

'Busy tomorrow? Come down and tramp around. No need to bring your wellingtons and crash helmet—we have abundant spares.'

'But I can't help wishing it was a real historic home.'

'My dear fellow—history is today! Who cares about the past, or could recognize its authentic artefacts? For almost everyone, history is two generations, at the most, enlivened by contradictory legends dreamed up by quarrelsome pedants.'

'Oh, no! History is traditional knowledge, from which lessons can be learned to shape the future.'

'With the consequences we see in the six counties? You're drunk with history, protestants and catholics alike.'

'But we have principles, and Englishmen have none.'

'Thank God for it—I mean in politics. Personal relations are another thing, of course. But political *principles*? When I hear that, I look round for plastic bombs, occult police, and gleaming gas ovens.'

'You're a cynic, Mr Rattler.'

'I am an Englishman, a nobleman, an Etonian, and a former member of the Brigade of Guards, if that's what you mean.'

'But not a catholic, I hope.'

'Me? Good God, no! Though I am a sort of fan...'

'You plundered the world, including Ireland, but you've lost the lot, even Orange loyalty, so you've only got England left to rob.'

'In which endeavour I hope you'll collaborate without fuss. For imperialism ends where it begins: the last natives are the native-born—not so? Meantime, glance over this, while I order luncheon. It's a creation of Lady Aspen's, for pre-plantation in the media':

Weary of Woburn? Bored by Blenheim? Know all you want of Knole? Prepare for the ultimate in Stately Homes!

The location? A mystery: for Otranto Towers is mystery incarnate. All we can yet reveal is that this Home's in the Home Counties, and—a Ruin!

Yes, a rotting, rambling, resurrected ruin! A verminous, viperous, venomous abode!

Who dreamed up this tops in tourist titillation? An old Etonian—who else? But not so old—'hitting the hungry forties' the Hon. Captain Rattler says, and he's a gallant ex-Guards officer to boot.

But how can a *ruin* please the paying public—YOU? Because a tour of the Towers will SCARE YOU OUT OF YOUR SWEET SOUL. There's nothing scarifyingly sinister the deft designers haven't devised for your delight.

Otranto Towers! Its very reverberation clangs as a foreboding bell! Come one, come all, to faint with fear this simmering summer in ENGLAND'S STATELIEST SLUM!

'All set, Mr McC? The banquet awaits its honoured guest. Ah! You approve the text?'

'It doesn't make any sense to me.'

'You have all that on your own doorstep, so you're blasé. This side of the sea, familiarity with horror hasn't yet bred contempt.'

*　　*　　*

A meal less ornate confronted the Adams family in the exiguous kitchen: presided over by a rare guest, the patriarch Grandad.

'Good meat: you didn't get cuts like that in HM Forces.'

'We had goats' tits and palm fibre salad, I recall.'

'And look what it made you, Dad. Smithfield doesn't produce males of your massive mould.'

'Don't cheek your father, boy.'

'Then don't you, Grandpa.'

'Belt up, Kik.'

'Nobody loves me: it's too much.'

'So what about this invitation, Soldier? We accept?'

'Isn't that decided?'

'Yes, but I mean for everyone? She said the family.'

'Hey—what is all this?'

'What is it, Mum?'

'Your admirer, Miss Aspen, has asked us over for supper this evening: to meet her ... well, what *is* he to her, Soldier?'

'Rattler? I'm buggered if I know; but there's some sort of intimate connection.'

'You said yes, Mum? I mean, for all of us?'

'Shut up: I'm talking to your father.'

'What about taking me along as well?'

'You, Dad? I thought you didn't like the upper classes.'

'If he's going to try to exploit my girl and son-in-law, I want to have a look at him.'

'Well, sod it, let's all go, Evie—the whole fearsome five of us. If Rattler survives the shock, and still offers me a serious deal, then he means business. Kids, give your Mum a break today, and help me tidy up.'

'No, I'll do it—you'll all only create a shambles.'

'Go on, Grandad—take her out in front, and let her be elegant and put her feet up. And don't you two groan so pitifully, or you'll have me weeping.'

His sons limply took utensils with distaste. Their father watched them, as a drill corporal moulding reluctant rookies (for whom, however, he has a certain abstract tenderness).

'Kik, tell me more about this Aspen.'

'No, no. You've every advantage, Pop, and you'll have to make her on your own.'

'She's not like that at all, Dad. She's no pushover, and she doesn't tease.'

'Hearken to junior. "Tease", indeed.'

'Did you find you trusted her at all, Mas?'

'Yes: sort of.'

'But not you, clever Kik?'

'Wrong, Pop—in a way, I found that I did too.'

'This Captain of hers might make a lot of difference to our lives.'

'Not to mine, he won't. I'd better give it to you now, Dad. I'm leaving home.'

'Any reasons?'

'You want them polite, or straight?'

'Straight.'

'No violence, then. In the first place, ridiculous though it may seem to you, there isn't room for two men in this cosy pad.'

'Agreed.'

'In the second, I think your mini enterprise is one vast fuck-up. Don't think I'm knocking your endeavours, but really—the operation isn't serious. Now, if you could get your Captain to finance it...'

'That's my worry. Any idea what you're going to do?'

'Move out first: inspiration I hope will follow.'

'Got a place to go?'

'A mate's: I've one request, though.'

'Go on...'

'If I get stuck, let me come back a while.'

'Any time. And I've got a request, too.'

'Tell, and I'll tell you.'

'Whatever activity you have in mind, don't use weapons until you understand them.'

'No promises, but I'll remember what you say.'

'All right, then. Mas, answer that phone. If it's anyone for a car, say we're closed down for the day.'

'Right. Oh, hullo Aspen. Yes, he's in—you want him? Okay—what message? Look, that's a bit complicated— can't you speak to Dad yourself?'

'Give me that, son. Fuck, she's hung up on me. What was it all about?'

'She says will you go over to her place now, and that Mr Rattler, who's out at the airport, will pick Mum up here about six and bring her over.'

'She wants me there first alone, is that it? She has got a sauce.'

'But you'll go, won't you Dad?'

'Kik, if you pack your gear, I'll drop you off at your mate's place on the way.'

*   *   *

The same lift ascended to the poised muslin abode. Aspen wore winter white, and a scarcely calculating smile.

'We meet at last: I feel I almost know you by now.'

'You would have, if you'd waited for me yesterday.'

'I lost my nerve a bit ... And besides, your wife thought it best you and she should see Rattler first.'

'Was that the real reason you disappeared?'

'Not entirely ... Did she mind your coming here just now?'

'I just sailed straight out. Why didn't you want to wait and see me?'

'It's hard to explain, but obviously, I've asked you here to have a try. It's difficult, because I'm torn between a conflict of loyalties ...'

'You haven't got any to me, that I can see.'

'In a sense I have, yes, because I've met your family; and then to you because...'

61

'What about leaving me out of it, and telling me of your loyalty to Rattler? Now you've asked me here, why not explain how you connect with his life and schemes? You're only a vague name to me, you know, but you seem to be trying to turn yourself into one that matters to me and mine.'

'Well, yes, that's so. Now, then—Rattler and I: shall I sort that out first? We're close blood connections, but not too close, strictly speaking, for a formal union, if either of us really wanted it, or could. But it's not that sort of relationship, exactly. He's more than twice my age, remember, besides which a sort of foster-father in a way, a sort of guardian, or partner. I mean he's always guided me, just as I've tried, with less experience, to help steer him a little.'

'I really can't make much of this. Do you mind a question? Have you been his woman?'

'Oh, no.'

'You could be?'

'I really doubt it: really do.'

'But he's devoted to you, and all that? And you to him? Is that it?'

'That's more like it. You might say we're inseparable.'

'I might say this is a relationship I just don't understand: or frankly, can believe is very real.'

'There I assure you you're mistaken. Rattler is the chief person in my life, and I in his: I know that, as does he.'

'All right, I take your word for it. So: what's all this got to do with me?'

'Rattler has plans for you, if you'll accept them. Big plans: he has large ideas for your whole future.'

'Nice of him. But suppose I just want a decent job, if he's got one on offer? And suppose someone starts telling me what all these large ideas *are*, before I decide I may forget about Rattler, and the whole notion of working with him?'

'He'll give you all the particulars, I know. But briefly, he wants you to manage a glorious garden.'

'I'm not a gardener.'

'*Manage* it: and a great big house as well.'

'What's this? A motel, or something?'

'A sort of a peculiar palace.'

'Miss Aspen, do come off it! What *is* all this?'

'To understand, you've got to understand Rattler, too. Oh yes, I know you do, in some ways, better far than I. But not the real Rattler, who I think only I do, and who's highly complex: really a deep, complicated person, whose nature I must just try to make you see.'

'Go ahead, then.'

'He's a prodigious force, potentially, is Rattler: but not a good one, necessarily.'

'I could have told you that.'

'I don't think you know how deeply he's thwarted, yet creative. Also a bit crazy, if he's frustrated.'

'You're warning me off him, then?'

'No, no—just warning, not warning you *off* him. Because I think he *could* alter your whole life, and Evie's, and your children's.'

'Land us all in the nick, you mean.'

'Land you, if you really understand him, almost any-where: the heights, the depths, depending on whether you realize what he's offering.'

'And that's money.'

'That, of course, but far, far more: the sort of life you all really might deserve.'

'The keys of heaven, then.'

'Oh, in a sense—yes: the keys to your own lives.'

'Can we come down out of the stratosphere? What's

Rattler really aiming at—I mean apart from any little plans for us?'

'Poor England is desolate, and licking its sad wounds. Rattler's intention is to heal them, and revive it.'

'All on his own.'

'Don't despise one man's capability! Truly, Adams, that's not worthy of you—it's mediocre; vulgar. It's always been one man who's turned the trick and worked the miracle. But he needs help: supporters.'

'Stooges.'

'Okay, okay. Sort it out with him, man to man, yourself. Be like all men of judgement are, and underestimate a woman's foolish, fallible opinion.'

'Now, don't get shirty. If I wasn't interested in what you have to say, I wouldn't have come, and I wouldn't have stayed.'

'All right. Wipe that male arrogance off your face, then, and out of your brain, and stop regarding me as a gorgeous imbecile.'

'You're gorgeous, all right.'

'I know, I know. You may not believe it, but it can be a pest, at times. Beautiful Aspen! Since childhood, it's a factor I've had to live with. It opens every door, but so often into the wrong rooms.'

'Yes, I can see that—vulgar and mediocre though I may be. But tell me some more: about you this time, and not the acting-colonel. In short: what *is* your interest not in me, but in my wife and sons?'

'I love your sons: I do: already.'

'Fancy them?'

'No, no—not that. They're both quite a bit extraordinary. Of each hundred English kids today, ninety-eight are professionally youthful: mini-stars, perfect little performers. So wild and pretty, and so vacant! Such narcissists! Such self-admiring exquisites! Beautiful and mindless

64

marionettes. And then, and then ... there are one or two marvellous young sceptics who've got the point, somehow, and whose sharp, sardonic natures can grip their young lives and transform them into a hard passion of creation and belief.'

'You see Kik and Mas like that?'

'Perhaps mistakenly, I do.'

'Me too: now isn't *that* peculiar!'

'No, because you love them.'

'A father loves himself in his sons.'

'Not you, I think: you expect them to be themselves. I can't tell you how rare that is in fond, or bullying, daddies.'

'All right—the kids, then. What of Evie?'

'Her life hasn't begun.'

'You blaming me?'

'Oh, Lord, no! I'm not a *blamer*! I like to see what, though—what about what is real. No: I'd say you've done all the right things, best you could, till now.'

'Up till now, when I've got her stuck in a slum, involved in a half-arsed business.'

'Why not restrain that masochistic tendency, which is only a form of sterile arrogance? You're a man, Adams, so you don't have to be just another male.'

'Well—what do you see for Evie? She should leave me for a Brazilian millionaire?'

'Oh dear!'

'Well—*what*?'

'Your wife is an intelligent, handsome, sensual, capable woman. She also loves you, though I'm beginning to think you're so conceited she may be mistaken, apart from your not deserving it.'

'I'm not fucking conceited: I'm a proud man.'

'*Be* proud, then, and talk proud, and don't whine at me!'

'Honest! Men take this sort of thing from you?'

'I don't give many the chance; I string them happily along.'

'So—sensual, capable and all that. And she needs an outlet.'

'Obviously. Well—doesn't she?'

'Yes. Yes, I know she does. And that means Rattler?'

'Not personally, need I say. She'll spot at once he's sexually uninteresting, to say the least; but she may also spot, in fact I'm sure she has, that he can enable all four of you to realize your full potential provided ... and this is my whole motive in asking you here, and *not* for the reasons you, or Rattler, might imagine ... provided, then, you all take his full measure.'

'In his plans for the peculiar palace. Not to speak of the joyous garden.'

'Precisely. You'll take a look at the whole set-up, a far closer look at Rattler, throw a suspicious glance or two on me as well, and make up your justly doubting minds.'

'I could do with a drink.'

'Sorry. It's all over there. Help yourself, as they say. I'm too exhausted.'

'Anything in particular for you?'

'A Vichy: lemon, no ice. Thank you, thank you. I'm glad to see you're a long-drink-in-the-afternoon man.'

'Most of the evening, too. The tropics put you off spirits, at least, in the ranks, they do. Officers manage somehow.'

'Their kidneys are trained from earliest years, I doubt not.'

'Lucky fellows. So what will he want me to do down there, to start off with?'

'There's a hideous cottage on the estate, about the size of a Kensington mansion. I expect, for starters, he'll offer you that, rent free, plus a Rover at least, plus credit at the local supermarket, plus various other seductive perks.'

'No wages?'

'My dear Sergeant: but of course! Sumptuous, and he'll fiddle them tax free.'

'He really has *got* all those resources?'

'He's working on that angle, and not doing at all badly. Not well enough yet, though, for the grandiose scale of his ideas. However: I'll let you into a secret I've kept hitherto from him. *I've* laid my hands on several times what he has.'

'You have? And how do you manage that, if I may ask?'

'Sorry to remind you of it, but I'm a highly connected, dazzling member of a decadent nobility. Loaded idiots still fall for that—the dishonoured name even more than the legitimate looks, it's sad to say.'

'Okay. So financed by fiddles and fans, I uproot my plebeian lot—or whichever of them agree to come, if any—and install them in this gigantic cottage. What do I *do*?'

'Half a tick. I suggest—and you'll see the force of this, once the whole crazy scheme becomes clearer to you—that you go down solo first and look the whole thing over: the great house, the park, the gardens, the rivulets and all. Also, that you take Rattler's measure, and try to pin him down a bit, if you think you can manage that. Meanwhile, to give you an idea of what he thinks he's up to, would you care to glance at a press hand-out he's asked me to cook up for him?'

'Hand it over: I can't wait.'

'Mind if I put on a little music while you peruse it? Something soothing, to calm your objections with gentle decibels?'

'Go ahead. My God, this looks peculiar.'

Aspen watched the frowning, astounded soldier, and sighed with hopeful resignation. He finished it, turned the page over, then back, and read it once again.

'The Captain's a maniac, I'd say.'

'Don't tell me I didn't warn you.'

'And *you* wrote this load of bollocks?'

'Not really ... It's his re-write of my milder and, I think, more rational composition. However: this evening, if we put our heads together first, we might be able to alter his ideas a little.'

'Only our heads?'

'You take after your firstborn. I'll have a little dance around with you, though, if you'd care for it.'

'I'd really prefer a bit more chat.'

'You would? But let's have a snack first—we could steal some of the tit-bits stashed in my groaning fridge for tonight's banquet.'

'Lead the way. My favourite room's the kitchen.'

'Mine too. I think all my brightest and tenderest thoughts in those encouraging surroundings.'

* * *

Evie was displeased at her husband's brisk departure. Her Dad, whom she'd learned to listen to in second gear, had now a rare chance of working on her feelings.

'In your place, I'd simply say to this fascist, when and if he appears, that he can bugger off again and, what's more, neither you nor Soldier's going to have anything more to do with him.'

'In my place, I expect you would. But you see, you're not; and if you don't mind it straight, Dad, you've never understood much about marriage.'

'You're legitimate, aren't you?'

'Only just, if Mum's version was correct. Not that that matters. What does is, you weren't all that faithful to her.'

'*Me?* What are you saying? Who did *I* ever deceive your poor mother with?'

'Joseph Stalin; though it used to be Leon Trotsky at one time.'

'I was *never* a Trot—not ever.'

'In your young days, so I've heard.'

'From agents-provocateurs. I was reproached, way back, with one or two deviations. But sound political education soon sorted me out, and since then I've never wavered.'

'Good old Dad. Ask one of the kids to make us a pot of tea.'

'I'll make it myself. I'm not going to grovel to those fellow-travelling anarchists.'

'Mas an *anarchist*?'

'Kik, then. Mas is a crypto-fascist.'

'This isn't getting us the tea. Kik! Mas! Wheel in some char, and yourselves, if you want any of your Grandad's rissoles. Thanks for them, by the way, if I forgot. But you really needn't have brought so many.'

'You wouldn't have all those savoury scraps go to waste?'

'No. But are you eating enough yourself, back at the buildings?'

'You don't need to eat much at my age. Nor to sleep. I've learned that. If you do, it's nothing but self-indulgence.'

'So what do you do in all that surplus time?'

'Study and organize. Boys! Not on the floor, put it on the table.'

'Apologies, Grandpa. Our generation's very Arab.'

'Very slovenly. Stir the pot before you pour it, and don't slosh. And don't both grab at those rissoles till you've offered them to your Mum, let alone to me.'

'*Excuzez* me. I say, Grandpa: you don't mind a question? What *were* you like in your own younger days? Were you obedient, smiling and thrifty, and all that?'

'Level-headed and a learner.'

'You were? Yes—I believe you. There's no question of

69

it: the younger generation's not what it used to be, it's grown shiftless and feckless. Mas, do you hear what I do? A purring, sumptuous, souped-up engine and a melodic horn? Can it, oh can it, be a Capri calling on humble us? My, my, it is! And out of it's stepping Colonel Crook in person, looking, I must say, posh, the bastard—I do envy him. Shall I admit the blighter, Mum?'

'Yes, and you and Mas haul your sweet arses into the other room.'

'Oh—ho! A tête-à-tête, I see. You're keeping Grandpa as a watchdog, though, I hope?'

'Get out, you two! Evie, as I don't want any part of it, you'd better see him alone. But I'd like to look him over before he goes, if you don't object.'

'All right—let's have him in. And if anyone's going to insult him, please leave it to me.'

'Yes, I think you know how, girl. I'll be out in the kitchen if you need me.'

'Mum—meet Captain Rattler, of the Brigade: the other one.'

'Sit down, Mr Rattler. And don't make a din, you lot, if you can manage it.'

'My thanks, Mrs Adams. And for receiving me. Also for your courtesy to my dear child Aspen.'

'She's your child?'

'In a manner of speaking—yes.'

'Could we have less "manners of speaking", and some straight talk?'

'Yes. I can offer your husband fifty pounds a week, tax free, a house, a car paid for by the firm, and a one-year contract with reciprocal notice clauses. Employment of yourself, on somewhat similar terms, if you desire it. Also funds for the further education of your sons, if that be your wish, and his, and theirs.'

'Why?'

'I'll *tell* you why. Because with all my gifts, and all my resources, and all my knowledge, I can't operate without him.'

'*Why?*'

'Because, like all strong men, I have a weakness.'

'What?'

'Mrs Adams, I can not do *any*thing, anything at all, without one man at least whom I trust, and who trusts me.'

'*Trusts* you?'

'Relies on me, then; and whom I can rely on.'

'A woman wouldn't do?'

'You mean Aspen? No. For one thing, she's too close to me. For another, she's a thinker, not a doer.'

'I see; or perhaps I do.'

'Would you mind if I have a cup of tea?'

'You wouldn't prefer a drink?'

'Well—yes. I've had a day with a greedy fool and it's wrung me out. Thank you, indeed.'

'This fool's one of your associates?'

'Yes; and there will be many more. That's why I must have Adams.'

'As another fool.'

'Mrs Adams! *Must* you be so hostile before you've examined this? And he has?'

'I suppose not. What is this idea that can pay that kind of money? Is it criminal?'

'It sails close to the wind. It skates on precarious ice. As so many novel enterprises, in this year of grace. But it is not illegal; or it won't be, by the time my lawyers and accountants have wrapped it up.'

'And what is it?'

'I'm going into the stately home business.'

'You own one?'

'I'm about to.'

71

'You lords and ladies! You're just showmen.'

'But we always have been, Mrs Adams! The style of the performance alters, but not the substance. We are, and always have been, bandits: not criminals, mark you, except in desperate circumstances, but plunderers. The mafia families, much admired these days, have taught us nothing we didn't know centuries ago. And I'd honestly say, so far as glamour goes, we outshine them still, though they're unquestionably far more affluent.'

'All this would please my father.'

'Might I enquire why?'

'He's a working class Marxist of the old school.'

'Let me meet him, and shake his hand, if he'll deign to do so. For his is the only class we have any respect for. As for the doctrines of Karl Marx, at least he fingered the chief enemy of us both, who are the middle classes; not to mention the unspeakable lower-middle.'

'Oh, you don't care for them?'

'Mrs Adams! If I visualize the lower-middle, I see the social orders of Adolf Hitler, Benito Mussolini and, in a diluted version, sadly appropriate to the decadence of our country, those of its two most recent first ministers. If I survey the middle classes, I see, under the guise of morality, liberal education, and responsibility, a proliferation of highly-trained life-haters and hypocrites. I mean, put it this way: can one say that, whatever their estimable virtues, either of these classes is, in any sense whatever, lovable? Endearing? Animally attractive, even?'

'But the workers, you're able to approve of?'

'Of course. Why do you suppose that males of our persecuted class, if they couldn't marry their own endowed with money, or, as second best, anyone whatever with much more of it, turned instinctively, for brides, to the Gaity, the Music Halls, and even to high-grade harlots?'

'That was nice of them, wasn't it?'

'Well, didn't the girls have a fine old time? And they certainly produced handsome children, with no nonsense about them.'

'I don't doubt it, a few score of them. But what about the numberless pregnant girls you didn't marry, and the thousands of decent lads you turned into flunkies?'

'Thousands! How many do you suppose *we* ever were, and are? At the turn of the century, less than half a thousand. Add our most distant connections, and you still have a minute fragment of the population.'

'You set the tone.'

'Did we? The middle classes have always feared, envied, and tried hard to despise us. And the working class: you believe they ever hated us?'

'No, I think they found you comical.'

'Well, then! And how right they were, because whenever there's a revolution, anywhere, who gets the chop? We do. But do the middle classes? Individually, some of them, doubtless. But what emerges, once the revolution's settled down? A social order of an even more resolutely bourgeois hue.'

'Without capitalism.'

'Capitalism, state capitalism—take your pick. But look at the type of man who ultimately controls either. Don't tell me they're noblemen, except perhaps in Spain; and don't tell me they're workers, unless, maybe, on Pitcairn Island. From the mid-nineteenth century until today, power has passed to, and been held by, men of the middle mind.'

'You don't think much of the workers, then?'

'I think they're personally, apart from ourselves, the only attractive human creatures in the land, but I think ... is it all right if I go on?'

'Now, don't be bashful, Captain Rattler.'

'...I think, politically, which means socially, they're

73

born losers, because they want to be, because they're frightened of power, despise knowledge let alone art, and conceive their destinies in terms of grabbing the chunk they can of whatever more adventurous and ruthless souls have stolen or created. In short, they're never revolutionaries, rarely authentic rebels, but formidably persistent and realistic as bargainers and hagglers.'

'I see. That, I think Dad *wouldn't* like.'

'Well, it's what's known as a "frank opinion". So: I've put you off the whole plan irrevocably?'

'That doesn't follow ... You're going to reveal it all tonight, is that it?'

'If you'll permit me.'

'Just one thing. Does sex come into your proposals anywhere?'

'If you mean do Aspen or I intend to try to seduce anybody, or contrive to get seduced by them, then no. If you mean do we hope you'll all have more fulfilled lives along those lines, then yes. Since you asked, that's our presumptuous intention.'

'That was why Aspen had to see Adams alone without his bothering to tell me?'

'Not in the sense you imply at all. Simply, so that she could tell him about me ... or what he doesn't know about me.'

'Give you a build-up, as it were.'

'If she has done. She's an incalculable girl, but I prefer her possible blame to anyone else's uncomprehending praises.'

'Then I think that's as far as we can get now. I'll tell you one thing, though. You don't learn, or get, anything, without paying something for it; so we have to be ready to pay a price for whatever's offered.'

'Obviously. That applies, I'd say, to everything. And so: shall we set off now, in my ostentatious vehicle?'

'Room for the boys in it?'

'Oh, plenty.'

'You don't mind if my old Dad comes along?'

'Delighted. We only glimpsed each other a second or two. I don't know your family name ...'

'His name is Angell.'

'But how reassuring: as of an ancestral guardian!'

'Tell him so, then. Dad, you ready? Boys! Come along —this is it.'

*   *   *

The evening was successful: how could it not be, with all the right ingredients? A sumptuous, discreet décor, an excellent yet modest meal, drink flowing without insistance or economy, and seven lively creatures, dubious and hostile, yet intensely curious of one another. True, there were momentary halts in harmony, whose shock they absorbed, and swiftly surmounted: rising, by common consent, from sudden snaps of discord to a calmer plane of intercourse. Or so it seemed.

During an interlude of that kind when hosts, without appearing to, may leave their guests a while without their feeling scorned or abandoned, Aspen took Rattler to her bedroom for a breather, and a showdown.

'Now then, my dear old fellow: are you pleased with the atmosphere out there?'

'It's surprisingly cordial, yet I feel thwarted. I sense they're suspending judgement to an alarming degree.'

'They're not yet in the hollow of your hand, you'd say?'

'I'd say not: yet how I've laboured!'

'Then do you know what you're about to do? Before you get down to details with that dear little lot, you're going to alter your tactics altogether, whatever may be your strategy.'

'May I know what this untoward terminology portends?'

75

'The Stately Home caper—yes. Otranto Towers and all that idiocy—no.'

'No?'

'Oh no, but no.'

'You seem unusually decided about this. Why?'

'The people who'll give me the money won't, for anything so absurd; and, as they see it, poor dears, demeaning.'

'Well, that's a good reason.'

'I have another. I don't know about the paying public, but our happy family won't see the point of your project, such as *that* is.'

'But they could be enticed—persuaded.'

'You persist in underestimating the Adamses, and the strength of their background. In their way, they're truly honest people.'

'That's why I want them.'

'I know, I know; and you can still have them, I believe. But only if you stop being so obviously diabolical.'

'You really think so? You think there's something of a ... of a, let's say, demon king element in my performance?'

'No, no, your performance is immaculate. It's just this Dracula Towers that strikes a discordant tone.'

'Otranto Towers: somewhat subtler, I'd say.'

'Just as silly. You *must* change all this, while there's still plenty of time, or, well ...'

'You'll not abandon me, Aspen, dear? You can't!'

'No ... lose my conviction: even some of my faith in your splendid star.'

'I see—that would be grave. So what does my Aspen have in mind as an alternative?'

'The Stately Ruin survives; so does the garden. But you'll make them the most lyrical, welcoming ruin and park the country's ever beheld.'

76

'But that will need much more ingenuity than what I had in mind.'

'Rise to the occasion, then! You usually do...'

'And what of the sinister hints we've been dropping everywhere? To the builder? My frustrated Orangeman? Even to stalwart Sergeant Adams?'

'You say that was just a jest, a cover story—anything.'

'I was so attached to the idea. And yet ... Aspen: you're sure you're right about this? Your profoundest feeling tells you so?'

'Absolutely so.'

'Oh. In that case, farewell Otranto Towers, and welcome —what?'

'We must rely, as one always must, on our beloved national sage and poet. So what do you think that you, the family, and the visiting public, would say to This Other Eden?'

'What a patriot you are, my dear! Yes, I see the force of your amendment, and on the whole, I must say that I agree. But will our family too, do you suppose?'

'Let's go in and discover. As to our countless potential supporters, time alone will show.'

Of the guests, it was Grandad, when the revised scheme, with improvised embroideries, was unfolded by their hosts, who first broke in on the silence of their astonishment.

'A *ruined* stately home sounds right to me,' he said, 'but whatever this lot decide, you won't see much of me there till it well and truly is.'

Tending the Soil

March 3

Dearest Great Great Aunt Clarissa,

Of course, you *never* interfere, and as for your being a 'doddering old relic' ... pray stop fishing, dearest, so outrageously for compliments! Relic, if you wish: it's not, after all, everyone who's thwarted the evil intents of Tum-Tum, and was presented, in the last days of her reign, to his august Mamma. But 'doddering' ... ah, well, thereby hangs my tale.

The Ruin is now doddering splendidly: that is to say, with our new plan, we've chiefly had to shore it up all over, to satisfy the insurance company. I hadn't realized, till I clambered all over it on planks and ladders, what a monstrous construction our dear madcap ancestor devised. Was he in love, and painfully thwarted, do you suppose —or know? The whole edifice sings of lament: but goodness, it's really beautiful. I didn't realize till I'd thoroughly examined it—both from inside, and from the sorrowful vistas of the park—how far more exquisitely melancholy a made ruin can look than all those dreary ones created by the neglect of centuries. (A quote about art and nature would be apt here, if I could remember who first said whatever it was.)

As for the parkland, it's a midsummer night dream, despite the season; though as to that, we can already offer primroses, and there's a promising profusion of bursting buds. The work on the building is as nothing compared with what we've put into coaxing and tidying wanton nature who's let herself run sadly to seed, with all these dire years of neglect. In a way, though, the wilderness quality of what must once have been a cleverly designed park, works in our favour: there's many a tangled acre where we've just had to comb and plait a little, and rediscover lost, mysterious paths. The trees look at their best untended, though later, we may have to lop. As for the pools and rivulets and nets of foliage, all we need is an Ophelia, or at least, her spirit.

Our head gardener and factotum—steward, I think your generation called them—the former Sergeant Adams I told you of, is in his element. Or rather, has made the elements his own, for I don't think he was knowledgeable about gardens in his army days, and still isn't, strictly speaking ... but why speak strictly, when he has such a manifest flair? And such a 'way with him' in spurring on our reluctant man and woman power—rather surprisingly, for his manner isn't 'military' at all; but then, I suppose, a real soldier's never is. He's not a bit bossy, but cordial and persistent, with a glint of amiable menace that seems to turn the trick. Anyway, they grumble about him in a possessive sort of way, and get upset if he sometimes isn't there.

For he goes up to London sometimes to see his family who, though they've made a tour of inspection, haven't yet moved into the neo-palladian cottage that our forebear amazingly constructed—I suppose impelled by that practical turn of mind that mid-Victorians blended even with their fantasies (or am I wrong?). I have to restrain his instinct to make things ship-shape, though ... no, that's navy, so is 'Bristol fashion'—what *does* the army say? ... anyway, get through to him that it's a romantic ruin. At such moments he stares at me, smiles a little pityingly, then does exactly what I asked, and even better. Another small difficulty is that, after his under-spending on everything the first week or so, money's rather going to his head—or is it to his family? I suppose when you're used to the army budgeting for you, it takes a while to get the hang of doing it for yourself. The only real tussle we've had has been over a swimming pool: I said yes, enlarge one of the natural ones by all means, but I didn't want a Lido effect. I told him it would be an anachronism, at which he looked cross, and called me for the first, and I hope last time, 'madam'.

Now, as to your remarkable great great nephew! Rattler, since we've all really got down to work, is almost a 'changed man', as they say: that is, both wildly energetic yet, at the same time, strangely subdued. It's as if all his frenzy, which usually erupts in antics I needn't describe to you, has been channelled exclusively into driving the scheme along. He's like a man purposefully possessed; and some of his ideas are so remarkable, they amaze everyone so much that they're apt to agree before seeing what they've let themselves in for.

For instance, the Council. We're Tory down here, as you'd expect, and rather unsure-of-ourselves Conservatives, at that: a bit flushed, and over-emphatic, and genteel. For dear things like this, especially their ladies, Rattler's background seems heroic and reassuring, the more so as they're short on stateliness in the county (or in our part of it), and it's for a prestige business proposition he's soliciting their support. But then we have light industry as well—gimcrack furniture, and caravans and so—which gives us an active Labourite minority, who represent the diverse immigrant groups employed there: we've even got Mauritians, and a south-sea islander or two. Well, with them Rattler's just as irresistible! Their delegates and councillors think he's 'one of the boys' (or ever ready to show willing), and the lost sons and daughters of the lost empire think he's a *scream*: 'he is a hu—man be—ing', as a Sierra Leonian lady put it to me. In short, he appears to be apt at the same Tory populist legerdemain dear great great uncle Tobias admired so much in rumbustious Joe Chamberlain, and that Carson was so clever

at, and even wanton Sir Oswald, in his way; though
I don't think he can yet be said to rival that hysteri-
cal Welshman you may have heard of, who speaks
Greek.

But that's not the end to his triumphs on the political
front: so necessary, these days—I mean the deception
and flattery, and manoeuvring—to get anything done that
needs powerful permissions, as everything, short of breath-
ing, seems to do. Mr Angell, our steward's father-in-law,
is a steadfast disciple of Joe Stalin: or at least, of his principles and, above all, practises, which he feels are sadly
neglected these decadent days, save in Albania, which is
his Shangri-la. Well, then—would you believe it? He's
growing fascinated by Rattler, who seems to him the living embodiment of all that needs overthrowing, and made
a thorough example of. And Rattler, though this naturally
annoys him a bit—for who, after all, wants to be thrown
into the ash can of history just like that?—plays up to
him, as a stoat does to a weasel, if I've got them the right
way round. Deep down, I think Mr Angell's rather riveted
by meeting at last, in the revolting flesh, what he sees as
the ultimate Grand Duke. This, in turn, flatters Rattler
in a perverse way, for he's not, poor dear, without his
vanities; and they have endless arguments together, like a
friar of the inquisition and an intelligent victim, just
prior to the burning.

Nor has Rattler neglected his recent army connections.
Peculiar field officers, with a look in their eye I don't think
even dear Sir Winston would quite have approved of,
arrive in a cloud of dust—no, trough of mud—and mutter endlessly with Rattler in the library, the only room
we've finished yet, though we haven't moved the tattered
tomes in—they're on their way in bulk from a rural
library that's been suppressed, since none of the immi-
grants can read them, and the locals don't want to, now

that they see it all on the telly. More useful than all this politico-military mutter, resounding with muffled guns, is that the officers send down huge lorry-loads of soldier 'volunteers' to help out in the garden: nice hefty lads who don't do much, except in bursts, and who have terrible tales to tell about Ireland, from whence they've recently returned with a poorer opinion than ever of all civilians.

Which brings me to another slightly disturbing point that perhaps I shouldn't bother you with, and about which I do hope Rattler knows what he thinks he's doing. Conspiratorial Irishmen, of I'm not certain which hue and persuasion, arrive and disappear like jacks-in-the-box, and leave carrying away crates I don't like the look of, the more so as this type of activity is nocturnal. We've even had a light aircraft landing perilously in the mist on the plateau beyond the park, and taking off overloaded, let alone, I'm sure, illegally. This doesn't seem to me to help the myth of a romantic ruin we're trying to create ... or, perhaps, does it? At any rate, I'm sure you, dearest Great Great Aunt, won't be alarmed, and will take this knowledge in your stride (I mean metaphorically—I really wouldn't come all the way down from Scotland, if I were you), since it will remind you of the heroic days of the Curragh, about which I've so often heard your vivid, emphatic recollections.

Let's look on the brighter side—to the ever youthful future! Did I mention that our steward (to whom I seem to be referring rather obsessively) has two appalling, highly delightful, sons? Called Kik and Mas (I think—I hope—I explained that bit about their names?). Well, now. Kik, the senior of the pair, thundered down here last week with scores of admirers on rather shabby but powerful motor-bikes, that didn't seem to belong to them, exactly. These lively lads were uncouth and shaggy, though bursting with ill-suppressed energy, save in their speech, which was monosyllabic. They looked like the advance guard of a horde that doesn't quite know what it's advancing on, or even why. They frolicked about a bit, and when they got tired of that, lounged angrily, and when that bored them, created such a tumult with their vehicles as would arouse the jealousy of the gifted technologists who designed Concorde. At this, I had to call for hush, and there were leery looks, and rapish glares and gesticulations, that Kik gallantly put a stop to. I consoled them with heaps of grub and booze, and they all said they'd come down again, bringing auxiliaries, to lend a helping hand. But at what, I wonder? And would they collaborate peaceably with the soldiery?

Then brother Mas brought his rather different delegation: less squalidly exotic than his brother's, but, I thought, even less seductive. These were orderly lads in neat overalls and boots, with strange gleams in their eyes, and gestures of controlled ferocity. He tells me they're interested in joining *organizations*, and they came down, and departed, by diesel train. But not before doing quite a bit of useful tidying and burning, and even some quite heavy digging. At meal-time, which they took out of doors around the fire and in the chill, they sang obscene, energetic songs. They also, apparently, will return in due course to offer their assistance.

From tales of brute man power now, to those of the higher spirit. The scholar and connoisseur in Rattler have also stood him in good stead, for he has enlisted the active sympathies of our national spokesmen for the things of the heart and mind. That charming, boyish poet with a Dutch name, and that lordship who can explain civilization (though what art, which he understands, has to do with *that*, I could never understand) have both, as have others impelled to salvage our vanishing cultural glories, come out in firm support of preserving so perfect a specimen of mid-Victorian eccentricity. Then the nature-loving people want us for a sanctuary: no, no, not imported wild life, but for our own fleeting, tormented beasts and birds. The gardening lobby (and I never realized how fanatical *they* are) are all for reviving a near-perfect specimen of organized horticultural chaos. Even the ecologists have pricked up their ears, and if we enlist their support, our cause will become international, I hope.

About one thing only, much as he hankers restlessly for publicity, Rattler had been absolutely adamant: and this is television. Crews have already appeared, but have been banished instantly, and patrols are out to thwart espionage by tele-camera. For Rattler's reasoning runs thus. Our opening, he says, will be the first historic event since the medium captured the national devotion which, despite its highly promising visual and 'personality' aspects, will be barred ruthlessly from the eager parlours of the people. All he will offer them is a single shot of our old ash, and of our limpid springs and streams: a suggestion rejected with pained astonishment. Don't you want to make this whole thing *go*, they asked him indignantly? Certainly I do, he answered, and by keeping you chaps off my turf, I'm going to assure maximum coverage on all the other media. I wonder: hasn't the whole telly lunacy gone so far that this bold tactic may backfire disastrously? But perhaps Rattler's tantalizing them, and will surrender expensively at the last moment.

So farewell for now, dearest Great Great aunt Clarissa, from the verdant battlefront. Rattler is sending you pages of figures that I hope you'll understand, because I don't, nor, I believe, does he, but his accountant, Mr Watson, does, and I'm sure your dear, reliable Mr Macpherson will as well. Much, much love from us both to you in your windswept castle from the soon, I hope, to be peaceful ruin and pleasance of This Other Eden.

Your own
Aspen

March 20

A freak, shrill spring sun shone prematurely for a day. Aspen and Adams reclined beneath the tree beside the pool.

'Back to the desert. You mind if I bare my torso?'

'Delighted. But beware of casting clouts. My, my, you are a hirsute fellow. And that rippling musclature—I say!'

'Nothing to stop you following suit, if you feel inclined.'

'Now, now ... you miss the desert, Soldier?'

'Everyone does—it's the old story. Hate the bake while you're there, best days of your life when you leave it.'

'You feel the same way about the army?'

'Not really ... Well, perhaps I do, it's too early to say ... It's a habit-forming existence, as you can imagine.'

'Indeedy. Is it that "comradeship" we girls get so bored hearing about, you hanker after most of all?'

'That and, in a way, the officers: I miss having something to resent.'

'Now, there's a confession! You didn't like them?'

'Up to Captain, yes, you couldn't help it: I mean shitting in the same ditch, if you'll excuse me. Target of the same democratic bullet, and all that.'

'But not the gentry stashed in their châteaux?'

'Don't mock, they still have their privileges, you know —I mean their super-privileges. All rank and responsibility deserve that, but beyond Lt-Colonel, or so, they start collecting civilian rights, as well as military.'

'Do they? I thought they all raced about in tanks these

days. So what special privilege have generals, for instance?'

'They write diaries, for one thing.'

'Do *what*?'

'It's strictly forbidden to all ranks: could fall into enemy hands, and so forth. But that doesn't prevent generals—they're great diarists. Or flogging their day-to-day accounts of their tribulations later on to the Sunday papers.'

'Well, that seems innocent enough.'

'Oh, does it? And then they have soldier-servants, known as batmen, who are supposed to be able to tote a gun as well, but somehow don't seem to do so.'

'Now, Adams! Don't tell me you never paid some swarthy gent to do your spit and polishing for you?'

'Oh, but of course. Not quite the same thing, though. And anyway, *I* paid them, not the army.'

'Heigh-ho, Soldier. You should have been bold, grabbed a commission at whatever rank, and found out for yourself.'

'Not in the British army, Aspen. It may be changing, but not in the army as I knew it, and as I was.'

'Well, anyway, that crazy career's behind you. What do you make of this new one in show business?'

'Have to see. The money's fine, the idea's interesting—though, between ourselves, I can't see us opening this summer.'

'Oh yes, we will. We're a *ruin*, don't forget, so can afford to be a bit haphazard. They'll think it's all part of a carefully designed effect. As to the cottage, you're making that so neat we'll have to camouflage it.'

'Well, naturally—they're moving down next week, or some of them. Evie yes, Mas I think so, Grandpa Angell I hope not, and Kik, I just don't know.'

'Evie's looking forward, do you think?'

'Yes, I think she is. She's always had a thing about the

country, though God knows where she picked that up. Also, she's never had her own house yet: or, if not exactly hers, one she could call her own.'

'How is she—I mean in general?'

'Blooming: blossoming like these daffs. She's looking smarter, more relaxed, and certainly sexier. We're in for a second honeymoon, I should say. Not that we had much of a first one . . .'

'Is that due to your coming back, the change of job, or Rattler's calculated generosity?'

'The money certainly helps a lot. I've bullied her into spending at least some of it on herself, and it's wonderful what the dress shops and hairdressers can do.'

'Good for her. Your bold sons haven't laid their eager paws on the whole lot, then.'

'I've seen to that. Apart from housekeeping, I've paid the bills—any bills she likes—till Evie gets down here. Kik has had a sub to go and make his fortune and get nicked, and Mas is moderate in his demands, anyway.'

'What of Mr Angell? Has he succumbed at all?'

'How did you guess? We've paid the deposit on a new engine for his car. Strictly a loan, of course.'

'I hope both the boys will come down here—even dynamic Kik. They'd be re-born in this atmosphere, I'm sure.'

'You may live to regret that hope.'

'Oh no, for I'm country reared, you see, and have a great faith in rural tasks and joys. I'd like to see dear Kik fall off a horse, for instance. As for your censorious Dad-in-law, I'm not so sure. He might cast a blight on the element of fantasy we're trying to create here.'

'He'll come and go, I expect. With Evie, even when I was away, it was always I won't come where I'm not wanted, and back again next Sunday dinner.'

'Well, I expect he's lonely.'

'Oh, sure. The Party's not a gentle bride.'

'Also, he may, in his way, be fond of you all. Seed of his own seed, if nothing else.'

'If so, I wish he'd show it once in a while. I don't mind for myself, but after all, the kids are his grandsons, and those two generations are supposed to be rather close, aren't they?'

'Usually, yes: the further the blood relationship, the greater the tolerance and affection.'

'Well—not with him. He treats them like delinquents, even Mas.'

'But they're not, really.'

'No, not Kik either, I'd say—he's just a performer. And if they are, it's partly that I've been away so long, and even more, the social set-up encourages delinquency.'

'It does?'

'Oh yes, it must do, it's quite simple. Unemployment, specially youth unemployment, plus television, and you've got delinquency.'

'You mean the violence of the programmes?'

'Oh, no! Their fatuous worship of luxury, their premium on envy. Put a kid out of a job in front of a telly for a week, and he says—why not me? ... and goes out and does a bank, or tries to.'

'Commercials for breakfast foods lure him to that wild life?'

'It's not the commercials—it's the programmes. Apart from token shorties on doss-houses that everyone switches off, the programmes always show people making, or rather, spending, at least twice as much as they can possibly earn, if not ten or a hundred times. That wouldn't matter in itself, I mean everybody wants dreams, but the programmes aren't shown as dreams, they're projected, with a wide smile of approval, as reality: the desirable life that's owed to every little you and me.'

'They are rather shitty, most of them, if you'll excuse the word.'

'I'm not unused to it. Never mind: old Mas may escape from *those* illusions in the army, if he sticks to wanting to go in. Though of course, they'll teach him others ... But he'll have a reasonable sort of an existence...'

'So long, dear Soldier, as he doesn't get caught up in that great big Episode Three we all sense uneasily on the horizon.'

'World War Three? My dear, it's begun: you haven't noticed?'

'Oh, come on! Don't try to alarm me.'

'Only to make you see what's staring everyone in the face, and some have spotted sooner than others. Korea was the last big, old-style, international battle. Since then, we've had political wars, dozens of them, not only us, but all armed nations everywhere. Then add to that minorities bombing for their rights, civil riots, hijackings, terrorists and what not, and you have the perfect pattern of World War III. And we're going to have a whole lot more of these disturbances, and bigger ones.'

'You think so? And we're building a ruin!'

'It's a sign of the times. In his way, the old Captain is a realist.'

'I suppose. Anyway: you're not bored with what you do down here? All this horticulture doesn't go against the grain?'

'I'm enjoying it, surprisingly enough. It makes a change to build something, even a ruined garden.'

'Not supposed to tell you, and all that ... but I think Rattler plans to let you run the whole thing, if you want to, when it gets off the mud.'

'He tired of it already?'

'Far from it, but I think it's just his base of operations: his jumping-off point to weirder things.'

'And what's he going to jump into? Politics?'

'What else? You know the man as well as I do. But of the modern kind, I expect: military-commercial, not debating chambers.'

'So long as he doesn't ask me to join in any of *that* nonsense. Pass me that T-shirt, will you? The sun's packed in on us.'

'You want it inside-out as it was, or right way round?'

'I want a bit of a kiss, as a matter of fact. How do you feel about that?'

'It'd be a mistake, but if it's only a kiss...'

'Now, don't go coy on me, and cock-tease. You want it, or not? I can't do much harm to you out here, in full view of I don't know how many nosy bastards.'

'Would you settle for swapping your T-shirt for this cashmere cardigan I've pinched from Rattler?'

'Aspen, you *are* a cock-teaser, you know. I wouldn't have thought it.'

'Yes, I may be, but not quite in the way that you imagine. Why don't we lurch through the mud and have a drink instead?'

'Well, it's a second best, but I can live in hope...'

March 28

The scraps of furniture had gone ahead by van; and by arrangement, Evie was to be driven down by Rattler to the Ruin.

'Ah, good-day, my dear. The last day in the old home! Are you all set for the hegira?'

'All ready. Dad's been in to say good-bye, and the boys have gone down by scooter.'

'So we are to have both brethren after all, and not just Master Mas?'

'Kik says he wants to try it out before he makes his mind up. Is that okay?'

'Entirely up to him and you. Now, then. You've done those little things that one forgets? Turned off the gas? Removed all the bulbs? Taken a last look round for precious items staring you in the face?'

'I'm glad it's the last look round, to tell you the truth. I've had enough of two rooms in Kilburn.'

'I know how you feel—it's true also of a soldier's life. One moment, a slit-trench or tin hut. The next ... well, somewhere preferable, if less familiar. So, now: shall we be off?'

The car fought its way from the city, Captain Rattler grim and dexterous at the wheel; and reached that tract of urban-rural confrontation which is, for miles on end, ambiguous neutral ground. The Captain lit an unexpected cigar, and Evie broke the silence.

'Now that we're going there, can I ask a few more questions?'

'Any. Please say on.'

'Lady Aspen: she's not thought of marriage?'

'Oh, I suppose so! What woman doesn't? But with Aspen, you see, it's not so much that she's hard to please, as that she's had one or two unfortunate experiences, I think.'

'Such as what?'

'That, I'm afraid, I mustn't answer, even if I knew all. But disillusioning: upsetting, I believe.'

'Perhaps she *is* a bit too hard to please.'

'Not exactly, I wouldn't say. It's more that she sets herself high standards, and therefore can't be at her best unless she can give of *her* best, and that she's unable to do with just anyone.'

'Isn't it that she doesn't want to marry beneath her?'

'I say, you *are* an old-fashioned thing, my dear!

"Socially" beneath her, you mean? Well, I'll let you into a dreadful secret. Among our exclusive lot, you can't *ever* marry "beneath you", even if you tried. Anyone who can lose caste just hasn't got any, is how we see it.'

'Really?'

'Really! I assure you.'

'So if Aspen married someone like Soldier, she wouldn't lose class, according to you.'

'Sorry to be arrogant and all that, but no. Apart, of course, from her not wanting to, and his being happily allied to our estimable Evie.'

'So if he's been flirting with her alone down there, it won't do him any good.'

'Oh, I don't know about that—flirting is always fun. But if you're thinking she'd try to steal him away, well, I just don't think it's on. For one thing, a girl like Aspen—and when I say "like" her, there aren't all that many who are —if she thought of an act like that, she'd do it openly. I mean, face to face with her furious rival.'

'Oh, would she!'

'Oh, yes. And what's more: consider Soldier. You admire him, I do for different reasons, but that doesn't mean *every*one's going to fall head over heels.'

'You're not denying he's attractive.'

'Of course not! To deny that, would be to question *your* attraction, wouldn't it, since you selected him? Oh, no. Adams has allure, no doubt about it. All the same ... hey, you don't think this chat's getting a little intimate? I mean, perhaps there are certain private doors that should stay locked, wouldn't you say?'

'"All the same"—what?'

'Oh, well—how about if we stop at a pub and have a glass?'

'I've got some beer here in my hold-all.'

'You have? You *are* resourceful. Well then, let's find a

secluded lay-by. Why! Here's one coming up—it's fate. There we are. You have an opener?'

'They're the pull-off kind.'

'Oh splendid! Ale out of a can—it takes me back to my days with Soldier. So: your husband: why *did* you marry him?'

'What a question!'

'I must remind you, Evie, that you began all this personal bit, and insisted on going on with it.'

'I married him because he asked me first.'

'Excellent reason! That wasn't all, though, was it?'

'I wanted away from home—which was a dog-fight; I won't go into that.'

'That all?'

'I fancied him: still do.'

'That *all*?'

'I was sorry for him.'

'Oh—you were?'

'That surprises you?'

'Not exactly; but it's not always the best basis in a marriage.'

'What is?'

'Ah—indeed. So: let's put it this way. Given other circumstances, you might have married someone else.'

'Most women might, given other circumstances.'

'Oh—of course! But I mean, he wasn't—how shall I put it?—the one and only possible choice, let's say.'

'He was the only possible one for me at that time.'

'Not what I mean. He wasn't, to you, *the* man.'

'Well—no. So where does that get us?'

'Oh, I don't know. Nowhere in particular, I dare say. It's just that it's always struck me, right from the start, that—dare I say this?—you were a cut above him, fine man though he is.'

'Socially above him, are you saying?'

'Oh, *do* free your mind from that obsession! "Socially", indeed! No, not "socially". In value; in quality; in style.'

'You could be the echo of my old Dad.'

'God forbid! Besides, he's prejudiced in your favour, I'm impartial.'

'You sure you're all that impartial?'

'Lordy me! Not content with suggesting Aspen's after your husband, are you now hinting I'm playing up to you?'

'You are a bit, aren't you?'

'Only insofar as any man would do to a handsome, intelligent, attractive woman.'

'Thanks for those words, Captain. You've made my afternoon.'

'It's a pleasure. But the fact remains: you could have done better than Adams, and what's at the back of your mind, though you're not admitting it, even to yourself yet, is that you still could.'

'Do better than Soldier?'

'Do differently, let's say.'

'And what if I don't want to?'

'Then the subject's closed. Our words are as empty breath on the polluted air.'

'Beery breath, too—mind you don't meet a cop car.'

'I'll be prudent. Shall we be on our way?'

'We'd better.'

A stretch of authentic country came into view and, amazingly, continued. No doubt about it, spring was hitting form, communicating an expectant tingle.

'You're a strange fellow, Mr Rattler.'

'No question of it: I'm an oddity.'

'I don't say that, but I've certainly not met anyone at all like you.'

'Not probable you ever will: I'm a pure eighteenth century type—the earlier period.'

97

'When your lot were lords of the whole damn creation.'

'Were getting to be ... digging in our toes. Less murder than in the older heroic days, but much more money.'

'And now you're only left with the corruption.'

'Absolutely! What else would you have us be? Well—what else? Who isn't after power and money, and who doesn't grab or cling on to both as best they can? You, for instance, who are so censorious: you don't like the idea of good, hard cash?'

'Oh yes—but on conditions.'

'Come off it! Once you admit "conditions", you admit that, potentially, there are none. For instance: for a million quid, say, you wouldn't hop into bed with almost anyone?'

'For a night, or is it forever?'

'Let's say for just one revolting session: certified cheque available on the morrow.'

'I admit I'd be tempted. But in my class, we don't quite see things that way.'

'You and your class! Honestly, Evie, you wave your origins at me like a banner! A woman, before she belongs to any class, is first and foremost a woman: more authentically so, I'd say, than men are really men, who are so apt to believe their own silly ideas.'

'Deep down you despise us, don't you?'

'Not all that deep down, if you mean your "class"! What's all the point of complaining, yet really grovelling, living in squalor, and envying what you're afraid to go out and get? What does that prove—that you've saved your proletarian souls?'

'No: that we cherish our integrity.'

'Cherish your arses, if you'll forgive me! A chief folly of mankind is rejecting temptations it's not been offered. The real way to test your "integrity" is to go out and get the best for yourself, and see if your integrity can stand up to *that.*'

'There speaks the capitalist.'

'My foot! You think there's *any*one adventurous in the world, in *any* society, who doesn't want to fight his way to the top? And whatever his notions are, essentially for himself? The only ones who can afford to do things "for mankind" are the defeated, like your old Pa.'

'I'd like to hear you tell him that.'

'Because it would challenge his complacency, or because I'd get a sock in the eye?'

'Both, as a matter of fact.'

'Well, at least he has in his favour he's an activist: I mean, politics is his life, if I've understood him. And if you're a Marxist, politics *has* to be your life, since there are no other outlets for your ambition.'

'All human activity is political.'

'I accept that, but not *party* political, as your Dad imagines. You, as a matter of fact, see it differently, though you won't admit it. You're a politically educated lady, but unfortunately for your orthodoxy, you've applied your experience and imagination to the doctrines, and found that, for practical purposes, they don't appeal to you. Am I correct?'

'Something along those lines, possibly.'

'Well, then. England, today, has produced a new class, which you might call the upper working. They want the money, they're not fooled by the middle classes and mean to keep to their own social patterns, and they don't kid themselves they want to rule the country—what they want is for anyone else, almost, to take on that tiresome chore, while they supply the permanent, effective, prosperous opposition. And what's wrong with that, as an intelligent strategy, at any rate for our lifetime? So—join them: hop aboard. Get what you can, and start a second life while you're at your peak, and still have the time to do it.'

'Ho—hum. You *are* a plausible fellow, Mr Rattler.'

'Well, what's so foolish in my analysis, if you'll condescend to tell me?'

'That you don't understand the working class, except, as your kind always have, as an exploiter, a slummer, a paternalist.'

'That strikes me as a bit text-bookish, but if so, then teach me. I like to think I'm something of a realist, and if I find I'm wrong, I'm almost the only man I know who can take it, admit error to himself, and learn again. So, all right: if I'm wrong, show me.'

'If you're not too far gone, I may take you up on that.'

The country gave way to another rural-urban bit of disconsolate cows and optimistic plastic.

'Our budding factory estate. I'll give you a quid for anyone you find there who knows the difference between Karl and Groucho.'

'How far to the Ruin, Captain? I don't remember.'

'Over the hills and beyond that secluded foliage—we're practically there. And with your arrival, we may say our great adventure here has really begun.'

*   *   *

Moonlight fell on the ruin, visible from the cottage through the trees: it was beginning really to look the part.

'Home sweet home, Soldier: or is it going to be?'

'Dunno, Evie: we'll just have to see how this lark works out. I'll tell you one thing, though. Now we're on the ration strength, we're going to save those wages, so we can start the car business again with something, if we have to.'

'Prudent, Soldier.'

'Nothing wrong with that, is there? You got to be.'

'You been prudent with her ladyship?'

'I made a sort of pass, but it didn't get me anywhere.'

'Oh, it didn't? Was that out of loyalty to me?'

'No, not interested enough, really. Nor was she.'

'You're losing your touch, Soldier. Or are you settling down to married life, now you're not wedded to the army?'

'Could be ... What about you and the crafty Captain? You had a nice ride down?'

'Chatty ... You know how it is in the front seat of a car.'

'Don't I! All legs and close proximity, cut off from the curious world.'

'We talked politics chiefly, as a matter of fact.'

'That's as good a subject as anything, when you're really talking of something else ... Or perhaps you *were* talking about politics. The Captain rather fancies himself as an expert.'

'You don't think he is?'

'No—not that I am. But he sees it as ideas and adventure, and I think it's really committees and deals. He's a pirate, the old Captain, in politics as in anything else.'

'Have the kids settled in?'

'God knows: they're out somewhere on their bike. Scanning the local talent down at the factory estate, probably. Kik seems girl crazy.'

'Quite unlike you at his age.'

'I wasn't so blatant about it.'

'You couldn't be. The social scene was more severe, and you were far more bashful.'

'I should hope so. You think he makes it with those mini-bits?'

'I'm not supposed to know, but he's had the clap.'

'He has? Why didn't you tell me?'

'I thought it would upset you, and make you try to come the father.'

'I hope he's got rid of it ... he has?'

'Oh, yes. He knows about those things.'

'Does Mas?'

'You mean has he been with a girl? No, I don't believe so—he's holding his horses. Any moment now, though, I dare say.'

'But he's a kid.'

'He doesn't think so. Nor do I, as a matter of fact.'

'We'll have to see about finding them a school.'

'Oh yes, if they feel like going...'

'How about a kip for now? It's been a day.'

'You want a bit?'

'It's not that ... Strip off, though, I want to see your arse.'

'By moonlight? You strip too, Soldier. It's been a while ... You're not putting on weight, are you? No—don't breathe in.'

'See? All rib cage—not an ounce of fat.'

'What about all this? Don't tell me that's all muscle...'

'No, gristle, but give it a rest for now...'

'You just want a cuddle—is that it?'

'Something like that—we'll see.'

*   *   *

'They've bedded down for the night, the happy pair. Or at any rate, "dowsed the glim", as he would say.'

'Stop spying, Rattler. You'll be using a telescope next.'

'I haven't had our Soldier under such close observation as have you. How have you two been behaving?'

'Easily, modestly ... He made the ritual advances, but chiefly as a matter of form, of what he thinks's expected of him.'

'And you spurned the not very eager fellow?'

'Put things on a more relaxed footing, I hope ... Spurning is fatal: it makes them bullish.'

'And you don't want that?'

'With Adams? No. You know I don't. We've been into all that.'

'Then I shall have to work my wiles on Evie.'

'That's why you've brought them here, isn't it? It's your plan, so it's your labour.'

'I know, I know. And that wild little pair of males are now coming into view: pushing their vehicle, I do hope it has at least a puncture.'

'Poor dears: when anything mechanical goes wrong, men get so cross.'

' "Poor dears", indeed. The elder fit for, at best, a pimp, and the younger for a male harlot.'

'Oh, but cynical! You're not in an imaginative mood.'

'True enough ... I confess to an unforgivable moment of exhaustion.'

'You've given yourself such a *lot* to do, dear, haven't you?'

'And it's only beginning ... Do you know, dearest Aspen? I sometimes even regret I banished myself from the haven of the army ...'

*   *   *

'No rumbling tonight. No creaks, no groans, no animal exclamations.'

'Belt up, Kik. You shouldn't speak of Mum like that.'

'The idea disturbs you, does it, her having it off with Dad?'

'Belt up.'

'You feel he's cut you out a bit, since he came home?'

'Lay off Mum, Kik.'

'Or on her? That's what you'd like, isn't it? But boy, it's forbidden. Why not turn your nasty thoughts to milady Aspen, if she shows willing?'

'You've got a mind like a sewer, haven't you?'

'Sure, but my filth drains off. Yours is blocked up in your festering brains and crapulous body.'

'You're vexed you couldn't make that Cypriot bird to-night.'

'You're quite wrong, as usual. I did, while you were listening to those moronic records.'

'Where?'

'Never mind where. You don't need a "where" if the chick's willing. She wasn't at first, because, despite my allure, she turned out a bit commercial: needed some bread, she said.'

'But you hadn't got any.'

'Not till I flogged your petrol to a mate, but unfortunately I miscalculated, which is why we had to walk part of the way home.'

'You're a liar, then, besides a thief.'

'Oh yeah—I get unscrupulous when the need is dire.'

'But you did get her?'

'Oh, yeah. Terrible. It always is. I wish some great big gorgeous girl would really fall in love with me, one day.'

'One with money.'

'Oh no, I might even work for her. She might be my inspiration.'

March 31

Beloved Great Great Niece,

So dear of you to write me, which few of the younger generation seem able to do now, thanks, I suppose, to the telephone, an instrument I'm far from abhorring, but I do think a letter's much more fun. One can re-read it and ponder, and think of a deliberate reply. Conversations on the telephone are so scrappy, so abrupt; besides being frequently inaudible, though my ninety-two year old hearing remains reassuringly acute. (It's only my digestion, really, that I suffer from, but one mustn't be greedy; and at least there's less of the constipation that used to weigh so much upon my spirit.)

You ask about the origins of the Ruins (plural, dear —you omitted to add an 's') built by your Great Great Uncle Tobias's strange cousin (they were all odd on that side of the family), at some time in the 'sixties, I think it was; and I'll gladly tell you what few legends I can remember. But before I do, Aspen, I must rap your dear knuckles for an inaccuracy, and a slight impertinence. Nice persons did not call the P o W 'Tum-Tum'—that was a horrid metropolitan vulgarity; they simply called him 'The Prince' (or, of course, 'Bertie', if properly entitled to). As to 'thwarting his evil intents', I did not, and this, I may say, with your great great uncle's connivance or, at least, tacit approbation. A great mistake, however; for not only was the experience unpleasant and degrading, but, more to the point, I did not succeed in securing the advancement your great great uncle coveted. 'Put not thy trust in princes', as somebody so truly said.

Now, the Ruins, and our distant connection who erected them. It was not, as you romantically suppose, because of a thwarted passion that he did so; for our cousin's only passion was, precisely, building, and at huge expense. The Ruins were thus preceded by some half dozen constructions in various styles, for our forebear was a restless innovator; and since he could find no architectural form appropriate to his dreams, he thought that a deliberate shapelessness, an engineered abandon, would best enshrine, in stone and greenery, his vision of an unrealizable Ideal.

Their chief feature, though, was to be the gardens, on which our cousin lavished far more thought and care than on the building ... a characteristic, even, of his earlier erections, wherein the house was conceived of chiefly as a pretext for the more intricate and perfect park. I first saw that of the Ruins, as a young girl, some time in the dear 'eighties, a decade or so after our cousin had completed, and abandoned, his last work; and even though fallen, by then, into a decay, the grounds were ravishing—a perfectly devised romance.

What a nice thought to restore them for the delectation of the public, after a century or more of sad neglect! How unexpected this intent in Rattler ... though it is manifest, from your dear letter, that it is not alone reverence for his ancestor that has impelled him to this jaunt. Still, no matter: if good is done, why importunately seek a motive? Tell dear Rattler, though, that whatever his purpose with the Ruins and their park, the whole effect, to be true to the initial spirit, must be of a place quite beautiful, however impregnated with a tincture of regret.

Ever your devoted Great Great aunt

Clarissa

PS Freezing up here, and wild. Never, dear child, ally yourself with an ancient Scottish family, or you'll find yourself one day, as I, in a windy dower-house set upon an ultimate crag.

April 1

'So, All Fools' Day, Aspen, and two months till our provisional opening. We must gird up our loins, my dear, and induce all our collaborators to do likewise.'

'Amen. Mr Timothy Botany arrives at any moment.'

'You're fully briefed for his enlightenment and instruction?'

'He'll steal the words out of my poor mouth: he's the prime stately impresario of our country.'

'And I must confront that human computer, Mr Leopold Watson: a nay-sayer, if ever there was one. Still: no one like him to understand how noble fantasy may be presented as solid, if alluring, finance.'

'You're pleased, Rattler, as to present progress?'

'On the Ruins front, I am, despite the predictable toils and troubles. As to our resident family ... yes, I think so, on the whole. Come May, they'll be ready to blossom on the espalier we're providing.'

'You're providing.'

'And you're tending, then. That looks like your Mr Botany. Oh—ho: chauffeur driven, and in uniform at that. Hired, would you say, to dazzle us? Go greet him.'

The driver opened the door, and even removed his cap.

'Hullo, Tim! How, with the traffic, do you always manage to be punctual?'

'By employing a driver, and paying him a bonus for being so.'

'Ingenious lad! Come, dear. Rattler's deep in high finance, and has deputed me to entertain you. Will it be warm enough in the pagoda? Let's try.'

'Well now, milady Aspen: personal things first. Are you well? Do you miss London and escorting?'

'Well and happy, if a bit anxious over Rattler's mania. Escorting I *do* miss, surprisingly. They were decorous, lonely males, chiefly, and so vulnerable to gentle flattery. Besides, I had some cherished gifts ...'

'But now stern Rattler has you under his command; and has involved you in this hare-brained project which,

I'm bound to say, will need near-miracles to get it off the turf.'

'That's why we've enlisted you, dear Tim.'

'Oh, I know: desperate remedies, and so; and God knows, I've witch-doctored some statelies far less promising. As to the Ruins here, you've three things in your favour. First—and I'm sorry to say it, for aesthetically it's the least relevant—your proximity to London and, I may add, that unspeakable factory estate. Urbanized trippers, you see, are terrified of real country, which they loathe, and reassured by the sight of concrete that's destroying it. Next, you have certainly an unusual theme, the Ruins, though I'm not sure Rattler's earlier, spookier plan wouldn't have been more promising—we'll just have to see what can be done with nostalgia and romance. Third and, in fact, foremost, there is yourselves: we must flog the mod-aristo thing for all it's worth. For example: I want every coronet and collateral you can raise down here for the opening.'

'Even Great Great Aunt Clarissa?'

'Specially her: she'll make a packet, incidentally, if she trundles down, or lets us air-lift her, for I can fix stupendous personal appearances. After all, she's one-woman stately in her own right. I can't wait to hear her telling the masses what the Kaiser said to Queen Victoria.'

'I don't think she ever met His Imperial Highness.'

'She will have, by the time I've done with her. Now— disadvantages: these are formidable, but I think, with a big splash at the right moment, and ingenuity, they can be partly overcome. First, the whole idea is a bit *dainty*, or will seem so in the suburbs. A *ruin*? I can just hear their adenoidal voices. So, following custom, we must have alluring ancillary attractions appropriate to our theme; I have ideas, and I'd be glad to hear any of your own.'

'What have *you* in mind? Perhaps a drink to fortify our souls?'

'Too early, but go ahead. Now, grub and booze: vital. I suggest we run up a railway-style châlet in ornate plastic wood, and serve the stuff in dozens of small rooms, half hidden from one another by gothic trellises and rambling vines. Each little hideaway will have its theme: Maiden's Prayer, Immured! Vain Regrets, Hope Frustrated, Foiled! and Endless Lament are one or two I've jotted down.'

'With personal service at the tables? No cosy cafeteria? Won't that alarm them, and come costly?'

'Ah, now, that's just it! The impression we must create, and moreover *sustain*, is that the Ruin just isn't for everybody: not a mere vulgar palace, or a hundred bedroom mansion, or anything as commonplace as that. Oh, no! To enter the Ruin will be a privilege: that must be our line.'

'Who will serve what in your railway châlet?'

'Girls, obviously: salaried lookers, to match the prices. I have in mind Victorian bunnies: bustles, corsets, crinolines and so.'

'The girls *will* need a bonus. And the eat and drinkables?'

'All very Victorian: b. & s., hock and seltzer, half quarterns for the vulgar. Steak-kidney-and-oyster, ortolans and sherberts ... that sort of thing. In fact, of course, it will be pork pies and pasties camouflaged and writ large; but they won't know this, and the tableware will be of unbreakable Lowestoft.'

'But the drinks *will* be authentic.'

'Oh, yeah: the s. and seltzer will permit legitimate dilution.'

'They'll come and consume all that?'

'Not at first, they may not, but they will when you've held a publicized banquet or two.'

'And who will be my guests?'

'All the habitual herd. Your lovely lot, who'll go *any*-where in my experience, hordes of cosmopolitan diplo-mats, who are the world's greatest freeloaders, the fashion people if we get the right photographers, the culture kings, though they're all a bit scruffy, and some ageing pops, if we can afford them. That sort of trash. Well? You don't seem enthusiastic.'

'Oh, but I am! I'm just thinking how I could help add to the heady brew.'

'Go ahead: ideas are money, rightly handled.'

'How about glamorous guides in the shape of tattered, but cleanly and wholesome, Street Arabs?'

'You can't trust the youth element, you know: their enthusiasm is apt to wilt, and they're so demanding, they've priced themselves out of all but the most crazy and lavish markets.'

'I think I can call on volunteers. We have some pictur-esque nubile fellows on the premises.'

'Well—up to you; but I wouldn't trust the little bas-tards further than I can see their hair-dos.'

'You sound disillusioned with the youth element.'

'No, dear. It's just that I've so recently stepped out of it.'

*   *   *

In the library, Rattler was ensconced with Leopold Watson.

'I can't see the function of such crazy cover, Captain.'

'It's not entirely cover, Mr W. I *am* devoted to this project, for personal and private reasons, and as cover goes, there's nothing like the limelight.'

'That can be overdone. Why don't you stop dickering with the factory people, since you're going to try to sell the property anyway? Then you could handle the other thing from somewhere more convenient, and safer. Scot-land's the obvious choice.'

'Next autumn, possibly. And it's not the factory folk I'm really after; my *dickering* is with developers in London who have insane notions of an upstart country club. Well, now: once we get those planning permissions in the pipe-line, that will be quite enough to stimulate their rapacity, and look on us with a more favourable eye.'

'Which developers in London? Am I allowed to know?'

'Some Japanese gentlemen, among others, are also interested: in light industry, for making electronic knick-knacks.'

'No other foreigners? No Pole?'

'Pole?'

'Or ex-Pole ...'

'What is this, Watson?'

'Nothing much ... Have you realized there'll be local opposition to all this?'

'From whom? People born round here? There are hardly any left, and the landowners among them will see the light, when they see the prospects of land values rising even higher. The conservation people are all ex-Londoners, and they don't matter, or deserve to. London is what they should have bloody well conserved: and look at what it's becoming day by day!'

'You'd better be sure you're right, then, about selling off here, because it's got you far deeper in than was estimated; and meanwhile, what you'll clear at the gates for your museum won't even be peanuts. Don't say I didn't warn you of all this.'

'Your function isn't to warn me, Watson: it's to do what you're told, and take your lavish cut.'

'I admit your retainer was generous, and in cash; also that you're a man of ideas and enterprise. But after all, Captain, I'm the professional; and as such, I must say I don't think you quite understand what business is.'

'A "professional"? "Business?" Now I'll tell you something, and listen hard. You're not a professional man of business, but an accountant, and a bent if an able one at that. As to business: what is all this mystical balls about business men being gifted with esoteric knowledge?'

'Not esoteric, perhaps, but plain...'

'Answer me this. Do some of our most experienced corporations make vital commitments to the United States, and then find they've under-costed and timed the entire deal? Do government auditors find defence contracts are grossly over-priced? Do shipbuilders blow hot and cold, and when it turns out cold, come whining for public funds as if of right? Do exporters deliver their products according to specification, and on time? And I don't mean little madcap businesses like mine, but great big enterprises stuffed with legal, technical and financial expertise? And if they don't, am I to be respectful and impressed by their performance?'

'You have a point there, Captain, in fact, you've got more than several. But there's another aspect I'd ask you please to not forget. Which is that I'm taking a chance on this, and I don't mean financial.'

'Then it depends if your greed overcomes your alarm; not to mention your scruples, if you have any.'

'Sometimes, Captain, you say things you oughtn't to.'

'Let me judge that. If I treat a shit in a shitty way, he usually merits it.'

'Meaning myself, Captain?'

'Who else? Stop provoking me, or take yourself off where you came from; you won't be hard to replace.'

'You seem to be certain of my silence.'

'Of your *silence*, Mr Leopold, one way or another, I'm absolutely certain.'

* * *

He also saw, later and discreetly, Adjutant van Nieuwen-huis.

'Do sit down, Adjutant. Forgive my French being so rusty, that I use my mother tongue.'

'French isn't mine either, Captain. I'm a Fleming, but not fanatical about it.'

'No mercenary, I suppose, can afford to waste time on tedious linguistic squabbles.'

'No—nor on mere patriotic squabbles either. We are the first true internationalists, in an hysterically national-ist age. Since technology, in its essence, is hostile to national groupings, we are the men of the future, I would say. But evidently, that doesn't help us for the present, or make us loved.'

'But you can dispense with admiration or approval.'

'We can dispense with everything except arms, loyalty of comrades and, of course, employers who deal fairly with us, and are certain what they want.'

'Precisely. To recap, then. You know where the con-signment will be from ... and the occult items it will contain?'

'As usual, I expect, from Czechoslovakia.'

'You have no objection?'

'None. Their material is excellent, its delivery discreet, and their dealings invariably correct, in my experience. I have fought for clients of the most diverse ideologies, and for those with none, but have never heard any com-plaint about Czech arms.'

'On this matter of ideology: forgive a question. You have no particular feelings, may I take it, about the vari-ous doctrines held in the six counties, and the republic?'

'My only feeling is, it is a pity men should wish to die for causes so dated and banal, but if they do so, then I am there to help them.'

'Yes, I see. Your function, then, will be, with your

assistant, to take delivery of cargo at Rotterdam, and accompany it to one of our north-western ports, where we will tell you of arrangements for trans-shipment to the six counties, or the south.'

'You cannot ship direct to Ireland, Captain?'

'Increasingly difficult; our clients prefer to use their own vessels, anyway, for the short, clandestine haul across the Irish Sea.'

'Nor air freight?'

'We've tried it, but it's ruled out now. Things are getting most military in the north.'

'So much the better for, with all respect, to me that always implies confusion.'

'Do I detect a note of disdain, Adjutant, from the mercenary to the poor old regular?'

'No, no, not disdain—sorrow, rather. For the undoubted military skills of regular soldiers are so often hampered by their inevitable bureaucracy. However: a mercenary learns not to question the conditions, but to adapt to them. And so—a question: who will be my contact in England, if anyone? Yourself, Captain?'

'No, not myself. It will be a former regular I'd like you to look at later, but only socially, since he doesn't yet know that he'll be doing this.'

'An officer?'

'Non-commissioned.'

'Ah.'

'May I ask the meaning of that "ah"?'

'I was reflecting, Captain, that if this man is to operate effectively on so delicate an assignment, then once you have told him his duties, neither you, nor any other officer, should accompany him. Excellent when on their own, British NCOs, in the presence of their officers, seem paralysed; at least, for any undertaking needing initiative and quick decisions.'

'This is not so in the Belgian army?'

'I cannot speak with authority of the Belgian army, since I was dismissed from it with ignominy after two months' service; and besides, the rank I at present hold, of adjutant, does not correspond to that of a soldier of this title in your army, who is, if I'm not mistaken, an administrative officer. The Continental adjutant is an ambiguous creature: inferior to officers, superior to other ranks, and loved by neither.'

'That was your last mercenary rank?'

'Yes: it is a convenient one, since it assures certain comforts without danger of becoming involved in desk-work, the bane even of a mercenary army. However, I might add that, except for a few commanders of outstanding talent, and a few soldiers of total depravity, ranks, in our army, were to a great extent interchangeable, and not given much importance except, of course, for pay.'

'I see the force of what you say, so far as my regular is concerned. As to a rank that is neither fish nor fowl, I fear this would never do in the British army.'

'Oh, no. Yours has a profound class structure, which has its merits, I am sure, in conventional warfare. But a mercenary army must be utterly classless, as you can imagine. This does not prevent, of course, racial snobbishness of various idiotic kinds. But so far as class goes, and nationality, we have created the dream of every fashionable philosopher, which is that of a classless, international society.'

'Quite so. But despite these manifest blessings you don't ever ... well, sometimes tire of so rootless an existence?'

'No, I do not believe I ever shall, so long as I keep my mental and physical faculties. It is perhaps hard to explain this to you, Captain. But to be able to express, in the most manifest form of violence, and by staking your very existence on the outcome, your utter contempt for governments and nations, and all their bureaucracies and hierarchies, affords an exaltation to the human spirit that I do not believe any other man, even the most committed revolutionary soldier, will ever fully experience. For us, there is no tomorrow of success or failure, since we expect nothing, except from our comrades and ourselves. We do not wish to smash one society to build another, let alone to defend any. We wish, simply, to destroy all societies. Manifestly, we will not succeed: even, as yet, make more than a fleeting impression on events. But in doing as we do, we at last feel free: our little song seems, to us, an anthem.'

'You saw service in Africa? The Near East? The Far?'

'In all such places; and now, I am glad to say, at last in Europe.'

'Ah yes: the ultimate colony, one might say.'

April 9

The Capri overtook the battered scooter; halted, as often by the wayside, the brothers battling not with the problems of repair, but with their own.

'Lift lads? Hop in.'

'We can't leave this here, Mr Rattler: it would vanish.'

'I doubt it, Mas, but why not camouflage it in the ditch, first removing one or two essential parts? A wheel, for instance?'

'You wouldn't let me drive as far as the factory estate, would you, Captain? I'd be ever so careful.'

'Alas, Kik, no; not that I mistrust your prudence or your skill ... Help your brother, lad: set him an example of initiative and responsibility.'

'Oh, he'll manage ... He likes clearing up other people's messes. It gives him a lift, a sense of superiority.'

'You're a veritable Mary, Kik, and poor Mas, a Martha.'

'Meaning?'

'Sorry ... I forgot your generation wasn't read in the good books ... Don't glower at me, boy; it was your social sense I was impugning, not your virility.'

'Your talk fascinates me, Captain. You really know what these expressions mean?'

'What of your own? When I hear you and your brother, it could, to me, be Chinese.'

'Here we go ... You'll be criticizing my clothes and hair-style next.'

'Oh no, I won't—I like them. Your picturesque abandon has a decidedly Elizabethan air. Of the stews, though, rather than the insanitary palaces. You're both heading for the Friday orgy at that alluring discothèque?'

'Why don't you come in with us and have a peep, instead of knocking it?'

'Do you know, I think I will. I feel I've been neglecting you two lads amid other preoccupations. Ah, here comes angry Mas. Pray don't slam the door, old chap, it's ingeniously self-shutting.'

The estate reared itself into anonymous perspective: not welcoming, not attractive, not even hideous, not here, not there or anywhere, particularly.

'Captain, there's just one little thing.'

'May I guess what it is? Your noble instinct to entertain is inhibited by lack of cash.'

'Do you have to be sarcastic?'

'Be fair, son; can't I purchase the right to be so?'

'That's not the attitude of a gent.'

'The remark comes oddly from your lips and is, anyway, irrelevant. I am assuredly *not* a "gentleman": a middle class concept, if ever there was one.'

'So how much do I get for taking all this crap?'

'A quid so far, only. If you turn on a particle of charm,

and stop being so tight-arsed and snooty, I might con-sider an additional sub.'

'You're in a strong bargaining position, Captain.'

'It's best to be. Here's one for you, too, Mas.'

'If you can spare it, Mr Rattler.'

'*Now* who's subjecting whom to irony? Don't you two manage to con something out of Adams, or your mother, let alone save a bit out of what I'm over-paying you for your languid labour?'

'Dad's getting very close-fisted, I'm sorry to report. Prosperity's had a bad effect on him. He even runs poor Mum on a tight rein.'

'She's always been generous with what she's got.'

'True, little brother; but she ought to be able to wheedle more.'

The Captain liked everything about the discothèque except the din.

'Care to jig around with any of the talent? I could fetch one or two lovelies over for you to examine.'

'Too kind, Kik; but I don't know the steps, and I fear I would lack allure.'

'Just shake your arse around, and leave the steps to nature. As to your greying hairs, don't worry; the *demoiselles* will sniff easy bread.'

'Mas is somewhat surprisingly adept, wouldn't you say?'

'Oh, no. He dances better than I do, because he's still at the stage of believing they come here to dance. He gets partners just like that, as well. I suppose the incipient mum in the girls explains his morbid attraction.'

'Mas *is* an attractive lad, you know.'

'You noticed that? Me too, and it makes me mildly jealous, at times. Oh, yes. Behind all those pimples and hair sprouting in the wrong spots, there lurks the makings of a winner. What's more, even the most freaked-out chicks spot the born father in him.'

'But not in you?'

'Now—come on! No, not in me. They sniff angry Mums, abortion clinics, and hopeless affiliation orders.'

'I say, you wouldn't consider it cowardice if I took off, would you? It's the perforating ear-drums, you know. The bogus-gentry pub was my original target—you wouldn't care to join me for a while?'

'You won't mind if I come back here later, and you finance the evening?'

'My dear fellow!'

'They'll let me in with this gear that costs twice theirs?'

'I'll say you're an honourable of some sort. Would you mind that so much?'

'I'll suffer in silence, and try to act the part.'

'Just be yourself; most scions of your age could be carbon copies.'

The estate pub, in the managerial sector, contrived triumphantly not to look, or even be, a pub: it seemed more a converted bank. Rattler was greeted deferentially, but with reserve; he was not, after all, of the factory élite. Kik won oblique stares that hinted he should not presume on present indulgence to return alone.

'Me, Captain? Oh, anything.'

'Really anything? One drink's just the same to you as another?'

'I'm on smoke, you know. A drink, to me, unless I'm thirsty, is just a liquid in a glass.'

'Hard to get what you want in these rural parts?'

'Easy. The factories have commonwealth contingents.'

'Perhaps we should grow it for you at the Ruin.'

'We're experimenting already, under glass. You don't mind, I hope?'

'Oh no, not really . . .'

The waiter brought a large brandy and some Malvern water.

'Bottled water—kinky! They'll soon be charging us for air and sex.'

'If they could, they would, and tax us too, I doubt not.'

'Since we're on the subject of bush, I hope you didn't mind I had a puff in your Capri. That's why I opened up the window.'

'You mustn't come the old soldier with me, Kik. I was inhaling and chewing hash when I was a subaltern; and in the London of my youth, there were all sorts of sniffs and jabs. Less publicized than now, and confined to the upper crust and dregs, like so many agreeable things.'

'No kidding. I thought all those joys came in with the Welfare era.'

'Far from it, my dear chap. In the last happy century, our freewheeling ancestors were on opium, or laudanum, of which even the most worthy persons took steady doses, when not overdoses, on the dear old family doctor's orders.'

'No stern objections to all that from Mr Gladstone?'

'On the contrary. You simply sent your footman round to the apothecary, or house-parlourmaid, as it might be. What is more, trade between India and the Far East was based on the export of the poppy, or its juices, from which many noble City fortunes were created.'

'You make my lungs itch. You wouldn't care for a puff now, out in the toilet?'

'No thanks, old bean. Alcohol in cool climates, plants and fungi in the warmer, I think's best. So tell me: how are you liking it down here?'

'Oh, my! You haven't lured me in to have a "serious conversation", have you? Never mind—you're paying, so you should get your money's worth. So—liking it. Mas does, that's obvious. He has useful things to do, and can practise his judo in the open air, flourishing his skills by hurling hefty labourers into the air. Me, I like it well enough: I even think the country life's making me a bit adult.'

'What about dear old school: have you arranged anything?'

'Not bothering: if you change address often enough, it takes the system centuries to catch up with you. That's the beauty of systems and computers, which are intended for the well-behaved. The anti-social lot just throw them.'

'Why more "adult", my dear Kik?'

'I can tell you, if you don't laugh. Apart from Mum, and Grandad if you count him, I've never really associated with any—I mean intimately, not like with teachers, and fuzz, and parasites like that. But here, we have Mum, Dad, you, Aspen, and all your bevies of collaborators. It's a real senior scene. And the curious effect, I find, is that the more you *do* associate freely with the older lot, the more independent you become of them; I mean, you don't have to rebel so much, as you do when they're just hanging over you impersonally, like a swarm of vultures.'

'Your mother has seemed to me more relaxed, as well.'

'Wrong word, I think: "herself" is what I'd say—doing a thing of her own, at last. It's a paradox that's not so flattering to Dad. Anyway, she's all for it; here for keeps, she's still affectionate and all that, but more beginning to think a bit of Evie. High time, I'd say. Of course, I needn't tell you that your bread makes quite a difference in that respect.'

'But she's still fond of your father.'

'Oh yes, and always will be, I dare say ... Women are creatures of habit, don't you think—or am I wrong? There is this, though. She comes in here quite a lot, on honest errands I'm sure, but she's making connections among the classier factory ladies. Also, she shoots up to town from time to time, ostensibly to see Grandad. I think she's branching out, in fact; but I don't think I need fear she'll ever threaten me with a step-father.'

'Soldier certainly wouldn't care for that idea.'

'Oh no, not he. Dad likes stability, you know—all soldiers do. They're curious people, really. They fly about everywhere shooting everyone up the arse and creating mayhem, while what they really long for is a cosy cot among the folks that live on the hill.'

'And how do you find you all get on with Aspen?'

'Ah—Aspen: that's another case and a half, isn't it; a mysterious one. *You* should really clue me up, not me try to tell you.'

'Believe me, though so close to her in so many ways, even I cannot always fathom her.'

'Oh, no? Well, as to the Adams family, Mas admires her in a dog-like sort of way, I think she's great but mean nothing to her because she's seen my kind before, Dad gets horny at the sight of her but is far too respectful, or indoctrinated, take your pick, ever to do much about it, and Mum ... well, Mum, for I expect no real reason, other than that Aspen is younger and classier, though not, I'd say, all that more beautiful, but, anyway, round about the premises ...'

'Draw breath, Kik.'

'... Yeah ... Mum feels slight pangs of jealousy, if jealousy can ever be slight. Not, of course, that her reason tells her there's any cause to be, for whatever she may think of Aspen, she does know Dad: I mean, his limitations. Will that do for a run-down, or would you like me to tell you what we all think about you?'

'You'd best let me find out for myself, you know.'

'Okay, if you can. All right if I pull out now? I mean, have I earned my keep?'

'Finish your Malvern water, lad. I have just one more question.'

'I say, you ex-soldiers can't kick the habit, can you? You just do like ordering the serfs around.'

'I'll tell you a secret, son. No commander, however good, can ever order any soldier, even the worst, to do *any*-thing effectively, unless the soldier really wants to.'

'No kidding.'

'None: not in battle, anyway. The trouble about civilians, if you're interested, which I doubt, because no civilian I've ever met *is* interested in the army ... the trouble is, you judge soldiers by those splendid balletic performances we put on for you periodically on the Horse Guards' Parade. Officers yelling, and automatons wheel-ing, isn't that how you see it? There is, of course, a con-nection between ceremonial and battle, but rather too complex for me to go into now: that is, unless you've got an hour or two to spare. But as for combat, you must, if you want to persuade men to risk death or wounding, ensure, somehow, that they want to take this risk. And if you think ordering them about, in itself, achieves that, well, my dear young civilian, I can only promise you you're wrong.'

'I'll have to take your word for it, Captain, won't I?'

'Or not, as you prefer. However, spare me your scorn a moment, and hearken to this: bearing in mind that you've got, with luck, fifty years ahead of you to play with, to find out whether what I'm saying is false or true. His-torical accidents assure, in a freakish way, that certain nations, for exceptional periods, are islands of relative peace in seas of conflict. Such is the fortunate state of England now—if we manage to forget Ireland, part of which is a reluctant portion of the United Kingdom—a reluctance shared by both parties to their quarrel, I may say. However: the rest of the country has a pacific appear-ance and mentality, despite the six counties, let alone a world which demonstrates that nowhere—not even, these days, the remotest coral atoll—is exempt from the eruption of sudden danger. So: what I am trying to whisper into your incredulous ear is this. One way or another, all young men should learn to fight; and I don't mean in amateur gangs at football matches. And if so, it follows that they're possibly foolish to sneer at those who have come to understand their epoch.'

'Well said, sir; but let me tell you something—do you mind? If my generation ever fights, it will be in a civil struggle of their own choosing, and never as conscripts ordered about by folk like you.'

'My dear chap: what is the difference? What "civil struggle of their own choosing" has ever ended up as other than conscripts ordered about by bullies far worse than I?'

'You should be giving Mas this line—he'd lap it up.'

'Has it ever occurred to you that your innocent young brother might be the greater realist of you two? And has it, either, that a temperament like yours would relish soldiering enormously—in time of war, I hasten to add, which is of course when soldiering really begins? And as for ordering anyone about, would you mind my saying I can see you enjoying it far more than your brother, or your father, even? Or even than I myself who, as a matter of fact, found it tiresome, since by nature I like to persuade, and not to command?'

'You're too good to be true, Captain—you really are. Still, I can't help liking you, as they say. Though liking doesn't mean trusting, I needn't remind you.'

'What's so untrustworthy about me, Kik?'

'Just about everything, if you want it straight. In the first place, what *are* you up to with this phoney ruin, and having all those odd-bod weirdos down here? Not my business, you may say, but I'm genuinely perplexed.'

'Is that all?'

'No, it's not all. Here it is, Captain, since you asked for it. I'm not an admirer of the working class, and believe if you come right out of it, as I do, the thing to do is keep coming out as fast and as far as you can. I mean: two thirds of the population, if not three quarters, and we're still perpetually fucked about. However, there's also this —two things, in fact. When I look at the other classes, about whom I may know more than you think, because I've taken the trouble to get around, I find them odious: detestable, and that goes for your fancy lot as well. I would willingly—but willingly, and I do mean it— slaughter every fucking one of them, except perhaps for a few chicks, if I thought I could get away with it. So: to move on from there. I believe this feeling's far more general than you may suppose; or know even—how could you? I mean, among our crummy, usually obedient lot. And that feeling isn't based only on resentment, as all you luckier ones believe and constantly remind us, but on a deep belief that we're the tops—more practical, more honest, not to mention sexier, than any other toplofty group. Also on a feeling that we rarely express, and even more rarely act on, and which I wouldn't be telling you if I wasn't stoned, and in any case rather feel like it, that one of these fucking days we're going to make it where you are, and stick there.'

'If so, you will become us; or any of you who "make it" to the top.'

'Yes? But wouldn't it be worth taking a chance on that misfortune, don't you think? I mean: if only just to see?'

'Up to you, then. In your place, I'd consider it a pushover. But I'm not in your place, and so...'

'And so, for one thing, you don't really *know*. And for another, we can only go up, but where can you go?'

'Oh—me? I expect I'll still be around in some form or another...'

The sun blinked dubiously on the swimming pool: the climate wasn't spring, but the shoots and blossoms were, and early birds. As if two figures in an impressionistic sequence of an otherwise gruesome film, Evie and Aspen, both in dressing-gowns, approached the water from the ruin and villa.

'You an early bird as well, Evie?'

'Always have been; first, out of sense of duty, later on, because I grew to like it.'

'In each twenty-four hours, there are only two bad patches, don't you think? Between two and four at either end are terrible. Hot countries solve the problem by a late night, so no insomnia, and a later siesta.'

'Lucky people; a sleep after dinner seems immoral, somehow, here.'

'We wouldn't like it, even with the climate right. We're a puritan people, after all.'

'With all this sex talk going on, you'd say so?'

'The perfect proof: only a puritan people could have the subject so much in the brain.'

'So you don't think, these days, they're right to say we're more permissive.'

'How I mistrust that word! "Permissive" in relation to what other era, may I ask? In my not-at-all-humble opinion, the upper classes were always "permissive", and didn't give a damn about it, provided only themselves and their servants knew. The middle class males, behind, or beneath, a stupendous front of decorum, to preserve which must have driven them almost out of their minds, knew a hell of a lot about child harlots, fallen nursemaids, weird addresses around Long Acre, and clandestine forays to the Continent. As to the working class—well, you tell me;

but I'll be surprised if you say that they weren't "permissive".'

'We usually had little choice about it, did we? Try living six in a room of mixed generations and sexes, and "going into service", or "going for a soldier", and you'd discover. But I think we were more understanding, more forgiving, and certainly less complicated about it all.'

'Well, then. Isn't the chief difference that people now, on the whole are franker? Even the middle lot or, at any rate, their younger generations? But the only trouble about that is, they don't seem able to relax their earlier hang-ups without making a terrible song and dance about it. Between clandestine forays to Long Acre, and a "frank and fearless" show today in Shaftesbury Avenue, I can't really see much difference.'

'Yeah. I'll tell you one thing we might agree about, though: the women of any bloody class got the raw deal, and still do.'

'Silly old us—of course! It's not for nothing there are con men, and no con women.'

'Even so, it's all a bit easier, isn't it, if you've got money and education?'

'The con is more polite, that's all. Those men who so admire your educated independence, and really only want your cunt.'

'Aspen!'

'Pussy, then.'

'That's better.'

'Well, I've seen enough of them in my young life. So many of them don't love women at all, don't even *like* them, come to that—they're just crazy about their own sweet stupid selves.'

'But that hasn't put you off it altogether?'

'Of course not, how could anything? I mean any misfortune due, after all, to my own bad judgement? Oh, no.

Sex is all right, it's a kind of truth, there's no kidding about it, and it's ultimately the only way to understand anyone. But I think for sex to mean much, there's got to be a bit of heart in it—more than a bit, in fact. Or at the very least, a bit of honest lust. But not just—my God!—"affairs".'

'Well, I might agree with that. Trouble is this: unless you're fucking lucky at the outset, you have to find out by hard experience.'

'Just so, unfortunately. Though even "experience" is much over-rated, I believe. I suppose if the search for it is prompted by hope, by desperation even, then it can be worth it, if you happen on the fellow in the end. But as for "experience" in the sense of shopping around and learning tricks ... well, I don't think that gets you anywhere much, except to further fruitless shopping.'

'Do you think men are more realistic about all this, as they make out?'

'No, I think we're both distorted and deluded, but that they're rather more so. I think women are better at sensing there's something wrong, if there is, even when they don't know how to put it right.'

'We're more honest?'

'No, I don't think we're particularly honest; just a bit more truthful with ourselves, even if it gives us pain. I don't believe it's a virtue in us, specially, but just that the facts about our beautiful bodies are just so damn obvious and important that they give us a closer grip on hard reality.'

'I've often thought, though, it's not all that easy for the boys ... You haven't sons, have you; but I can't help thinking of my Mas and his little problems...'

'True enough; and men change as well in a highly sensational way, and very pretty it is as we all know. But that sort of transformation seems to work more on their imaginations than their grip of fact: so that unless they're highly intelligent, or just plain nice, it can make them arrogant, or else dreamy, sometimes both. But I don't think it makes them realists, as our little adventures do each twenty-eight days, or if we find we're pregnant.'

'You've evidently thought a lot about all this.'

'Well, haven't you?'

'Oh yes—I have. And if you want my conclusion on the matter, it's that there's nothing—nothing whatever—men can do that we can't, given the proper opportunity. No job, I mean—I'm not speaking of sex. Nor anything, I'd say, we can do that they can't, really, if they wanted to. Myself, when I hear "men are this", and "women are that", I'm instantly suspicious: because what they really mean is "we like being this, and want to make you do that".'

'My own un-favourite male remark is when they praise us for our "intuition"; which is their polite way of saying they think we've got no brains. "Intuition", indeed! Men, or women, are, or aren't, intuitive, that's all, just as they either have, or haven't, brains. What it amounts to, really, is that childbirth is the only true distinction; and, of course, how we each behave in that old bed.'

'I wouldn't say I've worked out such extensive theories.'

'Oh dear, I'm sorry they sound like "theories"—they're just conclusions I've picked up on the way as a consequence, usually, of disasters.'

'But that's just it: I'm almost twice your age, but I haven't got half your experience.'

'Here we come, back to "experience" again! Isn't most "experience" just a name for getting it wrong again, whatever it is, when you might have got it right much earlier, or even at the first attempt?'

'What I mean is ... well, as a matter of fact, the only experience I've had is Soldier.'

'And you regret that? I mean, you love him, don't you?'

'Oh, yes. But I sometimes think it does seem ignorant to have reached the age of thirty-four, and known nothing between daft virginity and one man.'

'"Ignorant" of what? If he's right for you, and you for him, I truly can't see you've missed anything much that matters; except, of course—and I do see it's a large "except"—his having been away from you so long.'

'Yes, but even so: I sometimes feel I just don't know anything much about all that.'

'What is there to "know". It's a prick and a pussy, basically, always, isn't it? If they match up, and the feelings do, what else is there? I mean, Evie: You *like* him, don't you?'

'Oh, yes. Do you?'

'Like Soldier?'

'Yeah: "like Soldier". Do you?'

'Fancy him for a fuck, do you mean? If I say no, you may think I'm also saying I don't admire and like him, which I damn well do.'

'Okay, okay ... I just thought I'd ask you. That's all...'

'Then you have the answer: which it's up to you to believe or not, because I can't do much about *that.*'

'No need to get shirty.'

'Well, I am, a bit, quite frankly. Sorry, and all that...'

'Oh, it's all right ... I raised the question, and I got my reply, didn't I? It's just that, well, among other things that came into my mind, here you are, living down here in the same house as Mr Rattler, yet you don't seem, unless I'm wrong, to be interested in him in that sort of way at all; which made me wonder if you might not be in Soldier.'

'Evie, dear: do I have to have a lover just at present? I mean, I can't take a little holiday from all that, can I, without arousing dark suspicions?'

'Oh, I'm not suspicious, I'm just nosy, I suppose. I mean take us: Soldier and me; I wouldn't say we're ordinary, but we're usual, more or less. But you and Mr Rattler—well, that *is* a bit unusual.'

'I see that. But "I and Mr Rattler", or "I and Soldier Adams" don't mean anything like that. Rattler's an old, a close connection since I can remember, we know a lot about each other, and are very near; that's about as far as I can go to explain my relationship with that exceedingly odd person.'

'Now, he *is* unusual, I'd say.'

'And you'd be right. However, despite my loyalty to him which comes first always, and which I can't do anything about, I should tell you, perhaps ... and Soldier, who knows him well, in a different way, would bear me out, I think ... I should tell you he's a rather dodgy person.'

'Sounds exciting.'

'Dodgy people often are.'

'Oh, yes? And tell me this, then. All he's supposed to be doing for Soldier and the kids, is dodgy too, or on the up and up?'

'Even his gifts are apt to turn out ... well, conditional ... With him one has to be rather on one's guard. He's apt to give a lot, and then you find that there's a price.'

'I do?'

'Anyone might. His gifts are genuine, but they often have repercussions, complications. So, I'd say—be aware of this: I mean, more aware than I think Soldier can.'

'Because Soldier's over-trusting?'

'Because Soldier's a man, and we've decided which sex is wiser, haven't we? Or thinks it is?'

Rattler received the junior military historian, who came to him as something of a surprise: seeking witness material for his mammoth *Retreat from East Africa*, in preparation for which he had already interviewed five hundred participants of both races.

'Ah, Mr Venture, this is indeed an honour! Most certainly your name is known to me: for which of us soldiers of the egghead sort hasn't studied, to our advantage, your *Singapore*!? Yes, I can assure you the name and fame of Elwyn Venture were well known in the sultrier messes.'

'Too kind, Colonel; and dare I guess you thought "who does this civilian whippersnapper think he is"?'

'By no means! You want to test me out? Well, then! Ask me any question you like about your prior study! You'll find I know my sacred texts!'

'May I take your word for it, Colonel, and ask you about Kenya?'

'By all means! But first of all, let's have a drink to refresh my memory; and allow me to ask you, too, how you came to embrace this calling. And by the way: a small point of punctilio: I was an acting Lt-Colonel, retired with the established rank of Captain, and am now, though doubtless a military aura still hangs faintly round me, a mere mister like us all.'

'May I stick, at least, to "Captain", all the same? It's how I still visualize you, at the time of your exploits there.'

'If you insist. Now tell me: what is it that so fascinates you younger academics about our deeds of deering-do? For in truth, you have erupted of late in such scholarly profusion, that it's almost as if, by some subtle process of compensation, as our actual forces shrink, our military historians multiply.'

'That may be the explanation, Captain, as you say; for disaster may well attract historians more than success. As an example: could one visualize someone writing *The Rise and Apogee of the Roman Empire*?'

'Only with horror. It may also, of course, be that, for historians of the contemporary scene, a phenomenon on the wax, so to speak, is harder to define, since no one knows where it's heading to; whereas one on the wane has written its own final pages.'

'Yes, quite so. I found that factor a great help with my *Singapore!*'

'Did you indeed! Now tell me, kindly, further. A historian is, obviously, a historian, while a soldier's a soldier, a king a king, a pope a pope, and so on and so forth. But isn't it somewhat difficult for the modest scholar to wage battles, behead kings, and defy popes, even in imagination? Pray do not take my question amiss: but though a soldier of sorts, I confess I'd find it impossible to put myself in Napoleon's boots, let alone Caesar's sandals.'

'That is a difficulty, of course; the military historian of direct experience has a decided advantage, as is proved by the expertise of Liddell Hart or Fuller. However, perhaps one might say of both, that their real fame derives from subjecting themselves to the second discipline of a historian.'

'But that would scarcely apply to a writer like Caesar himself, would it, not to mention Charles de Gaulle? And what about Leon Trotsky, my own favourite generalissimo?'

'To that I can only rejoin, Captain, that one makes the best use of whatever knowledge and experience one may have acquired; which is one of my reasons for coming to visit you.'

'Yes, yes, I see the force of that. But could I, further, ask you this? Whenever I read, as I fairly frequently do, a contemporary history written by anyone who was not himself a participant or, at least, an eye-witness, I have the curious impression that he thinks whatever did happen, *must* have happened, just because it in fact did. In other words, when he rebukes this commander for this error, and that one for some other blunder, it's not so much because there *was* a blunder or error, as because the historian knows, in advance, what will subsequently occur. Do I make myself clear?'

'Oh, yes—indeed.'

'Whereas what strikes anyone most about a battle, I would say, and a strategic manoeuvre even more so, is that no one has the faintest bloody idea *what's* going to happen.'

'Your point is well taken, Captain. But what, after all, granted he *does* know, is the historian to do?'

'Perhaps not be so bloody snooty in his recital. I hasten to add I speak impersonally.'

'There is perhaps, in some cases, a fault of arrogance; of being over-wise about the fore-known event.'

'I should say there fucking well is! Another drink, Mr Venture?'

'Oh—thanks.'

'However, to proceed. When it comes to a history of the past, then we're all very much in the same boat, aren't we? I mean: despite all the historical bits and pieces, no one really knows, do they, what the battle of Waterloo was like?'

'Not exactly, obviously. One just has to try to put the bits and pieces together as best one can.'

'I see: so that ultimately, there's a large element of guesswork.'

'Of assessment, I would say; based on the documentary evidence.'

'But Mr Venture! Has it ever struck you that "documentary evidence" is so much crap?'

'It certainly hasn't. Why?'

'Why? Well, now. Forgive this personal question, but have you ever written an honest letter in your life?'

'But Captain!'

'Well—have you? Because I know I haven't. Every single letter I've written since I could put pen, or pencil, to paper, whether military, amatory, commercial or whatever, has been nothing more than a plausible presentation of a personal point of view.'

'One must, of course, seek to make the necessary adjustments for that factor.'

'I should think so, indeed! "Darling, I love you." Have you ever written that?'

'That sort of thing—yes.'

'And meant it?'

'Sometimes.'

'I see. And when you look up the files, and see I wrote "the enemy were repelled with severe losses", what would you decide *that* meant? It might in fact mean we didn't even see the buggers.'

'I take your word for it, sir.'

'You'd better. However: this all does lead somewhere—I mean my train of thought—even though it might not yet appear to. And where it leads me to, is to ask you another question, if I may, which is: why are historians so quarrelsome?'

'Aren't all professional men? Isn't it an indication that their subject matters to them?'

'But my dear fellow! I don't know any profession that quarrels like children as historical scholars do. And isn't the reason for it obvious? They just don't know, and they have to pretend they do. And the less sure they are, the shriller become their bickering scholastic voices.'

135

'I hope I haven't offended in that respect, Captain.'

'Not to me, you haven't. To your colleagues, it's doubtless another matter. Very well, then. Where's all that got us? Drink?'

'No thank you.'

'I'll tell you where. Historians are frustrated novelists. Since they lack the imagination to create characters, they make use of what they suppose to be the natures of real ones.'

'That's certainly a point of view, Captain.'

'Isn't it just! But wouldn't you say there's something ludicrous about such an activity?'

'Captain—be fair! Of course scholars have their comical aspect. Hasn't every satirist loved to portray pedants? But are we, as a profession, alone in being sometimes risible?'

'No, but you don't get shot up the arse if you make a mistake.'

'But we *are* sometimes subjected to verbal violence, Captain.'

'I'm not surprised. So, now then—this interview. Dare I hope you don't have a tape-recorder?'

'Of course not.'

'That's something. And could I beseech you, when you come to indict your final verdict on us all, to avoid any use of the word "crusade"?'

'I wouldn't dream of it.'

'Good. Unless, of course, you were referring back to the bloodthirsty plunder of the real ones. And you won't refer to my gallant troops as "boys"?'

'Captain! I'm just not that kind of writer!'

'I should hope not. "Boys", indeed! Boys don't drench one another in napalm, do they?'

'No, but some of them doubtless would if they knew how ...'

'True enough. Well, then: what can I tell you?'

The boys returned with their father drunk and bloodied; Kik driving his Dad's car, and Mas alarmed, but trying to be reassuring. Evie was frightened too, and wondered if she was ageing.

'Haven't seen anything like this since his private soldier days. What happened?'

'Little Mas heard a commotion over at the boozer, arrived to find two fellers being flung out on their ears, and one of them was you know who. So he fetched me, and I piled Dad into his heap.'

'Yes: but what *happened*?'

'Mum, how should I know? Saturday's a bad night at the estate. Friday is our night, but Saturday the senior soaks emerge. Perhaps Dad met an old comrade, and they got patriotic, and tangled with some Irishmen or colonials.'

'It wasn't one of your gang that had a go at him?'

'Who's ever seen any of us in that friendly inn? Besides, we're all barred there.'

'Well, I'd better go and sit by him, while he sleeps it off.'

'That's it, Mum. The wifely touch.'

'And don't you be fresh, or you'll get a clip over the earhole too.'

'Just hearken to that! I rescue Dad, bring him back to base intact, and look at the reward I get.'

'You didn't rescue him. It was me that fought the other fellers off.'

'Sure, Mas, but you had to fetch your brother Kik to help you. Why didn't you sail in on your own?'

'Now, don't you two start. Clear up this mess, and keep your voices down.'

Soldier had risen, made himself some tea, and was

lying back on the couch holding, but not drinking it. Bandaged and battered, he did look an old soldier.

'How you feeling?'

'Fucked.'

'You don't surprise me. Those lumps and bumps hurting?'

'Throbbing. Other heads are going to be, too. I'll be back next week to sort them out.'

'You will? So long as you don't try tonight.'

'I would have done, six months ago. That's what worries me a bit.'

'You're not in the Crater now, Soldier, you're not the greenhorn who used to get into this sort of thing when I first knew you, and you're trying to get settled into a civvie job.'

'In other words, I'm getting older.'

'We both are. You haven't noticed?'

'I've noticed just the opposite: you're getting younger.'

'I wish I felt it, then.'

'I think you do.'

'Let me make you some more tea.'

'A drink would be a better idea.'

'That sensible, you think? I'll get you one.'

The phone rang, a private line to the Ruin, which, though convenient, seemed somewhat to Evie like bells jangling in the servants' hall.

'Oh no, Aspen, he's okay. Yes, just a bit sore, that's all, when he fell over. I expect you saw the boys bringing him in, did you? No, nothing to worry about, really. So long. She was fretting about you, Soldier. Suggested she might come over. Should I have told her to?'

'No.'

'What did go on down there at that pub, Soldier?'

'What did was what always does when you get into a fight, which is it wasn't the feller you're quarrelling with who

138

upset you, but something or other disturbing inside your-self.'

'And what's getting into you?'

'I want to cut out of here, and get back to Kilburn.'

'Well, not Kilburn—not that, at any rate.'

'Somewhere else, then. Up north where I belong, or we might emigrate.'

'Is all this the booze, or the knock on the head, or is it you?'

'Me. It's been bubbling up inside me for quite a while.'

'Okay, what is it that's eating you, then?'

'The job, and this whole place are fakes; I don't mind that, but they're fakes I can't understand. And you've got into your head I'm chasing Aspen.'

'Have I? And have you got into yours that Rattler's after me? Or me after him, or any other complica-tion?'

'We're out of our depth here, Evie. These people don't think, or feel, like us at all.'

'Why should we expect them to? And is that a reason for running away from them?'

'Go and fetch him, Evie.'

'Fetch who?'

'Rattler. I want to talk to him.'

'When you're pissed, and your head's cracked open?'

'He's seen me like that often enough before ... Get him over here.'

'All right, if you feel like that, I'll ring him.'

'No—fetch him over.'

'What's wrong with the phone? I don't like to leave you.'

'I don't want anyone else to know.'

'And that means Aspen.'

'That means I want to talk it over, soldier to soldier, with the Captain.'

' "Soldier to soldier": you still stuck with that? I dunno . . .'

She took a torch for the alley through the trees. At the Ruins it focused on Rattler's feet, who was standing waiting.

'I thought you might come along. I mean, I heard the news, and fancied you might want to see me privately.'

'It's Soldier who wants to see you.'

'But you did want me too, didn't you? Let me take your arm.'

'It's not me that needs steadying, it's Soldier.'

'Ah, but the torch! Dangerous, really, a bright light in the gloom. See further when your eyes adjust to darkness. Stand still a minute, and soon the night's as clear as day.'

'Not to me, it's not.'

'Relax and adjust, and I think you'll find it is. There! Shall we take a step or two? You see your way clearer now?'

'I don't about what to do with Soldier. He's suddenly speaking of wanting to leave here.'

'No! Well, perhaps it's not unexpected. Just halt a minute, Evie—excuse the military word. We must find out what's upset him. Could it be, perhaps, in some way, Aspen?'

'I think there's a bit of that at the back of it. I think that's why, with him looking so undignified, he doesn't want her near just now.'

'Dear me! And *you* think there's any justification for what you suppose?'

'I don't expect so; but one never knows.'

'No, does one? Let's see! He doesn't imagine there's anything to foot, though, does he, between you, my dear, and me?'

'It's just that he's in a dubious state of mind.'

'But there isn't, is there, any ground for us to have such

140

a suspicion? Put it this way: quite evidently you're a handsome woman, and he knows it, and that I and every man of judgement's bound to think the same. But that's no grounds for his feeling I desire you?'

'That you what?'

'Desire you, my dear, and that you reciprocate? *That* thought couldn't perplex him, could it? I mean, has he any cause to imply we feel like that?'

'Certainly, up till now, he hasn't...'

'Up till now—exactly! Our conduct has been above reproach. No word has passed to express any other feeling.'

'No.'

'So, you see! It's fanciful! His thoughts are running away with him! But ours are not. Did you say something?'

'Oh, no...'

'The wind, the night noises ... I must try to sort out Soldier, dearest, if I can. But it's difficult: there are things he just doesn't understand. Choices: alternatives: grave decisions. That doesn't mean, of course, that you can't see all this. You see the world in simple terms, I think.'

'Did you say "dearest" to me?'

'I'm under the stress of some emotion. Soldier, in a way, is my only friend. My feelings are involved in all this, believe me.'

'Well, your friend's waiting for you in here. I'd best leave you two soldiers to yourselves.'

'Exactly! There are secret intimacies between each and every one of us, however closely we are attached to others. Would you agree?'

'Oh yes, there are, at times ... I'll go round the back door.'

'Right! Thanks for this chat, Evie. You've made things much clearer in my mind.'

'Have I? I don't know that I said much.'

'Ah, no, but your attitude was sympathetic to our

problems. Understanding. Well, now: on parade I go!'

Soldier was sitting up, in a sergeant-confronting-officer posture.

'Evening, Captain. Thanks for coming over. So this is it. I'm leaving.'

'All right, then, Adams.'

'It hasn't turned out as I expected, or I hoped, and doubtless I'm in part to blame.'

'No question of blame. This isn't the army any longer, Soldier, so I can't come "orders are orders" at you. Not that I would, anyway. Not that I did much, ever.'

'No. You made use of your persuasive powers, and don't I know it.'

'One does one's best. All right then—leave whenever you wish. We'll sort out the material aspects in the morning.'

'Of course, I can see what you're doing. You're trying to make me feel I'm letting you down.'

'Is it I who feel that most, Soldier?'

'There you go ... Rattler! I want out! This place disturbs me.'

'Mind if I have a drop? All right—I'll tell you. It *is* disturbing. Because what I'm up to here is very naughty. I dare say, being who you are, you've guessed it.'

'You've got an arms fiddle of some kind going on. Ireland, is it? Or is it further afield? Or here?'

'It's a fucking big fiddle, anyway, and I'll end up rich or in a fast plane out.'

'Or in the nick.'

'Or shot. Could be—they're those sort of people.'

'And you're doing all this for money?'

'What else?'

'You're not, you know. It's never interested you, except for spending. Other ranks get to know which officers are gentlemanly looters.'

'I see. So what am I after?'

'Influence, I expect ... And that's just what's disturbing me.'

'Nothing else?'

'Not really.'

'You think I'm aiming to be an Adolf Hitler?'

'No. The man behind him.'

'Hitler didn't have anyone behind him, or not for long. He beat them all.'

'An English-type manipulator, then. Your class used to be good at that, till recently.'

'My "class". You've been listening to Evie.'

'What's wrong with listening to her? I usually do ...'

'Nothing. But what I mean is, I just can't feel you personally object to anything I have in mind.'

'I do to this extent. If your plans, whatever they are, succeed at all, then you collect. If they fail, you've said it: you hare off to the Bahamas. And where does that leave me?'

'An officer's first duty is to his men.'

'Shit to that. Anyway, we're civvies.'

'Soldier: in my world, I come first. Then Aspen. Then you. Do you believe this?'

'In a sort of a way, I do ... I think you imagine *you* do, I'll give you that ...'

'Come right in with me, then. Let me tell you all I haven't yet, and see if you're attracted. Because I haven't asked you down here just to manage a fun-fair.'

'I guessed you had some other motive ... You haven't any further little plans for my future, have you?'

'Oh, no. Come in with me on this, when you see what it is, and it's shit or bust together, as you gents used to say.'

'Is Evie supposed to know about what you'll be up to? If so, I think you'll run into opposition.'

'She's too intelligent not to find out for herself, but I have hopes of winning her over.'

'How?'

'By showing her where her interest lies: in you.'

'And not in you?'

'In what way, Adams?'

'You know what way ...'

'Can I have this straight from you, Soldier? Are you implying I might try to seduce your wife?'

'I'm just asking you. And don't quote "officers never touch rankers' women" at me.'

'The answer's no. That satisfy you?'

'It'll have to, if I agree to stay ...'

'You already have.'

'Oh, have I?'

'If you hadn't, we'd not be having this discussion.'

'No—perhaps. Something else. Does Aspen know about your plans?'

'About some of them, she does: not others.'

'And she backs you, I suppose?'

'She opposes me in everything, and never judges me, or abandons me.'

April 19

This time, the military philosopher visited Rattler: a man of sterner metal than the historian, besides being a regular of medium field rank. Too open an expression of his notions had earned him a posting from active duties to a staff college, where it was thought his unorthodox views would matter less.

'Rattler, we won't forgive you! Deserting us at a time when the army needs its liveliest brains!'

'Colonel Peterson, sir, all I can say in my defence is

once a soldier, always one. But as a thinker, since you kindly allow I was one, I had one fatal defect—I never was quite able to hide it, try as I did. I kept interrupting even generals' gossip to talk of inappropriate whys and wherefores.'

'Ah—generals! What does happen to them all when they get a division, let alone a corps or army! Do you think we'd become as stereotyped if so promoted?'

'From what I hear, Colonel, you're in small danger, as yet. You appear to have managed to convince your superiors you're "too clever by half"—fatal words they use of anyone they fear might rock their comfortably leaking boat.'

'The rank and posting suit me for the moment: for in the present social context, this is the planning period *par excellence*. An officer of really senior rank would be too old, and hidebound, when the times are ripe.'

'They're ripening, you'd say?'

'Well—yes, I would; and the critical factor is, as it so often has been, Ireland. For centuries, that's where the plots and plans were hatched: from Leicester's expedition, to the Curragh. In the past, they always failed because the army in Ireland was, precisely, expeditionary. But soon we'll be reaching the point when the chief base of our forces will be there, or at any rate, the chief operative base, for the Rhine army's becoming, by comparison, a vast leave camp. Furthermore, by virtue of Ulster being, legally at least, a portion of the United Kingdom, the force stationed in the six counties is no longer expeditionary at all, but, technically at least, home based.'

'And this base will increase in size there or, at any rate, continue to exist?'

'Most probably; but it will at all events have served its purpose as a pilot project, a living war game, so to speak. From the point of view of the public's attitude to soldiers,

I'd say we have not been more admired since forty-four or 'five. The colonial disengagements, painful as they were for us, since the politicians surrendered our bastions even in the midst of battle, made little impression, really, on the public: Malaya, Borneo, Kenya, Cyprus—those operations bored them, I would say. True, we had a week's popularity at Suez, but once again, with incredible ineptitude, the politicians, having launched us on a venture whose implications they failed utterly to understand, with anguished cries obliged us to withdraw from it at the very moment when success awaited us. But Ireland is something different: the public impression is, we are guarding, at last, its hearth and home; or at any rate, the hearth and home next door.

'As for our soldiers over there, the training, and experience, have been salutary. To fight colonial peoples, even when in retreat, was part of a venerable tradition. True, the conditions, politically, had altered greatly: fuzzy-wuzzies were replaced by gents in spectacles, with excellent Chinese and East European contacts. But they were still, after all, to our soldiers, natives. It is also true that since operations in Ireland are more traditional, even, since far older, than any elsewhere overseas, these also seem, to our squaddies something vaguely habitual. Nor do they deem the inhabitants of either culture in the North, if not precisely to be natives in the colonial sense, to be other than "them", and certainly not "us". All the same, in Ireland there is an enormous difference. The battle is moving nearer home and doing so at the very moment when the traditional pattern of colonial warfare has seemed to have concluded. In other words, what was bound to happen, has, or is beginning to: the last battles of a decaying imperialism are likely, if not certain, to be fought at its very point of origin.'

'It's just as well, Colonel, from your point of view, that

146

we've been eccentric enough, among all European peoples, to rely on a regular army.'

'Oh yes, certainly; and it remains mysterious to me that politicians did not foresee what was likely to ensue ... except, of course, that, compared with Continental countries, we have, by ancient atavism, a revulsion against conscript armies in times of peace. But *are* these "times of peace", or have they been so since the end of World War II? I think not. However: be that as it may, a regular army suits our purpose best. Of course, all armies are, in a sense, political; and a conscript army can, in a time of crisis, be particularly so. Witness the collapse of the Russian, German and, almost, French and Italian armies in World War I. Witness, in recent years, the refusal of French conscripts to serve the purposes of their generals in Algeria, or the shattered morale of American forces in Vietnam. However, about conscript armies, there is this important factor, which is that when their activities become political, these are usually in the sense of laying down their arms, and saying "no". Although, of course, since even in conscript armies, the cadres are invariably regulars, this political negativism of the conscripts can usually be itself negated: counter-intelligence, battle police and so forth see to that.'

'Your analysis would surely not apply, though, to a revolutionary conscript army: consider those of France after 'eighty-nine, or of the Soviets, and China, in our day.'

'Very true: in an authentic revolutionary situation, conscripts show brilliant initiative, and fight like cats. But is that what we are considering in England? Is it not its opposite, rather? Are there, objectively, any real signs of a revolutionary situation here? And are there not many of events moving in a contrary direction? Events to which we may hope to give a more than gentle push?'

'You know I think so, Colonel. Which is one of the

reasons why I left the army, in order to participate more effectively in these developments, according to my modest lights.'

'Quite so: the liaison between soldiers and reliable political figures—I won't call them mere politicians—will be vital. And that's why a regular army is a godsend. For if less ideological than a conscript force, it can, in a political vacuum such as exists increasingly at present, be more effectively used, because of its disciplines, by those whose political purposes are clear. And these will be its habitual leaders, or the more determined of them.'

'You do not visualize, though, anything as clumsy as the Greek colonels' circus, not to mention those of Africa and Latin America?'

'Oh, dear me, no: that wouldn't be the English way at all. Perhaps our best model remains France of the late 'sixties when the leader, essentially a soldier however consummate a politician, had neutralized the military eccentrics, and was then able to use a purged and chastened army to overawe the country, as in the crisis of 'sixty-eight. A robust nation, such as we hope to see emerge from our present futilities, is one based firmly on its army; but in which political control, even if exercised by soldiers, will restrain mere military hysteria of the more extravagant kind. In this, we may take a lesson from the Soviets, as well as from Chairman Mao. Power emerges from the barrel of a gun, indeed; but a political philosophy must decide when it shall be fired.'

'And what of the opposition to our plans?'

'Let us consider our potential support first, since our attitude must be resolute and outward-looking. The middle classes, hitherto our governors, if not always our rulers, are on the run: petulant, disheartened and unsure. We shall cream off their élite, and leave the rest to write letters to what newspapers we decide may print them.

The lower middle classes, any society's small function-aries and traders, will continue to occupy the modest role for which they are so fitted; moreover, they will applaud us since, if their decorum is but respected, they are born grovellers. We must, of course, ensure that no demagogue emerges who can appeal to their resentments and their innate cruelty; as did the manic Führer so suc-cessfully until, most fortunately for the sanity of man-kind, he overreached himself.'

'That brings us, Colonel, to our chief opponent.'

'Does it? Are you so sure it is? Opinions may differ on this theme, but here is mine. The English working class, except for momentary eruptions of ill humour, has, ever since Cromwell taught them a salutary lesson in the use and purposes of power, been radical at most, and never revolutionary: radical-conservative would, I think, express it best—that is, radical as regards money, conservative in their social *mores*. Consider, Captain, what any group with the least sense of what they were doing, and of their potential strength, could have made of 1926! Of 1931, when the fleet was mutinous, the police dis-affected, and the City of London trembling in its gilded shoes. And what of 1945, when socialists were so obsessed with surrendering an imperial structure, that they failed to consolidate power where it really mattered, which was in their own back yard! Remember the Suez fiasco, a perfect opportunity for a determined, intelligent working class to assail the fatuous incompetence of their rulers! And what did they do? They cheered the bungled enter-prise to the echo! Consider, further, the rapture with which London meat-porters and dockers—that demo-cratic élite—applauded the crudest vilification of worthy Caribbean bus drivers and nurses! Consider most of all that, in nearly a century of overt political activity, the working class, as such, has produced only two tribunes of the slightest consequence, Aneurin and Ernie, of the same name, if not spelling or stature.'

'You're not forgetting the unions, I am sure.'

'You may indeed be. Well, let's consider them. The higher echelons, after losing their nerve in 1926, have never since recovered it. Thus, despite the radical vapourings of leftish union leaders, who end up invariably on governmental commissions or in the House of Lords, what do their mouthings amount to, save for a most understandable cry for a larger cut of the capitalist loot? This brings us at last, then, to the shop-floor, and to reality; where such political education and intelligence as the class can muster, are unquestionably to be found. And it is here that we must concentrate our most determined and realistic endeavours.

'Let us think, first, of the men on the floor, for whose loyalty their stewards will be our rivals. Now—mark this. If we can ensure, as we will do, since any economist who opposes us will be number one for the high jump, that, by a manipulated and thoroughly inflationary economy, we double their wages overnight, are they going to hate us? And if, after certain swift eliminations, we make of the most militant shop stewards, national heroes? And if, in all, our régime presents the face not of stuffy brasshats and derelict politicos, but of free-wheeling and bonhommous, albeit patriotic, go-getters, won't they soon learn— the controlled media assisting—to laugh with us, and to applaud us? The more so if we remove, overnight, restrictions that irk them in their drinking, gambling, and hire purchase of whatever their heart desires?'

'But back to the shop-floor, Colonel! Their stewards! Their resolute and literate leaders! What, to begin with, of the Party?'

'The Party is old, wise, sophisticated and reactionary: it will always make a deal. But the deal we shall make will not be with their apparatus here, but with their masters. This is an obvious tactic that all energetic régimes have grasped, when dealing with their Party internally. They simply don't: they send ambassadors eastward, with an acceptable proposition.'

'Trots, anarchists, and so forth?'

'They will constitute our real, and most dangerous, foes. In fact, I foresee that within a few months of our take-over, our sole opposition will be the authentic left, together with some staunch old whigs of the Bertie Russell stamp. When it comes to them, we will simply have to get tough, winkle them out, and forget any nonsense about judge's rules.'

'Rebellious youth, and all that?'

'My dear fellow, I can't wait to give them the opportunity to stop play-acting for television cameras, and prove their worth! However, I fear they will disappoint me, by joining us enthusiastically in droves. Witness the behaviour of their volatile generation in Germany and Italy, and now in the "emerging nations". Youth, Colonel, is by essence nihilist, when not authoritarian; and must merely be offered some opportunity—the more noisy and picturesque the better—to let off its excess of radical steam.'

'Urban guerrillas?'

'They will undoubtedly emerge; and we must make sure, by winning increasing popular support, that these fish have little water left to swim in.'

'I suppose we may omit the churches?'

'My dear Captain!'

'And what of the blacks, and other exotic minorities?'

'We shall completely reverse the odious and short-sighted policies of the romantic right, and welcome them with open arms. They will, in fact, soon constitute one of our several corps of praetorian guards. As you know, they make excellent soldiers, being by nature lazy, fun-loving and violent.'

'And to return to the nub of the matter: the Irish?'

'Here we must consider the categories that we shall have to deal with. There are the Irish of England and Scotland, some millions of them, of both faiths, but principally catholic. There are those of the republic, and its internal oppositions. There are the two cultures of the North, with their various schisms. Very well, then. We withdraw at once, and completely, from Ireland, and encourage in every way the triumph, and eventual alliance, of the provisionals and the protestant radicals. That is: assist them, if only by abstention, to overthrow the bourgeois régime of the republic, to master, or convert, the officials, and to make an end of the ludicrous vestiges of Stormont: so that catholic and protestant nationalisms, freed at last from the irrelevancies of bourgeois, marxist, and English imperial interference, may have a real chance to make the United Ireland of everybody's dream.'

'And our own resident Irish?'

'We encourage them in every way to move in the same fruitful direction. A united, nationalist Ireland would free England from that perpetual backward look over the shoulder that has haunted us for centuries, and made us behave, in their island, like insensate monsters.'

'Such a policy can scarcely be peaceful in its consequences, Colonel.'

'Initially, no: who said it could? But then, what English politician has emerged with any proposal that offers other than continuing, pointless bloodshed? Do not mistake me: this is not any "scuttle and let them fight it out" irresponsibility of English liberal opinion. It is a firm intention to create, by our prompt withdrawal and our subsequent attitudes, a situation in which celtic and saxon nationalisms in Ireland can at last speak realistically to each other, with a common interest on the near horizon.'

'There will not, as a consequence, be violence in England too?'

'Of course there will; but not, I think, beyond reasonably acceptable limits. You see, Captain, the English people have so long exported their violence overseas, that the notion it can arise at home, is still a somewhat novel one. But our first task must be to keep this to the absolute minimum; for a régime, though it may come to power through violence, loses credit if it continues to use it wantonly.'

'Unless it becomes an open dictatorship.'

'Of course; which doubtless suits nations wherein dictatorship is traditional; which is to say, the vast majority. But here, no; we would just not get away with it, even if we wished to. Ours must be a highly respectable revolt, whose leaders are manifestly eager to win the support of a consensus.'

'I must confess to a certain malicious pleasure in observing the reaction of the Westminster lot when it comes to the final crunch.'

'You wish for a prediction? They will crumple with ignominy, while preserving a perfect sense of their own dignity. With the possible exception of the Curragh, English politicians have not had to confront internal force, other than minor rebellions from below, since the seventeenth century. If not themselves born into a ruling caste, like your ancestors, Captain, or several distinguished nineteenth century prime ministers, then, in their heart of hearts, politicians have always feared and mistrusted warriors. But feared, mark you, the more! When threatened, Gladstone launched the fleet on Alexandria. David Lloyd George, the most brilliant and daring outsider hitherto, always baulked at a showdown with the generals he mistrusted. Ramsay Macdonald, that stalwart proletarian, positively slavered over soldiers. Churchill, of course, being an aristocrat and an American, was not over-impressed by anything much in England, except its history. Major Attlee showed a spark of fire ... he had, after all, been shot, accidentally, by our own gallant forces at Gallipoli; and this baptism, coupled with his middle class rectitude, gave him a certain authority in dealing with the fighting forces. But since? Well, I ask you! Consider those extraordinary conversations on *Fearless*, an appropriately-named vessel, if ever there was one! Who showed the greater realism, the fighter pilot or the cream of the educated socialist establishment?'

'Why didn't *Fearless*'s commander drop a depth charge or two, just to see what happened?'

'Why indeed? But Captain! We must prepare to launch our own!'

April 30

Aspen lured the boys down to the new pool for a picnic: a soppy idea, they thought, but the day was sparkling.

'It's just that it's so pointless, Aspen: what's *wrong* with chairs and tables?'

'Don't come the city boy, Kik, the grumbler. You've chosen the country of your own free will, so stop hankering for fish and chip shops.'

'You're not only bossy, Asp, you're snobby.'

'Everyone is, and you are, about city-slicker know-how. Give Mas a hand to unpack these things.'

'Can I have *no* privileges as an elder brother? Besides, he adores this boy scout scene.'

'Does he? I know who'll scoff twice as much as anyone when he's done complaining.'

'Gorblimey, Mas, you should be a clergyman—honest; that is, when you've done with your choir boy bit.'

'Kik, you want me to push you in that pool?'

'Try, little boy; and don't come at me from the rear.'

'Honest, you two! You *are* adults now, aren't you, more or less? I mean, can't you do better than this juvenile chat?'

'Oh, *pardon, Madame*. Of what would you have us brilliantly converse?'

'Your futures.'

'Oh, yes? And what interests you so much about our daydreams?'

'Despite myself, I like you both.'

'That seems to me a questionable statement. One or the other, yes, but how could anyone like us both?'

'Let's take you to begin with, and perhaps you'll see. So: what are your plans, now you come the adult thing so strongly, yet sit on your fair arse all day long doing absolutely bugger-all?'

'Hearken to her! I've told you: for me, a life of legalized crime.'

'Do you know what that really is?'

'No, and I don't expect you do, but I'll find out.'

'It's business. Not doing banks, let alone sweet shops staffed by elderly ladies, but getting to know about commerce.'

'Too much of a grind.'

'Not really, and no years wasted in the nick, and more money sooner you can spend openly.'

'All right. You see me doing what that gives me fifty quid a week for starters, and a gay life as part of the bargain?'

'Buying and selling for a classy garment shop. Selling to start with, to teach you manners and humility, then buying, which is far more difficult, though the commission's better, and there are more opportunities for acceptable fiddles.'

'You speak as if you really knew something about all this. Are you kidding, or are you making me a serious proposition?'

'I can fix something of the sort for you, subject to one condition.'

'Here we go!'

'Hold it, Kik. That you realize the lads and lasses you'll be working with are every bit as smart as you are, and know what you don't, which is how to run a store. I can get you turned on, but I don't want you walking in there and being so fucking clever you make a fool of yourself and me.'

'I see. And when do I start?'

'Give me a while to prepare the ground. You know, Kik, you *do* need a bit of explaining.'

'Thank you. And this isn't a dead-end job where I flaunt my charms flogging Indian beads to teenies for ten quid a week?'

'You give me no credit, do you? Nor to yourself. Despite your bullshit, I often think you're really a bit diffident.'

'You do? Try me out. This thing could lead on to something?'

'Oh, yes. I do have contacts, you know...'

'Lead to my having my own business soon? I mean, can you lay your hands on some capital for me?'

'Don't rush me. Haven't you to prove something first?'

'Okay—let's try it. There are no hidden angles, are there? I don't have to get raped by anyone, do I?'

'That's up to you, but it wouldn't be part of the deal.'

'I see ... Little Mas, look at him, all ears and gaping teeth. Haven't you any master plan for him as well? Provided, that is, wherever I go, he doesn't?'

'I'm not sure that Mas needs planning for. He still seems bent on HM Forces. That so, Mas?'

'More or less, it is ... what's wrong with that?'

'You do understand it means you've got to kill people, don't you? Including, possibly, some of us one day?'

'That's all part of the deal a soldier makes with society.'

'Listen to the little monster! What a cold-blooded kid he is.'

'The only difference between you and me, Kik, is that you'd kill for money if you dared to, and I would in the exigencies of the service.'

'He's even got the lingo all off pat! The little murderer!'

'Shut up, Kik. Mas: would you like to go round the world for a year before you join the army?'

'Do what?'

'Hey! Why didn't you offer *me* that? You could really fix that for a likely, willing lad?'

'You're signed on in the garment business, Kik, not a ship.'

'You could get me on a ship, Aspen? Doing what?'

'Mas, I'm the sort of girl who knows fellows who've got big boats—and I don't mean sailing boats. I could get you aboard as a learner, if you like. You could see some beautiful cities, master some lovely languages, and meet some not very beautiful people on the way.'

'You're having me on about all this?'

'Oh, come on, Mas! Do I ever? The idea is, why not try this, and get to be sure you know yourself before you plunge into the barrack-room?'

'I'll certainly think about it, if you're serious. Listen to what Dad says about it, too.'

'Yes, but don't make the decision your father's—make it your own. Decide for yourself first, then tell him.'

'You don't trust Dad's judgement, then?'

'About what he knows, yes. Not about choices that he may not understand.'

'I see.'

'And both of you: please keep all this beneath your untidy locks until I can get things moving further. Don't chat or gossip, please, to anyone.'

'All right, then.'

'That goes for you too, Kik, my dear old blabbermouth.'

'Oh yes, but how nice! There's you and me both fixed for the future, Mas! Think of it! You rolling down to Rio in your bell-bottoms, and me flogging classy schmutter to revoltingly over-publicized nits. I can't wait to see us both. And to celebrate the occasion, I'm going to be the first to try out Dad's murky pool. Stand back, everyone, and if you want to see a beautiful body, don't lower your eyes.'

'Keep something on, Kik.'

'Shut up! Aspen's seen all this before. Here we go. Christ! It's freezing! My bollocks are retracting into my bowels.'

'Not you too, Mas?'

'Aspen, for pete's sake! It's as cold as it's dirty.'

'Don't be bashful.'

'You think I am? Hey!'

Kik grabbed his leg, and pulled him in. The boys yelled and struggled. Aspen watched, feeling not old, but ageless.

* * *

At nightfall, Grandad Angell's car came putter-putter wobble to the Ruin gates. He parked on the verge, climbed clumsily over the wire fence and, for the next hour, prowled, like a wary hyena, round the premises; peering, loitering, hearkening, sniffing. Then he emerged, drove back to the factory estate and, with some difficulty, found a workers' caff (temporary, and due for demolition) to which he summoned Evie from its call-box. She arrived in a half hour, surprised, anxious and a bit flustered.

'And where have you sprung from, Dad? And why didn't you come up to the Ruin?'

'I did. But I don't want to see you there. Up there, you wouldn't have listened to what I have to tell you now.'

'Come off it, Dad! I've always listened to you, and you know it. And I'm listening now: what is it?'

'Come back to London, Evie.'

'Sure: but why?'

'Before that place corrupts you.'

'"Corrupts" me! Oh, Dad! What do *you* know of there that can "corrupt" me?'

'Fathers have instincts, Evie.'

'Fathers can also think a daughter of thirty-four's a child.'

'I grant you that. But I've been checking up on Captain Rattler and the Lady Aspen.'

'How have you? Through the Party, I suppose.'

'You can be as superior as you like, and sneer at the Party you believed in once. But you can't deny that if our men dig into any question, they find the facts. What they do with them, how they interpret them you can dispute with, if you want to. But if there's one thing Marx and Lenin taught us, and we've never forgotten, it's to *know*.'

'All right, then. What have they told you?'

'She's an aristocratic slut. He's a political adventurer, a tinsel bonapartist, who even the class enemy's security has got a file that thick on.'

'The Party's privy to those sort of secrets, is it?'

'You know it is; and you know how. I'm not going to speak about that here.'

'Right. May I tell you something? I've guessed all this, or something like it.'

'And you're still there?'

'Dad, we've been into this before. We've been into it, in fact, ever since I married Soldier over your dead body, as you used to say. I know the world needs changing; I know societies are rotten; I know somebody's got to do it, and good luck to them. But it isn't me.'

'All right. Stay neutral then, like millions of sheep bleating for their slaughter. But don't side with your own murderers.'

'I've got nothing to do with Rattler's plans, whatever they are, and nor has Soldier.'

'No? You think he'd have you down here if you hadn't?'

'We've simply got a nice, crazy, easy job with a bit of money in it at last, and a bit of variety. What *you* want to do, Dad, is to punish me. Because I became a soldier's wife against your will, you want me to pay penance as the helpmeet of a pensioner in the Corps of Commissionaires.'

'You're quite, quite wrong. If it was your own little business, I wouldn't mind that much, and I've proved it to you, because I tried to help you. What I don't want to see, is my daughter helping counter-revolutionaries; and I can't believe you really want to do that either.'

'I think I know what's really at the back of this, Dad. You've got into your head I fancy Rattler. You were jealous of Soldier, and now you're jealous of him.'

'Perhaps I was, and perhaps I was right to be, and am. Not because of their being men, but because of the kind of men they are.'

'Well, I'll tell you this about Rattler, anyway, if it'll set your mind at rest at all. He's smart as a snake, but he doesn't deceive me for a moment. But I *am* a woman, Dad, which is one thing about me you've never really managed to get into your dear old clever head. And when a woman's been through a life which she may very well have chosen, and which hasn't been strewn with roses, but has been hard, monotonous and drab, when she reaches my age, which means ten years to go before nature starts playing her kindly tricks, well then, she wants a bit of *life*, for God's sake, even with risk attached to it, provided it's not absolutely wicked, as you're trying to make mine out to be, but which it isn't. But there! How can a man, let alone a father, be expected to understand a thing as simple and basic as *that*?'

'We'd better have a cup of tea.'

'That's not an answer.'

'No. Well, here it is, then. Contrary to what you suppose, and always have, because you never listen, and perhaps I put it badly, I have *no* objection to a woman's having a full, and rich, and varied life. The exploitation of women is one of the very evils the Party's hostile to. But what kind of richness, what kind of variety—that's the point. I know it's difficult, in a capitalist society, for a woman, even more than for a man, to live in a way that fulfils her legitimate aspirations, and yet which is decent, healthy, forward-looking. Don't think I . . .'

'Dad, you're just tumbling into Party jargon. I haven't got any "legitimate aspirations", for heaven's sake! I want to *live*.'

'Yeah. "Live!" And you don't think women do in lands where the Party has control?'

'I just don't know, because I'm not one, I've never been there to have a look, and I've not even met any coming here to tell me, except for some high-powered female comrades you've taken me to hear who, frankly, scared me stiff and bored the pants off me.'

'You lack faith, Evie. You always have done.'

'But not you, Dad. I'll give you that . . .'

'No. Oh no, not me. I know the case against us, I've heard it put brilliantly a million times by false friends as well as enemies. I know all about bureaucracies, and purges, and prison camps and famines, and suppression of internal and external oppositions ... I know about changing lines, and disappearances, and I know I myself might vanish, any moment, without a trace ... But two truths remain, that only the Party ever can make reality. There is no other idea whatever, search as you can, that still holds within it the practical possibility of the world surviving as a living unity. And as for the English working class, I know, in the marrow of my bones, that whatever the present weakness of the Party, none other, however seemingly powerful or seductive, is ever going to rescue us, without betrayal.'

'Good old Dad.'

'But you don't think so; you think poor old obstinate Dad.'

'Not really.'

'Well, let's have that tea now, then.'

'I've ordered it. You were so busy lecturing me, you didn't notice. Here you are.'

'Ta, Evie.'

'You know, I often think, Dad, you should have lived a hundred years ago.'

'You do? That would put you somewhere in your seventies.'

'What I mean is, I see you more as a Wesleyan, really, or a salvationist.'

'Put me back earlier, and I dare say I would have been. But by 1871, I think I'd have got around to reading the Manifesto.'

'Marx didn't think it would all start in Russia, did he?'

'No; and don't quote me, but historically, I think it's a pity it did. The Russians had a fine revolutionary tradition,

162

true enough; but they also had a traditional taste for suspicion and autocracy. However, they're a great people: endlessly patient, tough, persistent, which we might remember, since if anyone thinks we defeated Hitler, then they're idiots.'

'Where should it all have happened, then?'

'There are no "should its" in history, Evie—you've forgotten your training. All you can say is this, though. Most revolutions come at the end of a war, often a lost one. The French didn't, which still makes it one of the greatest. Nor did the Cuban, which is why it makes everyone rather anxious, even its supporters: it doesn't conform to type, and it may be the new one.'

'And you really see anything like that happening here?'

'Evie, that kind of crystal-gazing's liberal talk. We're taught analysis and action, not speculation. Clearly, the English working class is one of the most corrupted, hence deceived. Popular imperialism, secret worship of class, and national contempt for education of *any* kind, have seen to that. However, deep down they know they're being sold a con, a fantasy they don't believe in. If they're really pushed, they're militant, or could be. I think you'll see...'

'I just don't see our lads as revolutionaries. Protesters, yes, and activists, and fighters for their rights. But revolutionaries?'

'Evie, in the core of every decent man and woman, if they're pushed to an extreme point and beyond, there's a supporter of revolution, whatever the consequences. Not for intellectual reasons, like the middle lot; but because, in the end, their dignity's involved.'

'And you see an extreme point coming.'

'Your friend Rattler does, doesn't he? That's why he and his kind are making ready.'

'But Dad, you've dismissed him as a fake.'

'I have, but I don't under-estimate him as a symptom;

163

and he's far from being the only one around.'

'Okay, okay. I'll think over what you say.'

'You might, for once. Remember this, Evie, please. I don't deny you can learn a lot in a set-up like that Ruin; I wouldn't even deny what you find might make you wiser. Nor do I think you're in danger, yet, or that anyone's going to try to do away with you. But when you go back to that place tonight, just pause, and sniff the air; and I think you'll smell a sewer, and all its evil.'

May 1

Oh, dearest Great Great Aunt!

What a May Day, what a catastrophe! The opening of the Ruin was itself one!

To begin with, it poured: those warm, steady, saturating sheets, that usually don't drench till June. Then the reception, and the visitors—oh my! Hear my dirge!

Nothing was ready at the Ruins, which even themselves, because of the scaffolding and builders' huts, looked less ruinous than when we came. The gardens weren't so bad, because nature's hard to spoil without resources we've not got, but our gravelled, winding paths were mud, and anyway, no one fancied a romantic stroll. To receive the guests of honour, Rattler had fixed up a marquee: but it must be so long since the soldier lads erected tents, that they forgot drainage, and there was a dreadful dripping sag just overhead.

I warned Rattler May would be too early, and Saturday a bad day; a week day, for openings, I said, to give the sense of an exceptional occasion. But no, Rattler replied; he'd like our workers to be there, to celebrate. Need I say none turned up?

To create an atmosphere by appropriate melodies,

Rattler had engaged a venerable string band. Where, oh where, did he dig them up? Their resurrection was his only triumph! They were all over sixty, of each sex. That may not seem old to you, dearest, but sawing away disconsolately with wet bows and strings, they looked despairingly antique. But ancient in the wrong way, surely; a period setting is one thing, but weren't you Victorians a lively lot? The women buxom and brassy, the men raffish and given to high jinks? Or so I imagine. Not our poor band, though; I think they must date from the tail end of the silent film era.

All this might have been saved from wreckage, had Rattler paid attention to the catering. Our Ranelagh, our Vauxhall, our exquisite Cremorne weren't ready yet (need I repeat?); so Rattler, never one to be daunted in emergencies, called in a Chinese caterer of his acquaintance... a Singaporian gent of reassuring calm and affability, but the food and waiters—dozens of them, I admit—just weren't quite right. Rattler, who's usually sensitive about such things, struck the wrong chord absolutely, by asking them to don mandarin robes and pigtail wigs he'd hired post-haste from a costumier; he thought this would establish a *fin de siècle* flavour. Of course, they just shook their heads, and blinked. Quite right of them.

The visitors, or what there were of them, consisted of mini-groups that wouldn't talk to one another, even when fortified by bamboo shoots and thimbles of tepid rice wine. Some councillors of both persuasions turned up late, and each seemed embarrassed not only by our débâcle, but by the presence of their rivals; their ladies, in particular, stood aloof, giving us two little frowning knots of damp, furled parasols in purdah. The humbler locals who honoured us, not many, seemed to think the Ruin was still a ruin; and as they'd never come here before, save in their courting days, they didn't see why they should pay to now; though they liked the idea of charging the Londoners for the privilege, and were the only ones who probed, with gusto, into their oriental bowls. We had a coach-load or two from the capital, but it turned out they'd lost their way to the races, and were offended we hadn't any tea, or petrol pump. Heigh—ho! If we want to wow the metropolis, we'll have to do better than this! We had a darling American, though, who was a fan of E. A. Poe, and, save for a pilgrimage to Stoke Newington, is visiting nothing else in England except ruins. So we had at least one appreciative guest, and he promised to present Rattler with ravens.

Of course, the Ruin residents rallied round! Our boys brought some charming ragamuffins, who crashed about everywhere, and delighted in the rain. They made a splendid mud slide, near our pool. The friends and acquaintances I'd appealed to were most loyal, on the whole—I had girls of my age familiar with disasters, who brought with them snappy males. What was touching was, some clients of my escort days arrived; supplying the only flashy vehicles for our quagmire car park, so I didn't myself feel too forlorn. As for Rattler's band of desperados, they were an assembly and a half! Plotters and odd-bods, with grim clandestinity written on their truculent faces, and darting mistrustful eyes.

What rescued the afternoon from utter disaster, was Rattler's speech; so vehement and weird, it should be recorded for posterity. True, it betrayed a manic, hysteric note, and the amplifiers, fixed up by our military, first slurred and crackled, then didn't work. But the controlled hysteria—my, oh my! He said the past lay in the future, and the present was a waking dream! We must arise, he cried, and take a grip on everyone and thing! No one knew what he meant, I think, yet the message came over loud and crackling clear.

Tim Botany, alone among the throng, preserved his cool. He'd told Rattler, he revealed to me, that May was futile, and has secretly fixed everything for June—a dull, formal, news-worthy affair, with artificial eccentricities, not real ones like today's. For this, he's got the media sewn up; their absence today was to underline his power.

So roll on flaming June, to mask this setback; myself, I have lingering faith for, after all, our balls-up was on an imposing scale! Nothing can come from nothing, Shakespeare says, and whatever today might be, it wasn't that. I do hope so, anyway, after all our far from effortless stress and strain. One way or another, I feel in my bones that things here are moving to a climax of some kind. Who will live, will see, as the French say.

Beloved Great Great Aunt, farewell!

Your

Aspen

PS Re-reading, it's apparent that gin accounts for half this letter, if not all. I'm sure you will 'understand'.

A

May 9

Kik walked enlaced with Aphrodite through the woods; his hand sliding on to her rump, allowed to stray, then jerked pettishly to her waist again. He stopped, and confronted the dark factory lass.

'For fuck's sake, Aph! You'd think you and me had never had it off.'

'Do not say "fuck": is bad.'

'Well, that's what we've done, and more than once. What's the matter with you?'

'It is Sunday, and we are visible.'

'Of all the tales I've heard a chick tell yet! "Sunday", indeed! Don't Cyps screw on the sabbath?'

'Do not say "Cyp": it is offensive.'

'Well, don't they? I mean, not even after church?'

'I do not know. I was not born there.'

'Well, in St Pancras or wherever, then, they didn't? Not even after gallons of retsina?'

'At home, of course, but not where it can be seen.'

'My dear girl, look around! We're in an impenetrable jungle. Isn't that just why I walked you down here?'

'I do not wish your mother to know, or brother.'

'Look, we're not Latins, Aphrodite! My Mum...'

'Nor are we, but Greeks.'

'Okay, okay, whatever you are, your ancient traditions oblige your over-populated family, down to the last second cousin twice removed, to slit any suitor's throat, if he even blows you a kiss across the village street, unless your troth is pledged in due and legal form. I *know* all that. But here in...'

'You know little of Cyprus customs.'

'More than you'd think. But here, my mother wouldn't say anything, or anything much...'

'Because you are male, not female.'

'Because she'd know she'd be wasting her breath.'

'As you are wasting mine, here in these trees. You said you would ask me to your house for tea.'

'All in good time: don't go all impatient on me.'

'You are a patient person?'

'How can I be, with a Mediterranean belle like you beside me?'

'Now you will flatter.'

'Oh—come on! I know for a fact your dates are quite okay...'

'Your brother might also wander in this wood, and be ashamed.'

'He'd certainly be envious—not that there's much for him to envy yet.'

'He is less talkative than you.'

'He's certainly not with chicks ... Hey, listen, I'm beginning to think you fancy him. You do?'

'Later on, he will have better looks than you.'

'Okay, okay! You like me to give him a yell, and see if you can turn him on? I can't wait to see his alarm and horror.'

'Do not be so certain of this. I would be gentle with him.'

'All right! All right, then! Go ahead—I'm all in favour! The boy's so repressed he'll be raping a donkey soon, if he can find one. He gives everyone round the place such odd, furtive looks, I think he's developing a vicious streak.'

'He is yet too young. Children should have only sex with children.'

'He's not all *that* young, and I can vouch for it. Come on, why not have a go? It might make the little bastard less superior and snooty. He's so virtuous at times, he isn't real.'

'You should not speak so of your own blood brother.'

'I know, it's disgusting of me, isn't it? I tell you what: I'll give you a nice little gift if you can tear off his grubby jeans.'

'Be serious, Kik.'

'I am. And what's more, you can bugger off home if you're barring the whole fucking family.'

'I shall do so. Your speech is bad.'

'See you round, then. Sorry I can't take you back to the estate, but I dare say a truck will give you a hitch if you hoist your mini.'

May 11

The publican councillor, and ex-regimental sergeant-major, had summoned Soldier to the unfriendly inn at the factory estate, whose landlord was a tenant of his own brewer. Though a less dashing figure than Rattler, it was clear the management considered the councillor the more imposing man. The service of stodgy food on the first floor was positively deferential.

'I asked you out here, lad, and without the wife—or mine, for that matter—because I wanted a few words in your private and personal ear. And I won't beat about the bush when I say to you, are you satisfied with what you're doing because, if not, I have a proposition that might interest you.'

'It's good of you to remember me, Councillor.'

'Remember you as a boy soldier, son, when I was no more than a corporal, though as proud as a peacock with six arses. Took a fancy to you then, and you never caused me to change my opinion after.'

'Were those happy days, would you say, or were we kidding ourselves they were?'

'We were too ignorant to know *what* they were, lad. I came in at the end of that great, big, wonderful war, and you did before the glamour had all faded. Soldiering seemed a natural way of life for most young men, unless they were one-legged, or smart enough to tuck themselves away in some reserved civilian occupation. We never guessed then the opportunities there'd come to be outside, or that we'd be reduced to a small professional force again.'

'You regret you served out your time, then?'

'Too late for regrets, in my case, isn't it? But this I do know: if I had a son who wanted to go in now, I'd belt his hide off.'

'They'd have been shook rigid in the mess, if they'd known you thought like that...'

'First thing the army teaches you, is to shut your trap, and keep your thoughts to yourself.'

'Yeah. So according to you, I've got to belt my son, have I?'

'It's your younger who's dead keen, isn't it, if I remember?'

'Yes: Mas. But I don't know, though. The older, Kik, was lost to me anyway, so I've not bothered to try to interfere. But Mas seemed more my son until—well, he seems to be changing now.'

'Growing up, is he, I suppose?'

'Growing away from me, is how I'd have to put it. In fact, I don't want to burden you with my problems, but it seems to me...'

'Go on if you want to, lad...'

'It seems my whole family's coming adrift, or I am...'

'Wife trouble too, son?'

'When I was away, she wanted me. Now that I'm back, specially lately, she's kind and all that, but who wants just kindness?'

'Yes. Now, may I tell you something about my wife, that may surprise you? Between ourselves, needless to say? Did you know, just after I signed out, she went missing for two years?'

'She did?'

'Two bloody years before I managed to persuade her to come back, or she persuaded herself ... And I think I know why, quite apart from my own well-known defects of character. Soldiers' wives have a hell of a life, far worse, really, than their men's. A hard, petty, stupid existence, is what it is. So: if they're good women, they curb their restlessness, for his sake, and the kids', and their own self respect. When it's easiest for them to be untrue to him, they're not. But once *he's* free, and out and about, these years of restraint and frustration bubble over, and often cause the woman to run wild. Can't say I blame them.'

'You would have, if she hadn't come back.'

'Could be. We had another kid, though. Don't look at me like that, it was her idea.'

'I don't think Evie's ever wanted another.'

'Or you don't, really: is that it?'

'As things are getting to be, we don't see much of each other, that kind of way.'

'Yes, I see. Remember this, though. I've told you why I think it's hard for soldiers' wives to settle, once their men are out; and now I'll tell you why I think it's hard, too, for the men. What sort of sex life does a soldier have? A mess! Harlots and short spells with his wife— what sort of continuity is that? What is there to build on, like other men and women do? Rickety foundations, I'd say. When a soldier leaves the army, he has to begin his marriage all over again.'

'When he's older; and she is.'

'That's it, unfortunately. So give yourself time, and her.'

'If she'll let me.'

'That, I admit, you can't altogether control. No man can. Still—that's the nature of your problem, I believe. Which brings me to mine. I'm leaving that boozer near the airport and moving up north to your part of the country. I need an assistant manager I can trust, who'd take over when I retire, or get his own pub from the brewers after a while, if he prefers it. That's my proposal. Will you have a chat with your wife, and think it over, and let me know? It won't be till the autumn, but the sooner I'm fixed, the better.'

'Thanks, Sergeant-major. It's a good offer, and I'm grateful to you. But it may have come too late.'

'You sure of that? When things aren't going well, a change of circumstances can sometimes put them right, or make them better. Perhaps the trouble isn't only with

172

yourself and Evie, lad. It may be with the life you're lead-
ing down the road there.'

May 13

On that no-day, Thursday, and that no-time after three
in the afternoon, Mas wandered, sighing for a farewell to
adolescence: through the park, aimlessly across the fields,
down into the no man's land of the estate. Few were about,
the adults at the factories or indoors, the kids at school,
the shops half empty, and the drear caffs closed; one of
those instants, far from rare in England, when it seems the
bomb has fallen, or the plague returned. The sky, to en-
hance the scene, yielded grudgingly a drizzle.

'Hey—you!'

'Me?'

'Come over here! Jump to it! Right. Turn your pockets
out.'

'What's all this, mister?'

'Shurrup. Hip pockets too. Turn round. What's *this*?'

'A bayonet sheath.'

'I know that. Where's the bayonet? Where you dropped
it—hid it?'

'I've never had one.'

'Never had one. So why you wear that sheath? To put
drugs in? Let's have a look.'

'It's looped on the belt.'

'Undo your belt, then.'

'Fucked if I will.'

'Oh! Abusive language, is it? And loitering with intent
—*I* know.'

'Intent to what? I'm having a walk around.'

'I see that. And how old are you?'

'Sixteen.'

'You're an effing little liar. I know your age, and I know where you should be. Which is your school?'

'I'm a boy soldier, like my Dad was. I'm home on leave.'

'Just as I said: an effing little liar. Now, look!'

'Take your hands off me!'

'Quiet: listen to me. You want to get nicked, or you want to take a hiding down the road there? Which?'

'I want your guv'nor to phone my Dad and check it's like I say. Stop that! Stop!'

'You can't take it, boy, can you? Great big fellow like you? All of sixteen? Come on, you're for a belting down the recreation. Nice and sadistic. You'll enjoy it.'

'You'll break my arm!'

'Shouldn't be surprised—now, walk! If you yell, I *will* break it for you: that's a promise.'

Guardian angels, in the unlikely form of squaddies heading for the Ruin in a lorry, slowed down, halted, and reversed. Two jumped down with that *clank* which takes years of training.

'I thought it was our drummer boy, tangling with the fuzz.'

'We don't care for that word, soldier.'

'No, I suppose you don't. What's our little mate done that's so bad you have to be so rough?'

'He's under arrest; and if there's any interference, he won't be the only one.'

'Fancy that! You hear that, lads? We're in danger of the dungeons. Right, copper: hand him over.'

'Like hell I will.'

'Language! And six witnesses, with only your word against ours ... Why didn't you walk round with a mate?'

'Move along, now, or I'll have to use my walkie-talkie.'

'Try. Go on—try. Because I might use my booty-wooty in your fucking facey-wacey.'

Jostling, grunts, scuffles close on kicks, and Mas was

174

hoisted over the tail-board of the truck, falling flat on his face when it accelerated.

'Pick yourself up, lad. The boy's bent on doing himself an injury.'

'What was he on about, the man in blue?'

'Said I had an offensive weapon, and should be at school.'

'Dear me! Well, I don't know about the weapon, unless he meant the other one, but perhaps you should be giving the teacher that, or else an apple, shouldn't you?'

'I want to get in the army.'

'Oh, no! Not that again ... Haven't we all tried to cool your ardour?'

'At least, lad, wait till you're older. Honest! Be warned by us.'

'But you helped me, because you're soldiers, and you know my Dad's one.'

'The boy's trying to work on our feelings, and make us blush. You didn't mention your Dad to that copper, did you?'

'Well—yes.'

'Shouldn't have, lad. Never land another soldier in the shit—although we all do. Fight your own way out of it, is the idea.'

'But my Dad's retired.'

'That's what *he* thinks; but they never do. Once in the nick, always a criminal. Once a brave squaddie, always a sucker.'

'I could have mentioned Captain Rattler, but I didn't.'

'You're fucking right about that, at any rate. Rattler? He doesn't give a bugger for any of us—and least of all for you, because you can't hit back at him in any way. Believe me: you could even trust that fuzz better than you could him.'

'But those in authority are supposed to help you, if you do your duty.'

'Yeah? Honest, lad—I give up. I pity you.'

May 18

The genius who controlled the factory estate was Mr War-saw. He did not own it, nor want to, but held a large enough piece of it to manipulate the whole. He knew more about its material assets than anyone, since he was gifted with a freak electronic brain: he never made a note, yet forgot no fact—he couldn't. To the human element that ran the factories he was largely indifferent, since he believed inspired efficiency was so rare that, provided he was in remote control, an adequate performance by underlings was enough; and that those unsure of their own expertise are more malleable and alert.

He has not hitherto visited the estate, since he saw no need to; accounts and blue-prints made it crystal clear to him. There was, indeed, throughout the country, many a Warsaw building where he had never been seen, though he was always nervously expected. He did not even often telephone to these places; others did this on his behalf, which made his unheard voice even more compelling.

But now he had come to the estate, impelled by an instinct that rarely failed him; unheralded, and admitted by astonished cleaners to head office, an hour before the earliest clerical staff. He gazed with distaste at the chief managerial room, and yet with pleasure; aesthetically it revolted him, but for economy and meagre status, it was just right.

Sipping some tea—a rare concession to the land of his adoption—he removed from his wallet a slip of paper wrapped in perspex, bearing only the signature 'Plock'. The letter itself he had long ago memorized and destroyed, yet the sight of the name of his dead and only friend, reminded him of its message:

Before I leave you, I think an analysis of yourself may help you to an ultimate lucidity. It is, in any case, all I can bequeath to you, and is written with that truth which comes with knowledge of a fast approaching end.

You have often asked me why, when we both left the Polish forces in this country, I did not stay, as hitherto before the war and during it, beside you; and preferred the modest existence of a cab-driver in Scotland to sustaining you in the endeavours which, beginning with so little save faith in your own star, have come to make you what you are.

Here is the reason: my best way to help you was to remain the one man who knew and understood you, and whose views, in consequence, would disturb you, and spur you on. Had I remained with you, as in the years of our imprisonment and subsequent release to Anders' army, you would not have hearkened to me as you did then. And I will tell you why this is so. You are not a coward, yet are not blessed, as I have been, with the simplest kind of physical courage, mysterious even to myself. Therefore, in those years of perpetual danger, you needed a stalwart presence to support you; but one which, in times of peace, was no longer indispensable to you. As for my judgement, proceeding from an intimate knowledge of your nature, you would have hearkened to it less, once peril ceased to make you conscious of its value. (There is also, perhaps, dear friend, that I prefer the life of a cab-driver to that of daily counsellor to a tycoon.)

Very well, then. I did not desert you, since my counsel was ever available to you when you wished for it, as was my belief in your high capacities. And I do not desert you now; for leaving you, I give you the key to man's most precious gift, which is self-knowledge.

Like all Slavs, you are immensely proud, and yet contemptuous of Slav passion, vehemence and irresponsibility. Thus, you believe a formidable self-discipline is necessary; and admire those Slav leaders who, in recent years, have imposed rigid rule upon their peoples. You are a profound student of Marx, and admire him because he is both dogmatic, and international in his outlook; yet your admiration is coupled with an equal determination not to endure life in a marxist society, since your personal, not intellectual, inclination is towards the individualistic activities of a capitalist entrepreneur. You have, in fact, made use of Marx's brilliant dissection of capitalist practice in order to become, yourself, a more efficient man of affairs; for you also believe that, whatever the future holds (which, since you will not be there in this flesh, fails to interest you completely), capitalism will conveniently last out your present years.

Your admiration for catholicism is, I would say, identical; that is to say, you respect its dogma and claim to universality, and are impressed by its capacity for self-renewal and survival. I do not think its declared essence interests you—the salvation of souls means as little to you as does the eventual emancipation of the proletariat, since you believe both may be frustrated. Your attitude, in fact, is devout in regard to forms, and politely indifferent as to doctrine.

Like all Slavs (and indeed most heirs to any Christian culture), you are instinctively anti-Semitic, your attitude being both racial and religious in its impulsions. But the realist in you admires the longevity of Jewish cultures, and your direct experience of the inefficiency of European militarism has given you a wary respect for the Israelis. In your personal relations, since your arrival

178

here, you have been invariably courteous to Jewish people—which is just as well, considering how many favours you have asked of them; and you are intelligent enough to know that they are never deceived as to your real attitude towards them.

Your style in relation to the English has, I think, been excellent; and here only I make bold to claim that my counsel has been of service to you. For regarding them, as you do, with profound contempt, yet realizing how dependent you are on their goodwill, your tone of modest deference—of one reliable, well-intentioned, and ever willing to learn—has been exactly right. Anonymity, yet availability, have been your watchwords in all your dealings with officials, and how rightly so; for you have convinced them that your refusal of any honours, or public advancement, are due entirely to your feeling of being unworthy of such privileges.

Perhaps what has seduced them most about you, is your manifest optimism about their country's future. When, after World War Two, they licked their wounds in disarray, who was one of the first to proclaim, albeit in a most minor way at first, his faith on England's resurrection? Who, in more practical terms, contrived to secure options on derelict corner sites in half devastated cities? Who, earlier than all, saw the harvest to be reaped in shattered London?

Your critics say you have littered their urban landscapes with dehumanized monstrosities. This I deem doubly unjust. For what native entrepreneur has done and differently—and which, indeed, has occasionally built, as you have, commercial palaces designed by the most advanced of architects, frequently at a loss (except to the favoured designers), and to the universal indifference of the populace? The fact of the matter is the English of all classes, save for a minute minority of aesthetes of no consequence, are incurably, indeed resolutely, philistine. The concrete image of their culture which you have erected in their cities is the very mirror of their souls.

You have, then, done brilliantly, dear friend. You have made a lasting mark upon a corner of the world, and on a society. You have proved that the forlorn exile, be he resolute and intelligent, can bewitch the natives, and transform himself into an indigenous culture hero of a kind. This, hitherto in the Old World, has been the achievement of regal dynasties; and in the New, of alien adventurers with far vaster opportunities at their command. You have also, personally, remained unchanged: rejecting the trappings of the ostentatiously affluent, you have stayed aloof, austere almost, and true to your only truth, which is to prove to yourself and others your own inborn distinction, and the inane banality of the majority of mankind.

One word of warning, though. Although you have met many obstacles and opponents on your path, you have not, I think, yet met your match, and grappled with him. I do not fear, for you, that megalomania might convince you such a one could not exist or, if he did, you would instantly, and readily, outwit him. Perhaps, indeed, there is no such person; it may be all potential rivals have by now accepted you as one with whom to negotiate, not to seek to overthrow. However, to meet an ultimate adversary, you may have one fatal failing; which is that, though you believe in little, since you do still hold fast to some few, well-tried conceptions, you may, in any encounter with a nihilist more absolute than yourself, discover that even you believe too much.

This weakness, however, my dear friend, I do not fear in you too greatly. For have I not taught you this: what profit is it to a man if he can gain a whole world without losing his whole soul?

The managing director appeared, considerably disturbed. Word had reached him, the instant he entered the gleaming gimcrack building, of the brooding presence sitting in his upholstered swivel chair upstairs.

'Good morning, Mr Warsaw. How nice to see you, if I may say so.'

'Have you the files on the country club deal or, as I hope, the whole matter in your head?'

'The "Ruins", sir? I think I know the circumstances.'

'Who are we dealing with?'

'A Mr Leopold Watson: the accountant.'

'No, no. Who is the principal?'

'A Captain Rattler: the landowner—or nominee of his family's rights.'

'And who is he?'

'The Captain, sir? I must confess I don't know that much about him, since all negotiations have been with Watson. He's a gentleman, sir, a former officer, who's thought of opening some kind of stately home, but seems to have changed his mind.'

'A gentleman? An officer? A *stately home*?'

'Yes, sir.'

'Fetch Watson here.'

'Yes, sir. But I don't know where he is—in London, over at the Ruins ... he might be anywhere. Shouldn't I arrange an appointment at a time and place convenient to you?'

'*Please*: will you have him here within an hour?'

May 22

Mr Timothy Botany had connections other than those with public relations for the Ruins, or elsewhere. His activities being parasitic upon parasites, he thrived on getting, and more rarely giving, 'inside information': usually valueless in itself, yet infinitely attractive to the tribes of spies who, free-wheeling or official, flourish increasingly in evolved societies.

The Contact met him, by appointment, on the quieter road that led from the estate out to the Ruin. Tim reluctantly obeyed the Contact's signal to leave his own more lavish vehicle, and come to sit in discomfort beside his interlocutor.

'Well, now: Rattler and his Ruin. What's the latest, from our point of view?'

'As I'm not working for you fellows, I think chiefly of mine: which is that there's still a hell of a lot to be done before we really open up in June.'

'The usual energetic confusion?'

'Worse. We've got wildcat building strikes on our hands, and most of the volunteer help has faded away. But that's not all—far from it. Voices are whispering in my ear that Rattler's up to some deal with the factory people, and may abandon the project altogether.'

'Leaving you, after all your labours, without your luscious fee.'

'There's more than that troubling my soul. According to my contract, I have a cut on all the attractions at the Ruin; and an income, however small, is so much nicer than a fee, however bountiful.'

'Yes. I feel for you. Could you wrench your mind away, though, from these personal considerations, to our own? You're not working for us, you say; yet in a sense you have, and are. So, in brief: behind all this manic cover at the Ruin, we know what Rattler's handling, and we know its intended destination. But we must have more precision at this juncture. Maybe you haven't Rattler's confidence on these matters, but you do nose about the place a lot, and should have picked up something less vague than the details you've given us hitherto.'

'I wouldn't say you're very grateful.'

'We're not an organization given to gratitude. So?'

'What little I know direct from Rattler has come from what he doesn't say, not does: his smiles, his silences, his changing of topic when I ask what strangers in the park are doing, or what this or that mysterious consignment may be. Also, of course, I've asked around among the people living and working there. And my guess, but I'm not sure it's right, and after all, it's up to you with all your resources to find out ... my guess is, he's simply out to spread confusion.'

'In Ireland?'

'Everywhere. I think Rattler would flog a gun to anyone in the six counties, even down to criminal psychopaths. I think he wants the British army out of there: to do another Palestine, or Cyprus, or Aden—you name it—so that they're back here on their native soil. That's what I believe he's after.'

'Why?'

'Why? My dear fellow, you tell *me*. You chaps are supposed to know these things. I mean: if anything like a military plot were brewing in this country, I expect you'd hear about it; or even be in it, perhaps, for all I know.'

'Botany, we're not asking for your counsel about strategy. What we want to know from you, is facts. So: will you please get your nose back in there rather more frequently, and start sniffing around to more immediate and direct effect? Do you think you could do that for us, old chap?'

'Look, I've got my work to do: this Ruin's far from being my chief account.'

'We know quite a lot about your accounts, don't we? Well, don't we? You'll do as we say?'

May 31

Summer shivered its arrival round the Ruin; cold May, still fresh, before there came tired foliage, and thicker air. The building, in late twilight, looked ridiculously right— too 'romantic' for survival to be possible. The sky was an instant blend of sun and stars; a soft rain fell, then stopped so fast it left unnatural dew. Windows gleamed here and there, but the park hid most. It seemed a peaceful place to welcome June.

Reaping the Fruits

'Hey there! Move your arse over, you'll have me out.'

'You been awake long?'

'Lying thinking, and watching your pink bum edging nearer. You never could sleep straight.'

'Nice for you, was it?'

'Not really, Soldier, and I don't have to tell you why.'

'What time is it? Six yet?'

'About that.'

'Reveille. Oh, well. Some tea?'

'You're going to make it?'

'No, you. You're still my darling wife, aren't you?'

'All right, all right.'

'Put on a gown.'

'Why?'

'Why? Well, you always used to when you got up.'

'Is that a reason?'

'No, it's not, but put one on.'

'It doesn't seem to make much difference to you whether I'm dressed or naked.'

'Out of bed, it does.'

'I'm not speaking of out of bed, for Chrissake! What's the matter with you, Soldier?'

'You're the matter. Or I'm the matter. Or maybe this bloody life's the matter.'

'Well, well. That makes a lot of matters, doesn't it? Here's your tea. I hope it revives you a bit.'

'Thanks.'

'Hey, Soldier.'

'Yeah?'

'What about we have another child?'

'What for?'

'What for! What a question!'

'Well—why?'

'You don't see why? To stop the rot. We're getting near the edge.'

'You think so?'

'I know so. Things are getting fucked-up between you and me.'

'Or not fucked up.'

'That's it exactly.'

'And do you know why?'

'I think so. But tell me your idea.'

'You don't fancy me any more.'

'You say that to me after what I've just said to you?'

'You never said it with Kik and Mas—we both knew it, and it happened.'

'But we're older now.'

'Oh, sure. And different together.'

'And do you know why I think that is?'

'Go on . . .'

'Well, perhaps I'd better not tell you.'

'Don't play tricks, Evie. Say your piece.'

'All right. You just don't fancy fucking at all. And the excuse you make for yourself, is that I don't fancy you.'

'That's what you think.'

'I'm sorry, I do.'

'Well, you know something? You may be right, for all I know.'

'Well, then. Another tea?'

'No.'

'You know something else? You're wrong about Kik and Mas. It didn't just "happen".'

'No?'

'Cast your mind back. I wanted to put it off till you got posted back to England. You were on leave and in a hurry, and practically raped me.'

'It wasn't rape: it was unwilling consent.'

'All right, then. But Kik didn't just "happen".'

'Mas did . . .'

'Yes—he did. He was a love child, wasn't he, if ever there was one.'

'Yeah. We worked on him for about a fortnight solid, day and night, if I remember.'

'Solid's the word . . . And he came easy, too. But then the second often does, or so they say . . .'

'And now you want a third, is that it?'

'Yes, if you do.'

'Just to prove something, or because you want to?'

'Oh, for God's sake! You want me to take this gown off and we start now?'

'No. Not after a row like this.'

'What "row"? We're just discussing, aren't we? All men and women do at times, don't they?'

'Yeah. But when they do, they're often really talking about something different from what they seem to be.'

'Honest, Soldier! You're turning all complicated on me! You use'n't to be like that.'

'Nor you. Perhaps our lives here have made us complicated.'

'Let's get out, then. You want to? Back to Kilburn, and all that?'

'You see! It's you who don't really want to leave. You like your new life here. It's given you ideas.'

'Meaning?'

'You're looking for a second youth, Evie; and in a different world.'

'And you're not? It wasn't your idea to come here?'

'It was, until I found out what it's like. We're getting out of our depth in these surroundings. Or at any rate, I am.'

'I see. You don't think, Soldier, it could be you're getting a bit cowardly?'

'Me?'

'Yes: you. What do you think about that, truthfully?'

'What I think is, I'm finding out about myself, and so are you. And what we were six months ago, isn't what we're turning into now.'

'Oh, well ... What a stupid conversation on the start of a lovely summer's day!'

'Is that what it's going to be?'

'I dunno, Soldier. We'll see. Mind if I use the bathroom first?'

'Oh, sure. Wash all your sinful thoughts away.'

'Oh, fuck you, Soldier.'

*   *   *

Rattler and Aspen breakfasted meditatively upon the terrace.

'Try an avocado, dear. They add an exotic touch.'

'Too early: it's the only fruit that's meat.'

'You'd say so? Oh, I don't know. They add substance and inspiration to the morning; and salt and pepper, oil and vinegar, combined with their flaccid pulp, provide a symbolic taste of man's condition here below.'

'You *are* talkative early, Rattler. It's unusual. Your greetings to the dawn are often sombre.'

'Chatter, my dear, is a sure sign I'm thinking. It's only when I'm silent, and appear to ponder, that there's really nothing in my head at all.'

'But the chat bears little relation to the thought.'

'Indeed—except obliquely, I suppose. I see you looking at me, Aspen, with those steady, searching, yet revealing eyes. Questions are hovering on your fine, arched lips, I feel.'

'Just the same old, eternal question, Rattler. Do you

think you'll get away with whatever your imagination tells you that you're doing?'

'I don't know, but I must try—it is my destiny. Some coffee, dear?'

'No more just now.'

'Later, then, perhaps. How June-ish June is looking, don't you think? The perpetual English miracle, the annual transformation scene. Even that ancient ash has flowered at last. A late-comer, a reluctant tree, indigenous too ... so obstinate, but when it yields at last to the kind old sun, how rich and flourishing its foliage.'

'You're quoting something, Rattler. What's behind these wanton words?'

'Ah that, all that ... well, lots of things. For instance, the true nature of this lovely ruin. It began as one. Neglect made it even more so. I encouraged the process somewhat artificially. Traitor to my own device, I then decided to dispose of it, ensuring its final and effective ruination. And what now? From out of a clear, blue, metropolitan sky, appears one Mr Warsaw, who informs me —or rather, doesn't, but does through his Mercury, honest Leopold Watson, who appeared to be scared out of his scanty wits—who tells me, then, this Mr Warsaw, that the deal is off, unless.'

'Unless what?'

'Now this is what's incredible: even my tortuous brain can't fathom it. He wants me—so far as I could get the gist—to be his seneschal.'

'You must make it simpler for me, Rattler, if you can.'

'Would that I could! However, I hope to be able to, since the distinguished fellow's coming down today, he says, to have a chat. Says that *he's* coming, mark you, and not asks me if that's convenient, or if I might be playing golf this Saturday, or polo, or something equally habitual and ridiculous.'

'I see. And you've said yes?'

'To his visit? What else to do? The imperious chap won't take no for an answer, nor indeed wait to hear of any such; so courtesy, as well as curiosity, impel me to wait humbly his arrival. Besides which: I don't want the purchase of the Ruin to fall through, if I can avoid it. It will have served its purpose soon, and then I'll need the money, and not this almost incredible white elephant.'

'Yes, yes. But what is this seneschal thing, so far as you could get the gist?'

'You must regard this as a translation of dear Leopold's translation of whatever it was Warsaw said to him. But this seems to be roughly it. The fellow's a Pole, British of course, because valiant warrior with old Anders and all that, who's amassed, by brains, guts and imagination few others had when he did, a fortune of no one knows how much—probably not even he, let alone his forty accountants of as many companies. All this he's done in a most unostentatious way, so that, except in the financial columns, and even there, one doesn't hear much about him: I mean as a person, apart from a hovering presence in the commercial firmament. You with me so far, my dear, or am I boring you? Your eyes look glazed and vacant.'

'Pour me a coffee, please, and carry on.'

'Permit me. Well, then. The company that controls the companies that control most of the factory estate—excuse all this—was ready to do a deal with me to buy the Ruin, or its grounds, to erect thereon an adult play-park complete with appropriately revolting country club for the local executive lot. So far so dreadful. But now it appears, which I should have discovered, and Watson certainly should, and I'm going to tear his balls off because he didn't, that the controlling company is itself controlled, at some remote, inaccessible, but no less effective distance, by Mr Warsaw.'

'I expect you'll soon be coming to the point.'

'Patience dear; weary irony's unlike you. So, to proceed to what I've been able to extract from Watson's garbled, tortured tale. It appears Mr Warsaw likes the idea of a bogus stately home. It appears he likes even more the notion of an authentic resident exhibit, to wit me. And his proposal would seem to be that he finance the whole place on a lavish scale, and reward me, even more outrageously, for sitting here like a cunt, or prick if you think I'm prejudiced, doing sweet bugger-all except existing.'

'But why?'

'My dear, you're asking *me*? God knows, as usual—though I think I can hazard a guess. Everyone has his favourite mania, his lunatic fantasy; and the immensely rich can even afford to gratify them—or try to, at all events. I would guess, then, that Mr Warsaw has by now achieved all he wants in our fair land, except to feel he controls our spirit: or even one single spirit of our kind. Even that one.'

'I begin to see the light, though dimly. Please continue.'

'Well, then! If this is so, and it sounds crazy enough to me to be so, then I can see how I might appear to him the perfect candidate. Venal, decadent, and picturesque, old blood turned bitterly rancid, would be about his idea of me, I think. And more: rather dangerous, since a soldier of a defeated fighting tribe, and the soldier in him will see this as a further challenge. So, if he conquers me, he's won his final symbolic victory. Something like that is in his mind, I'd say.'

'And the idea annoys you? Arouses your indignation?'

'But of course! Fascination, too, a bit, I must admit. However: I don't, need I say, intend to be Mr Warsaw's plaything. I shall meet him, and see who turns out to be more devious and more dangerous.'

'I know you like danger, Rattler, and courting it; but aren't you over-tempting tired providence a little? All this, besides the other fires you've been stoking here?'

'If you mean my para-military projects, they're subsiding for the moment, so far as the Ruin goes. The deeds are done, or already in pipelines far from here. Your Mr Botany, and all the bondsmen using him, are welcome to snoop and spy to their hearts' content. In that respect, the place is clean.'

'And in other respects? You're still determined to involve innocent Adams in all this?'

'Yes, and I told you so; it's the poor man's destiny. Soldier's going to become a soldier again, when he least expects it. His family are in for some surprises too, but these perhaps won't shake them quite as much—their woman, at any rate. As for the dear lads, we'll see.'

'Could it be, dearest, you might be in for a surprise or two yourself?'

'The possibility always exists, of course. I can't control events, but try to shape them, as you know. And so do you, Aspen, in your way—which however close we are, isn't always mine, unfortunately. But there it is: I just can't do without you. Nor you, I think, dearest, without me.'

*   *   *

The pool, now gravel-lined, and fed by one of the four streams, had cleared. The boys stood on the edge, Kik sampling with a cautious toe.

'No. A nice idea, but on the whole I think it's no.'

His brother plunged, and Kik stepped back to dodge the spray.

'My word, Mas! You're getting absolutely Olympic.

Just look at that aboriginal crawl. I feel quite envious.'

'Come on in, then.'

'No, I think I'll have a smoke, and sit on the edge and paddle, clocking your energetic act.'

'It's not so cold once you get used to it.'

'I *knew* you'd say that, goose-pimples.'

'I'm coming out, though.'

'You see? Pray accept this rather grubby towel. Fag, little brother?'

'Ta. It's nice once you've been in, all the same.'

'Oh, I don't doubt it. And indeed, you look a picture of glowing health, like a telly commercial for something.'

'But you're getting skinnier, Kik.'

'What's that mean, midget?'

'It's because you're growing faster. You're going to be tall, like Dad.'

'But not you, boy. You'll be the stocky, sturdy type, like Mum's lot.'

'I know. I've warned you of that.'

'All right, all *right*. You won't be able to pull muscle on me for another year or two, though.'

'You want some tea? I've brought a thermos.'

'I say, you are an enterprising, thoughtful lad, I must say. No, no—after you, sir.'

'Go on.'

'*Merci*. Here! Have you put something funny into this?'

'A drop of Rattler's gin.'

'You have? Well, well. I'm not sure they go together, but I dare say the stomach will sort it all out somehow.'

'Can I have a drop?'

'Oh, yes, yes—sorry. Where did you get it, anyway? Did you nick a bottle?'

'No, I asked Aspen for it.'

'You did? And she gave it to you just like that?'

'It was half empty, and she said she didn't mind.'

'It's your boyish charm, Mas. It's that honest lad look that gets them all.'

'Don't keep on about this "boyish", Kik. I've told you.'

'Yes, I know you have. But you see, you *are*: the word springs to the lips of itself at the very sight of you. But don't be annoyed, some chicks adore it.'

'Can I have that thermos?'

'Don't sulk, now. You know Aphrodite? The Cyp chick at the discothèque? She thinks you're just peaches and cream; she told me so.'

'Very funny.'

'Cross my heart! Ask her, if you don't believe me.'

'Let's get back.'

'Oh Mas, for fuck's sake! I do wish you'd just grow *up*, so that I had a brother, like I used to! I do wish you weren't such a mother's boy.'

'Leave her out of it.'

'Don't be so touchy—it's just a phrase.'

'Don't needle me, then.'

'Okay, okay. So—Aspen. Is she hustling on those deals for us, do you think?'

'I don't think—I know. This month we'll be hearing something.'

'Oh, so you *know*. And if you do, what the hell does "something" mean?'

'She hasn't given me details, but she's promised, and I believe her.'

'You do, do you? You on the high seas, and me in a super-boutique? Well, we'll see. What *I* want to see, though, is whether she'll be able to handle Mum and Dad. You think she will?'

'She'll talk with them.'

'I'm sure she will. But if anything legal's involved, there's the laws of our land concerning infants, which is what you and I are, believe it or not.'

'I think she'll know how to handle it all.'

'Well, I hope so—I really do. Because in my opinion, old chap, the scene here's getting throughly screwed up. It gives me weird vibes, and I like it less and less.'

'Then tell her so.'

'No—you. You seem on a wave-length with that dainty lady.'

'I wouldn't call her "dainty".'

'No? What, then?'

'The trouble with you, Kik, is that you go for push-overs. Aspen's not like that.'

'Listen to him! You'll be turning me on to something, next.'

A springing step was heard on the path towards the pool, and the lads turned to see the lithe form of Rattler and, as he drew near, his gleaming grin.

'Good-day, young men! Let it not be said the youth of England lacks in valour! An early summer swim? You both deserve a medal! Wrap up, though—'ware pneumonia.'

'Care for a dip yourself, Captain?'

'No thank you, Kik. In high August, possibly, though I doubt it. I've lived too long in the tropics to enjoy swimming unless you don't feel the water when you immerse yourself.'

'It sure gives you an appetite. I was almost thinking of eating Mas when you appeared.'

'That would never do. Cannibalism is an ancient and worthy tradition among all peoples; but of rival warriors —brothers are tabu.'

'Then I'll have to settle for whatever Mum's got, and keep Mas as emergency rations.'

'You haven't breakfasted yet? Well, Aspen and I just have, and since she's withdrawn after eating nothing,

there's lots left on the terrace if you'd care to help yourselves. Unless, that is, your mother is expecting you...'

'Oh no, in our household you cook your own breakfast
when you feel like it. Mum only supplies the makings.'

'I see. Well, what do you say? And you, young Mas?'

'I don't want to trouble you, Captain Rattler.'

'No trouble at all. I'd be delighted to entertain you
two lively lads—we see all too little of one another.'

'Thanks, but I'll have it over at the cottage.'

'Oh, come on, Mas. Don't disappoint the Captain.'

'I'd be glad if you would, young fellow. I have, as a
matter of fact, something I'd like to ask you both. You
accept? That's fine! When you've adorned yourselves,
you'll find me awaiting you at the Ruin.'

'He is a bullshitting old arsehole, isn't he?'

'Quiet, Kik, he'll hear.'

'Oh no, he won't. His military footsteps are receding
through the elms: left, right, right, left ... off he goes.
Well, shall we stroll on up? He might have more of that
silken gin.'

'Be careful what you say in front of him.'

'Mas, little man! I *have* been around, you know ...
have you? Come on, let's go.'

The Captain presided on the terrace all at ease and
beaming, without, apparently, a care in the wide world.

'Sit yourselves down, gentlemen, and tuck in. An army,
Napoleon taught us—or was it Caesar?—marches on its
belly; and that's equally true, I think, of civilians over
whom we keep watch and ward.'

'They don't get grub like this, though, Captain.'

'Better, sometimes, after looting sessions. Generally,
though, it's as you say. Still—hunger flavours all dishes,
does it not?'

'Since you seem in such a good mood, Captain, could I
ask a favour?'

'The answer's probably no, Kik, but go ahead.'

'You wouldn't let me drive that round a bit, would you?'

'My sleek and treasured Capri? No, dear boy, I fear not.'

'Just round the grounds a bit.'

'Oho! You are a crafty fellow! Were you a soldier, I'd make you quartermaster instantly.'

'That's not quite an answer, is it?'

'Well, all right—effrontery, in my book, brings its own reward. One condition, though, old chap. If you damage that vehicle in any particular, *or* if you go out on the highway and I detect you, you take six of the Dr Arnold best on your Youth Power Delinquent Lib bottom.'

'Christ, you're a sadist, Captain.'

'Yes, of course.'

'This needs reflection.'

'Reflect, then. And don't forget, your honest brother here is witness to the agreement.'

'I don't want any part of this. You can both leave me out.'

'So be it. I will have to take your own dubious word, Kik. What do you say?'

'It's a deal. Let's have the keys.'

'I want them back, too, intact, if you'd be so kind. And don't think I'm kidding about our bargain; or that dire force will not be used if needed.'

'Okey-doke, Marquis. See you in Sade Castle, maybe. Or maybe not, 'cause I really am a rather classy driver.'

'That's just what I fear; and you, most of all, of course. Good fortune, lad, and don't be more than half an hour.'

Kik made a creditable, if somewhat over-speedy, start, and vanished with a slick gear-change among the limes.

'A fine lad, your brother. It's sad to see such talents wasted on a sort of social masturbation.'

'What does that mean, Mr Rattler?'

'Kik is just like that Capri, deprived of gears. The car looks promising, the engine races admirably, but the whole contraption fails to move in any practical direction. How unlike you, my boy, with your steadfast determination to serve your queen and country.'

'You like being sarcastic, don't you, mister?'

'It's a failing of my class, I must admit. Your own prefers to be sardonic, which is just as wounding in its way.'

'You think we can wound too?' .

'Oh yes, indeed I do! Even with silence, perhaps specially so, you can. I have sometimes faced a file of men whose blank eyes and closed lips spoke volumes. The officer class, to deal with that kind of situation, which I confess rather throws them since direct disobedience is not involved, have invented, to cover it, a crime they call "dumb insolence". But at best, this can only be applied to individuals; to accuse a whole platoon of it, would merely involve the poor officer in additional humiliation.'

'You never served in the ranks, did you?'

'No, and I must say I think, in our present social set-up, that the exercise is pointless. Officer material, planted like an exotic bloom among the men, behaves, and is treated as, what it is: a sort of spy, a princess pretending to be a dairy-maid awhile. No: officer material should be trained as such right from the outset.'

'And what do you call "officer material"?'

'You mean in its essence? Irrespective of political and social pressures?'

'I mean the real man for being that.'

'Ah, that I think's an easy one to answer, despite such men, even in the most favourable circumstance, being rather hard to find. He must be brave, obviously; I don't mean rash, but consistently and naturally brave or, at least, able always to control cowardice. He must be able to handle men—and this I believe to be entirely an instinctive matter: a born pack leader, as among animals, children, people wrecked on rafts or desert islands ... the one the others turn to instantly, and without knowing why, to take control of a situation. And last—and God knows it's often forgotten, or worse, taken for granted, or worse still, "taught" as if it ever could be—he must be practical: just that. In any crisis, he must weigh all factors instantly, and know exactly what to do.'

'And you're all those things?'

'My dear fellow—please!'

'Well—are you? After all, you've been a colonel.'

'The best—or the worst—I can say, Mas, is that I am, and I am not. Don't frown, I'm not dodging your question, or presenting you with a paradox. But let me say this to you. I think my only weakness is, I'm perhaps too conscious of my own processes: too much aware of what I am. Does that make any sense to you?'

'I'll have to think it over.'

'A good answer, if I may say so. And what about you, young fellow?'

'Me?'

'You. What resounding qualities, or dreadful failings, do you esteem you have? And if you think I'm being sarcastic, you needn't answer.'

'I'm not sure I want to, anyway.'

'Then don't.'

'Though I'd say the best thing I've got is that I'm English.'

'My dear fellow, you surprise me! Isn't that a rather conventional remark? One that is echoed by countless india-rubber patriots and mindless xenophobes?'

'*Must* you use all those words?'

'Sorry. Well, now—English. What do you see as the virtue in being that? After all, the mere cosmic accident that you were born that way, doesn't prove anything in particular, does it?'

'We're a fine people.'

'Peculiar, certainly; remarkable, possibly. But "fine"?'

'I think so.'

'I know you do, old man. But why?'

'Because starting from next to nothing, we've made our mark on the entire world.'

'A large claim, indeed. Yet valid, I would say, provided you admit that the world has not liked this "mark" very much, and that we've ceased to make it.'

'Who's trying to explain what I think, Mr Rattler? You or me?'

'Sorry: proceed, then. I am all ears.'

'You can't be if you're still yapping. All right, then. "Starting from nothing." How many were we in Queen Elizabeth's day?'

'I may speak?'

'Oh, for fuck's sake!'

'Possibly four millions. Five, maybe. Thereabouts.'

'And what power and riches had we?'

'Relatively, I suppose, quite a lot. Absolutely, next to nothing.'

'Right! So that's how we started, isn't it? And in four hundred years, we were everywhere.'

'I say, you are a scholarly fellow! But this, my dear chap, is ancient history. Our most recent conquest, may I remind you, was of the peak of Rockall, the size of a nut, and inhabited by seagulls. Elsewhere, we've tended to vamoose in a most slattern and slovenly fashion.'

'But you can't deny a minor people made themselves major, and left their mark.'

'Historically, I agree. But now?'

'How many people in the world speak English?'

'Good God, I must confess I don't know. In various

versions, many incomprehensible, hundreds of millions, anyway. But I don't see that you've proved anything much. For after all: if you say to an Australian he's speaking your language, he'll reply that he isn't, or alternatively, so what?'

'But look, Mr Rattler! The fact remains we *did* invent it, and all those millions who speak it, didn't. A sign of a great people is to invent its own language, and then make it universal.'

'Even if that were so, dear boy, the feat is far from being exclusively ours. There are the Spaniards; the Arabs; the Chinese could make an excellent case, in terms of numbers.'

'All right. But is there any other people whose words were once spoken by fewer, but now are spoken by more?'

'You're a shrewd, if somewhat Churchillian, dialectician, I perceive. Yes, I think you've made your point. But what does it show?'

'That every time millions of people open their mouths, we're influencing them. And a people who know they've done that, know they're great.'

'Even if the alien races don't admit it? And even if most of our own people aren't even aware of it?'

'You try to put down the classes you don't know. Book education isn't everything; people learn more in families than they do in schools.'

'There, I rather agree with you. But what of this people now?'

'Well, what of them?'

'We are a defeated people, my dear Mas.'

'You think so? Well, haven't we been defeated before, and started again?'

'Yes, but the defeats have been minor, and the reconquests, major.'

'You think the loss of America was a minor defeat?'

'That was so long ago, Mas!'

'You think the loss of a million of our youngest and best after 1914 was nothing? But didn't we go on?'

'We tottered on.'

'You think we fell flat on our faces after we lost so much in the last big war?'

'On our arses, I'd say—and are still in that undignified, recumbent posture.'

'You're a defeatist, Mr Rattler—and you know why? Because you confuse your class with the people. Because if you've lost, you think we have.'

'Indeed? And who is this "we" of your fantasy—so robust, so indestructible, so forward-looking? A resentful, greedy, whining, idle mass—is that it? Enlivened with the colourful castaways of an abandoned empire? Is *that* your great English people?'

'You know, Captain, I'm sorry for you.'

'Oh, *are* you!'

'Yes, I fucking am. You're here, but you've been left behind.'

'Oh, I have, have I!'

'What you've never understood is that the people invented the speech, not universities. That we built up the wealth, and you took it. That our sort went out as soldiers and sailors everywhere, and yours claimed the victories. So when a knock comes, you're lost, and we're still there.'

'Any nation needs leaders, child.'

'Oh, sure. But you've lost the skill and confidence: we're just beginning.'

'I see, I see. However, I'm speaking of what has been proved, and you of optimistic, and rather vainglorious, surmises. My own diagnosis is rather different, though it has points of similarity with yours. I also sense the greatness you refer to, but one that is lost, and turned in on itself to become a species of febrile, if lively, decadence.

But this very wreckage can, I believe, be organized into fresh and productive patterns on a more limited scale.'

'By you and your lot.'

'By me, and by anyone from any lot who understands our status and how to manipulate it.'

'I don't like the smell of that, much.'

'Indeed!'

'It sounds to me like yet another con.'

'You *are* a subversive lad, beneath your dutiful exterior, I must say! You'll be saying next, perhaps, that I conned you all into coming here.'

'I wasn't speaking personally, Mr Rattler, and I don't see why you should.'

'I merit your rebuke, dear boy. We were, it is true, discussing generalities. And now, since I see your reckless brother approaching, it will be a matter of examining the particular—I mean the condition of my Capri. So thanks for our little chat, it's given me food for meditation.'

The Captain arose, and strolled over to the car; the thought entering his head, 'I must eliminate that little bastard.'

'Here we are, Captain. All present and correct.'

'Move over, Kik, but don't get out yet. You and I are going on a tour of inspection.'

The Captain drove five hundred yards in silence, then stopped the car in a glade, and cut the engine. He laid an arm behind his companion's shoulder, then turned and stared at Kik.

'Your brother seems to be somewhat uppity. What do you suppose has got into him?'

'Fuck Mas—what about the car? Is everything to your satisfaction? It should be, because I handled it like an angel.'

'Your own cheek I'm used to, even welcome; but what's

made young Mas so full of himself? Just growing older,
would you say? Patterning his conduct on his senior's?'

'Oh, Mas is a mystery to me...'

'I don't think so, lad. I sense someone's put new notions
in his head. What can they be? And whose? Any ideas?'

The Captain's hand gripped Kik's neck tight, yet lightly.

'Hey—take it easy, Captain! The car's quite okay, and
you know it. If you think anything's wrong with it, say
so—and get your fucking claws off my spine.'

'Answer me, boy. *Answer*, I say.'

'He's not going to be a soldier now.'

'Oh, no? What, then?'

'He's going to travel, or something.'

'How? Join the merchant navy? Hitch-hike to Aus-
tralia? *What?*'

'Oh, hands off, fuck you! Take it *easy*! Someone's trying to fix it for him.'

'Who?'

'Don't *you* know? *She* is.'

'Oh, I see. Yes, yes—I see. Well, well. Thank you, Kik.
The car seems quite in order. You want to drive it
back?'

'No thanks—I'll walk.'

'Get out, then. The stroll will do you good.'

*　　*　　*

Aspen, meandering through the valley, stopped cautiously
when she heard a shot. Approaching and peering, she saw
Soldier on his belly, taking aim towards a cliff. She waited
till another crack, then called from behind an oak. He
lowered the rifle, and looked round about.

'Hullo there!'

'Oh, it's you! Well, come on out: you're in no danger.'

'Why this military display?'

'That's it exactly. I was checking if my eye has lost its cunning.'

'And it hasn't?'

'Hard to say yet, till I go and inspect my target. You like to have a go?'

'I wouldn't mind ... What are you aiming at?'

'That stump with two twigs—see? But you'd better choose something different, or we won't know who's hit what. So here you are.'

'You haven't put it "safety", Soldier. Is that according to the book of rules?'

'My word, I *am* slipping, aren't I? You used to these things?'

'Don't tell a soul, but my sort are reared on weapons. At ten, I was allowed out with an air-gun. Light rifle at twelve. Ladies' shot-gun, so-called, shortly after.'

'Deeds, not words: down on your belly, madam. What's your target?'

'I don't like hitting trees ... I'll try two at the rock beside your stump. Here comes the first.'

'... bull, I think. Nice. You look very pretty down there, by the way.'

'Shut up, I must concentrate. Here's number two.'

'Not sure of that one. We stroll over and have a look? Let me give you a hand up.'

'Thank you, sir. And here is your weapon, rendered harmless for a while. So: how have you been, Soldier? We haven't met much since our longish chat about the lads.'

'It wasn't a chat: you lectured me.'

'Not really ... I was asking you; if what I said might not be better for them.'

'Yeah.'

'You decided anything? Talked about it with Evie?'

'No, not with Evie. I don't discuss much these days with Evie.'

'Your own ideas, then?'

'My own ideas? You want to know what they are? I can sum them up for you in just two words, really, and they're "fuck them". Okay—so look at me like that! But it's my conclusion after six months home: everyone wants to go their own way, so let them, and I'm going mine.'

'And what's that?'

'I'm planning to work for a former mate of mine. If Evie likes it too, that's fine; if not, it's up to her. As to the boys, or former boys, they've got so many bright ideas, and everyone's adding others, they might as well try them, and see what happens. But me, I want to stay with what I know, or more or less do.'

'Well, all right, then. Don't shout at me.'

'Women always say that when you talk sense to them. But it's sense for myself I'm talking now. I've served this country twenty-two years, and from what I've seen of it now, it's not worth fighting for. I've reared a family as best I could, and it's all falling apart. So from now on, I'm looking after number one.'

'Okay, then. Are you on to something good?'

'I hope to own a boozer one fine day. But that'll need bread I haven't got yet.'

'You find out how, and I might find some cash, if you care to keep in touch.'

'Oh yeah? I can't quite make out whether you're Lady Bountiful or Little Miss Nosy.'

'A bit of both, I expect. But if you're going to do it, don't delay.'

'Oh? What's the hurry?'

'Fortune's a woman, Soldier—you have to chase her. You need an idea, to work at it, and then she smiles, sometimes. Besides which: I think this scenery's not right for you.'

'This place, or the whole Ruin?'

'All of it. Another thing, if you'll allow me. You're feeling sorry for yourself, and that's not like you.'

'Now, don't *you* start, Aspen!'

'Oh, excuse me.'

'Excuse you! They insult you, then say that! Well, there it is—just look! We've neither of us done brilliantly, I'd say—each only one shot on target, and one lost.'

'You don't think I've hit this rock twice in the same place...?'

'That old trick! No, dear, I don't. Let's sit down and have a fag to soothe our nerves.'

'All right—it's a nervy day. The first real one of summer always is: everyone, everything changes; it takes a day or two to get adjusted.'

'Correct. In the tropics, you don't notice the sun, except as a nuisance; but here, it turns all of us slightly mad. Speaking of which: you wouldn't feel like a fuck, would you?'

'Mad indeed, Soldier. No thanks, no thank you. And kindly wipe off that rapist glare from your honest features.'

'Now, that *is* an insult! Only cowards and sadists are rapists, in my opinion.'

'And you're neither, I'm sure.'

'Sadist, no—even with raw recruits, I hadn't that reputation. Coward, I hope not, Aspen; but you never, never know. Or rather—you do. As a soldier, I think I have been once or twice, and can I tell you something that I think you'll understand, in spite of being "only a woman", as they stupidly say, who in my opinion are far braver, and make less fuss about it? Well listen, it's this: in battle, a situation can arise when you do enough—enough to get by in front of the lads—but not what you should have done. Now, is that cowardice? I know one who thinks it is: and that's Rattler.'

'Rattler's too vain, not even proud, to be a coward.'

'Perhaps that's it. But this I know, there are some decisions I just can't take. Now Evie, she's not like that—she can, if she feels strongly, and whether her action's right or wrong. And perhaps that's why, deep down, she despises me a bit; or pities. And fuck that—it's worse.'

'In a way, she doesn't really know you all that well, perhaps—or am I wrong?'

'In twenty years, we've never spent one together—I mean consecutive, and day by day. It's been barracks, or foreign postings, with spells of leave between like unreal honeymoons.'

'Soldier, you'll have to sort it out—her way or yours.'

'I know, I know. What you bet I can hit that nest up in that tree?'

'Nothing: I like birds. Come on, let's go.'

'Me too, and I'm not getting much these days from mine.'

*   *   *

A cordial cry and wave from Rattler summoned Evie, bicycling through the park, towards a table underneath the spreading ash.

'A word of counsel from you, dear, I pray. Perceive this groaning board, on which I'm rashly proposing to take luncheon. Now tell me, please, first glancing skyward. You, more familiar than poor exiled I with the vagaries of the English climate, would you say to eat outside is rash? Foolhardy to the point of lunacy? At the crux of the banquet, will the heavens open, mid a clap of thunder, and deluge us as in the days of Noah?'

'Have you been drinking, Captain?'

'Well—just a bit. Have a tipple too, please, to relieve my troubled conscience. Guilt, like misery, seeks companions.'

'What are you on, at this early hour?'

'Rum punch, an old favourite of mine, and of my own concoction. The recipe I learned while on service in the Antilles. The amiable locals call the brew "White Man's Evil".'

'Just one, then. But why eat out doors at all if you're unsure?'

'Ah, that's just it, you see. I must entertain, today, an alien gentleman—or one, at least, of extraneous origin. And I thought to impress him by a display of that hallowed English institution, the al fresco repast amid the wasps and rain-drops. So I chose this *echt Englisch* site neath the shade of these venerable leaves. Observe this sturdy trunk, and branches rising like suppliant fingers to the sky! Does not this ancient tree, well-known to our most distant ancestors, embody the antique wisdoms of our race?'

'Frankly, Captain, I'd say you're a bit pissed. Let's hope the foreign gentleman doesn't take advantage of you.'

'If he attempts anything so vile, I shall call on your stalwart husband for timely succour. How is he, by the bye? I haven't chatted with him yet this sunny morning, but I caught a glimpse of him, escorted by dear Aspen, and bearing, as was erstwhile his wont, a rifle.'

'Are you having me on, Mr Rattler?'

'By no means, unless my eyes deceived me. Mayhap they were out shooting conies, or on such a magical day as this, a unicorn—who knows? Your sons, however, I've already met with, and had a delightful word with each. The lads seem fired with ambitions of the noblest and most daring kind.'

'And what does that mean, if anything? At their age, the wildest ideas are always running through their heads.'

'True, true; but I fancy their infant projects are becoming more specific—such was, at any rate, my impression.

They seemed inspired—perhaps, indeed, by she who, although so young, has ever been my own dear guardian angel. I refer, of course, to Aspen.'

'And what's she been inspiring them to do?'

'I mean to ask her: you might too, I think. A mother, I know, instinctively can detect the influences on her off-springs' native genius. So seek her out! And you and I, too, dear Evie Adams, might have a further word on this, perhaps this afternoon. I feel for those boys as I do for my own sons, almost, and while I wish them their every hearts' desire, however foolish, I think we should seek to inject into their projects the quavering tones of a mature sagacity. Do have another whitey's punch.'

'One knock-out's enough. And you'd better lay off too, I'd say.'

'Then try, instead, one of these rare and delicious tropical globes of succulence.'

'Is it a plum?'

'A marriage twixt plum and peach, and called a nectarine—the consequent blend as tastefully rarefied as both. Come, take another, your family might care to sample them; and the bowl can easily be replenished, for I have a generous and costly crate inside. Don't gaze at it as if I'd handed you a lemon—be bold, my dear, and venture at least a nibble.'

'It tastes peculiar, but nice.'

'Exactly! 'Ware stones, though! As roses have thorns, so do nectarines contain a stubborn nut—and yet, once cracked open, an acid core within that's an acquired taste, as they say, but lasting.'

*　　　*　　　*

The confrontation of the girls was brisk; and odd because, beside the tool-shed, each clutched a mechanism of bicycle and rifle, which last Aspen was found cleaning with a pull-through.

'Could I have a word with you?'

'Say on.'

'You mind putting down that artillery a moment?'

'Not a bit; it's a tedious task, that Soldier seemed reluctant to perform. Do park your bike, too, and let's hear.'

'And don't talk down to me.'

'And don't get shirty. You want to speak, Evie? Unload it, then.'

'You been out firing guns with Soldier?'

'Yes.'

'Why?'

'Have you got a point, or points, to make? If so, let's hear them.'

'What have you been saying to him? And to my kids?'

'That they should organize themselves. And not be washed around like driftwood.'

'That's not my business?'

'Obviously. You doing it?'

'You telling me how to run my marriage? You? What do you know about marriage, Lady Aspen? Or having children?'

'Nothing. But I do know a bit about Soldier, Kik, and Mas, and about Rattler, and about you, and most of all, about myself.'

'What does that leave you *don't* know?'

'Exactly what you're going to do next. That is, to spell it out: either re-build with them, as best you can, and taking account of what they *are*, or become the Cleopatra of the Home Counties.'

'One more crack like that, and your face is slapped.'

'Do try, Evie, if you feel like it. Let's see what happens.'

'Don't tempt me.'

'It's not me who's doing that, and you should have

213

spotted by now who is. Also, who's getting indignant because they're thinking of succumbing.'

'You're hand in glove with him, and you know it.'

'I do. But I'm warning you, and not enticing. Not that a warning ever did anyone much good, in my experience.'

' "Experience"! Yours, little miss! Experience!'

'Yes, mine. Do you want to get out of the way, or would you like to see my experience with a rifle butt?'

'You're a toffee-nosed slut, in my opinion.'

'Just about that ... Why don't you stop your sweet mouth with that nectarine? It might save anyone else getting indigestion.'

*   *   *

Bearing a bottle of white rum, two sliced limes, an ice bucket with glasses and a forlorn appearance, Rattler came suppliant to the Adams cottage. He found Soldier 'out the back', sunning himself in a deck-chair.

'Old friend, I need your help: but first, have you got a corkscrew?'

'They don't put corks in nowadays, do they?'

'This is a rare Barbadian brew, whose distillers haven't caught up with the march of progress.'

'Try cracking the neck off: I've seen you do it more than once...'

'Ah yes, but in the desperate desert days of "needs must" ... However, let's see if I still can neatly, without filling our gut with deadly slivers. Close your eyes—here goes! Ah—victory!'

'Pour a bit on the ground for safety's sake.'

'Provident as ever, Soldier. Besides, it's an ancient tribal custom—did you know? The natives thus greet their ancestors, before imbibing: too reverently, I often felt, as I saw the precious fluid sinking in the sand.'

'So what's this state visit for, if I may enquire? You know? Purpose of manoeuvre always comes first in a competent officer's briefing.'

'Indeed! Soldier, I need your aid and succour.'

'So I imagined. Well?'

'All the indications are, alas, you're tiring of me and my madcap schemes, and want to move on to pastures new.'

'And so?'

'Since you came here kindly of your own free will, and are thus under no duress, I shall not speak of desertion in the face of the enemy. Nor would I seek to involve you in any para-military plans of which I sense you increasingly disapprove. However, I do have a crisis on my hands, and to help me solve it, I come to appeal for your voluntary aid.'

'What's happening now? You're being sold up? The Law is on its way?'

'Nothing so desperate yet, though perhaps, in the long term, more menacing. I have to entertain, to lunch, a Mr Warsaw.'

'And what am I supposed to do with him, whoever he is? Slip a grenade in his pocket—your way of disposing of unwanted prisoners?'

'Nothing so radical as that. Warsaw is, in brief, a man of enormous substance, and growing influence, in our land and my more modest affairs. I foresee he's coming here to bully me, and I want an ally.'

'Yes, sure, but to do what?'

'Just to be present at the luncheon.'

'It can't only be that.'

'Oh yes, indeed: to lend me your moral support. For that, Soldier, whatever our past differences may have been, is what I've always needed most from you. For there is a sense, dear fellow—a profound sense—in which, since

I've known you, I've not been able to function fully without you.'

'Captain: you really believe that shit?'

'Adams! I do, I do!'

'You know what you're doing—indirectly, of course, because I know you? You're telling me I have a debt of my life, out there in the desert, that you'll always be asking me to repay.'

'Perhaps, perhaps ... Repay it just this once, then, and the debt, if it was ever one, is no more.'

'I see. So what do I have to do: wait at table? Or just sit there, looking loyal, fairly tough, and with my wits about me?'

'But you are all those things, and don't I know it!'

'And isn't your Aspen all of them and more? Isn't *she* going to lend you any moral support on this occasion?'

'It's a man-to-man situation, we both feel. Women are often best kept in reserve ... hidden down in the *wadi*, behind the sand dunes ...'

'Captain, you are a wonderful old fraud! Unique, I'd say—really!'

'And so you've not turned me down—is that it?'

'Not yet, I haven't, Rattler ... But after this, we'll have to see.'

'Ah yes—ah yes, we will.'

*   *   *

Mr Warsaw arrived modestly, as befits the great, and driving his own Rover. Rattler's first impression, as they shook firm hands in the Ruin's portico, was of contained, almost indifferent, calm. One would certainly not have spotted Warsaw in a crowd! But perhaps, if one had, his distant assurance might have seemed increasingly disturbing.

'Welcome to our folly, Mr Warsaw. If you'll step this

way, under the loggia, we'll find a drink awaiting us on the sunnier side upon the terrace, which commands our most sensational view; and also an old comrade-in-arms of mine, whom I hope you'll not mind meeting, by name of Adams, a former sergeant of our army days.'

'Certainly, Captain—thank you. A Saturday drive is always an exhaustion.'

'A waste of spirit in an expanse of fumes and nervous energy, as our national poet failed to say.'

'He said "shame".'

'Oh, yes! You're a fan of gentle Will's, like so many, Mr Warsaw? It's true his opus has almost been annexed by those born outside this blessed plot.'

'The less happier breeds may find his words more relevant to their present experience, Captain Rattler.'

'Ah yes, indeed ... Though we, too, may soon be re-entering a Tudor era in contemporary guise ... Sergeant Adams—Mr Warsaw. You were an army man, too, were you not, in those distant days? I ask, since so many gallant Poles were pilots.'

'Yes, a soldier. I reached your own rank, though I believe you have sometimes attained to higher.'

'You've been reading me up, I see, and my modest attainments. Yes: the British army delights in human vicissitudes. One goes up and down like a veritable monkey on a stick, depending not on military expertise, but on "establishments" as they're so quaintly called. Now, then: do try this refreshing over-primed rum punch.'

'Thank you. To your health, Captain, and your prosperity. To yours, Sergeant, no less.'

'Do please be seated on this not very reassuring, yet entirely reliable, wicker chair: an authentic item of our great-grandparents' day, that has honourably upheld many a stately Victorian bottom. Luncheon awaits us, in a moment, on the sward—we thought you'd enjoy a *déjeuner sur l'herbe* or, at all events, be ready to risk one. Meanwhile, Mr Warsaw, do please tell me more about yourself. I've heard infinite rumours, of course—who, indeed, has not? For it seems that, since William the Conqueror, you are the most potent invader of our shores.'

'He was not a financier, Captain. Figures, not arms, have been my weapon. Or rather, shield. For it must not be thought—and I, of all people, know it best—that you are without your own financial wizards.'

'A childish question, for I have, in many ways, a simple mind: how *does* one make lots of money, Mr Warsaw?'

'Given talent, as in anything: you think constantly of nothing else whatever; or of nothing not relevant to amassing it.'

'But we're all obsessed with money, surely! Or most of us most of the time, at any rate.'

'Very far from it, I assure you. Most think of spending it; some of getting it; few indeed think perpetually of creating it.'

'I see, I see.'

'I doubt if you do, if you'll excuse me. For instance: you have driven down here often enough from London?'

'Of course.'

'So: can you tell me the current value, and date at which their leases expire, of every vital site and building on the journey?'

'My dear fellow!'

'I can. I have made it my business to find out, and to remember.'

'I see! And so—forgive the somewhat personal note—you've precisely assessed the value of our Ruin here?'

'No, *not* precisely; and that is why I've asked you kindly to receive me for a conversation.'

'You're not saying it has *no* value, I dare hope...'

'Oh, no; but much of this value lies in its intangibles.

Such cases are rare, as a matter of fact, though vendors, let alone officials, elected or otherwise, do not realize this ... until too late. They all suppose *their* land or building is a special case. There are few such, please believe me, Captain Rattler: the laws of the market, properly understood, are quite inexorable.'

'But we *are* a special case, I take it. Well, that's reassuring ... or perhaps it isn't? Well—we'll see! Do take your glass, Mr Warsaw, and let's step over under those spreading boughs, for our collation. I thought trout would be nice—it comes, incredibly, from a local and little-polluted stream. Then a host's selfishness—some goose; an under-cherished bird I relish greatly. Salad, of course, and from the estate, what's more. Early raspberries, and not their cruder, fatter cousin, then await us. Wines, as they say, to taste. I hope you'll not be disappointed.'

'I rarely am, Captain, and am sure I will not be on this occasion. You really are most kind and thoughtful. You too, Mr Adams, for I know how the sergeants do the work, and the officers claim the credit.'

'Not my doing, as it happens, but the Captain's cook's. If you'd come to my place, it would have been roasts— the warmer the day, the hotter.'

'Mrs Adams is a traditionalist, I would guess. But I admire this; a people's customs are a very proof of their existence, their survival.'

'Quite so—and here we are. Take the chair, Mr Warsaw, please, while Adams and I range ourselves with deference, as befits us, round about you. For let any say what he will: everyone, in his heart of hearts, respects a millionaire.'

'Or a nobleman, Captain Rattler, as it may be.'

'But there's no difference at all, Mr Warsaw, or rather, wasn't! All noblemen of any authenticity began as men of substance—whence, indeed, their initial enoblement.

Surprisingly, a fortunate number still survive enriched; but if they have lost their lands and gold, they are not respected at all, and merely accorded the interest aroused by any privileged mountebank.'

'This trout is excellent, may I say. You don't quite believe that, do you, though?'

'Your compliment to the fish, or to my tattered vestiges of glory?'

'Captain Rattler: what you say is evidently so. I am far from being impressed by the supposed qualities of those noblemen, having witnessed the manic irresponsibility of their conduct in my country, where I regret their disappearance not a whit. Nor do I esteem that in England, since the last century at any rate, they have earned their keep, socially or morally, as other classes have, save possibly in the matter of physical bravery which, considering their surviving privileges, was the least that could be expected of them. As for the vast majority of their lord and ladyships who, since 1900, are mere political creations, they are pensioners in fancy dress. And yet there is this. In some of the older families of this country—though not really old, if you will excuse me, by the standards of Continental Europe—I have found that there are men and women who, whatever they may *be*, do understand a great deal most do not: do have a rare apprehension of certain realities in their nation.'

'Which you do not have: is that it?'

'How can I? There is a limit to what one can learn of a country, whatever one's gifts and application, if one reaches it late, and with such a different background. There are things, Captain Rattler, which you knew at ten, that I shall never know.'

'Unless you're told—I see. But Adams here could tell you just as well.'

'I do not think I under-value Mr Adams, for I am not

conceited, nor a fool. But his knowledge, which I'm sure is deep, cannot be, in the nature of things, what yours is, or what I need to know. Are you acquainted with horse racing? Probably so. Forgive this comparison, then. In an old and well-established stable, whatever its present fortunes, there is knowledge that cannot be found elsewhere. I don't simply mean of present winners, or of past achievements; but of the whole what, why, when, how, where and who of breeding.'

'I congratulate you on your idiomatic turn of speech.'

'Captain Rattler—please! I know I have an accent: don't turn the knife in the open wound.'

'I see, then; at least, I vaguely do. You are in a position, if you wish, to move the little pawn of my modest property off your complex board, but will spare me from oblivion if I consent to be your counsellor on the equal complexities of the English temperament. Is it something of that sort you have in mind? Do try this goose.'

'Thank you—no, no, I offer more. Counsel is useless without involvement. It is something in the nature of a partnership I have in mind.'

'Oh, come, come, Mr Warsaw! You with your millions, and I with my brains and Ruin? I'm not a modest man, thank God—but really! What have I to give you?'

'A political collaboration, also.'

'Indeed?'

'Oh, yes. I see the way things are moving, Captain Rattler. You must remember, please, I have lived in the most intimate way, which meant in perpetual danger to my life, amid political upheavals in Europe during the last forty dreadful years. This makes one sensitive to trends, to tendencies, to under-currents—please believe me.'

'And what do your instincts tell you about the land of your adoption, Mr Warsaw?'

'Much the same as yours tell you, Captain, I believe.'

'Mr Rattler, I think I'll fall out now, if you don't mind. Thanks for the meal, and all the rest of it, and nice to have met you, Mr Warsaw.'

'Now, Adams, really—there's no need to go. Our friend here and I are merely discussing generalities.'

'Yes, and you're getting down to particulars I don't want any part of. I know just what you need from me, and this time out, you're not going to get it.'

'And what do I need from you, Soldier?'

'An honest witness to dishonest talk, just to test it out on him, and see which way it bounces back. You've always used me like that, Rattler, since I've known you. I've been your sounding-board, your moral stooge, just for you to find out how far you could go in any direction. But the trouble, for me, is this: the further you've gone, the more you've carried me with you, and this time, at last, I'm crying "halt!"'

'Soldier, my dear fellow—really! Still, just as you feel. Fall out, as you say, and we'll chat about all this later.'

'I doubt it. Good afternoon, gentlemen.'

'Well! Forgive that little episode, if you will.'

'It is understandable, and revealing. I know the sergeant's mentality, only too well: any duty whatever faithfully performed, provided the ultimate responsibility is his who gave the order.'

'I suppose that's it: yet I *am* attached to that fellow—deeply so.'

'I, also, had a subordinate to whom I was devoted, and on whom I utterly relied. I understand such affinities of men who seem so different.'

'Exactly! Now: what are these notions of mine you know so well?'

'Would it make things simpler if I told you I have often discussed such matters with Colonel Peterson, whose military-political theories are much like your own? For

Colonel Peterson has understood the importance finance will have in his undertakings; internationally, as much as within these shores.'

'You foresee a stronger government here, Mr Warsaw?'

'Realities are breaking through the crust of dying forms and notions, to reshape the structure of societies. The choices are narrowing fast, the patterns forming into few. I mean to assist the process here, and profit by it.'

'You can't need much more money, surely! Do you want that old bugbear, power?'

'Politically, no. I wish to see reality recognized and respected: it is almost the only thing I love.'

'You might be backing a wrong horse, to coin a metaphor: history never repeats itself, and politics are, at best, a chancy matter.'

'It never repeats itself, and yet conforms to shapes that can be studied and assessed ... Why do Grand Masters pore over contests of the past? Or soldiers learn from dead men's strategy? Or even sportsmen, review games that are played out and gone? Not because they suppose such events will ever recur; but to find out how those of now might do so in the future.'

'You know these events may be dangerous: will be lethally so, for some.'

'Do not try to frighten me with what I know as well as you.'

'Well, I see, Mr Warsaw. Try a brandy, will you? We might drink, might we not, to our better understanding of each other, and to such graver matters.'

'Just an instant, Captain: there is one thing more. I need an associate to plan, to succeed, in this with me.'

'Other than myself, you mean?'

'I mean Lady Aspen.'

'Do you! Oh, do you! Well, well, well!'

'I need a woman for a hundred reasons, the least of

which is sexual. There are tasks in a venture of this scope and scale that only a woman can perform.'

'But my dear Warsaw, you leave me breathless! You wish to encompass a social upheaval in our peaceful country! You wish to enlist my services to this end! And now you want Aspen to serve your purposes too! But what of my feelings in the matter? And what, even more, of hers? What, in short, do you *know* of Aspen?'

'Little and much. You must please understand I would not have approached you without profound reflection, and profounder study. Any knowledge, other than personal, about you both that can be acquired, I now possess. If this should appear effrontery, it is that I am telling you the truth. This I can make plain to you by saying that what I can offer you both, which is much, and potentially everything, is less than you, and especially she, can offer me: to help me make my thoughts of reality, reality itself.'

'Just that!'

'Just that.'

'I see.'

'So?'

'Pray don't be impatient, Mr Warsaw! No English family, however illustrious, will refuse the hand of its dearest and fairest to anyone, if the recompense be commensurate. But still: Aspen is Aspen and, quite apart from the altered conventions of our era, not mine to dispose of as I might wish, nor anyone else's other than her own self. Therefore, it seems to me: your peculiar proposal, embellished by greater precision, must be put to her plainly for her answer.'

'I ask for nothing else.'

'And who will perform this delicate task? Will you?'

'I should prefer it to be you.'

'You do me much honour. Well, we shall see; although

I think I should warn you I can tell you what her reply will be.'

'Tell me that, please, and not your prophecy.'

'So be it; shall we go in?'

*   *   *

Rattler brooded long after Warsaw's discreet departure. Then, sending for Aspen, as if he were indeed 'the head of the family', he installed himself in the traditional setting, the library. There, looking rather distraught, she soon appeared.

'My dear: something bizarre has just come up. Guess what.'

'*Please*, Rattler.'

'Warsaw wants to make you his concubine.'

'Oh yes? Isn't it usual to ask the girl direct?'

'He chickened out, and left the job to me.'

'I see; you haven't yet sold me into his clutches, then.'

'Dear Aspen!'

'I'm fascinated: do tell me what you thought of him.'

'Physically? Well, middle fifties, presentable if not distinguished, virile in a neutral sort of way. Manners impeccable and poised, if lacking grace and polish. Intelligence extreme—so much, he hides three parts of it. Temperament, I'd say audacious and implacable, yet patient or, at any rate, can bide his time. No charm, if that matters, but considerable dignity without imposing it. As to his moral, spiritual, qualities and so forth—well, need we go into that?'

'And what does he offer?'

'The earth. Or as large a chunk of it as anyone could reasonably digest.'

'And what would I have to do?'

'Be helpmeet in all his undertakings; he didn't insist on the sensual aspect particularly.'

'Not flattering. And why me?'

'Why, indeed? Except that he's somehow discovered, or surmised, that you are, dearest Aspen, nothing less than unique.'

'And did you tell him to go and screw himself? Courteously, of course, as is your wont?'

'Hardly, my sweet—he was, after all, my guest for luncheon; beside being capable of ruining me or, if so minded, helping me enormously.'

'And do you suppose if I say him nay, he'll ruin and not help?'

'No, to do him credit, I don't think he's petty to that degree; yet I doubt if his neutrality would be benevolent.'

'I see. So what next?'

'Please tell me, my dear.'

'I exercise my woman's privilege of delay: I coyly string things along while we wait on developments in all directions. How about that?'

'Most wise, I feel—and as I most expected; it is your finest quality, my dearest. As to "developments": word reaches me you've been exercising your wisdom on the Adams family, especially its younger generation. I hope you'll remember you're my ally in relation to the projects I have for them.'

'Your reluctant ally, Rattler, as you are mine, poor dear fellow! How simpler, by far, it would be for you, I've often thought, if you didn't have to rely on me at all.'

*　　*　　*

Agitated, though, Aspen walked down by the woods, sticky and sultry; and came to a dell where she found Mas at his Spanish grammar.

'*Buenas tardes, señor*. How you getting on?'

'*Malissimo, señora*. But I'll learn this fucking language if it's the last thing I do.'

'Picture your joy in Lima, though, or sauntering through the Andes.'

'You think it'll be soon?'

'You'll be off this year, matey, if I have anything to do with it.'

'I can't wait: this place gets me double-down.'

'Me too, at times; but I've had four more years than you of singing the blues. Stick it out, though, *Señor* Mas —you're going through the most dreadful age of all: don't frown, I mean for anyone.'

'It is, you know. Can I give you a kiss?'

'Two, if you like ... Don't eat me, Mas...'

'I want to, Aspen.'

'Yes, yes ... I know.'

'Now, then?'

'Come on. Don't stifle me, let's make it sweet.'

'Help me out a bit.'

'We unzip this, get all that lot out of the way ... Hang *on* Mas, a tick—that's it! Now, off we go.'

'Gee!'

'Steady up a little.'

'Christ!'

'That's nice.'

'Blimey, Aspen!'

'Matador Mas.'

'Fuck me, it's good!'

'Not you, it's me.'

'Oh, Gawd!'

'Yeah!'

'Oh!'

'Yeah, yeah, yeah!'

'Oh, Christallfuckingmighty, it's delicious.'

'It's a sweet invention.'

'Oh yes! Oh, yes, yes, yeah. You got a fag?'

'Slacks pocket. Mind if I have one too?'

'Oh—sorry. Thanks, Aspen.'

'It's a pleasure, as they say.'

'You like me, Asp?'

'Shut up, you delightful idiot.'

*　　*　　*

Evie soon noted, when he came in late alone to eat, that Mas seemed absent and elated.

'Why you looking so pleased with yourself, anyway?'

'It's the weather, Mum. Isn't it delightful?'

'Don't be cheeky, and wipe that superior smile off your ugly mug.'

'Now, what's got into *you*? You feeling the heat?'

'The sooner we get you in the army, the better for everybody.'

'Except the army.'

'You *are* getting smart, boy, aren't you?'

'Lay off, Mum. And thanks for the grub.'

'Hey—you: what's that on your jeans?'

'What's what?'

'You been playing with yourself, Mas?'

'No: I fucking haven't.'

'Don't *speak* like that! What was it, then?'

'What was what?'

'I'll slap you, boy! Hey! You haven't been with that woman, have you?'

'What woman?'

'Mas!'

'Take your hands off me, Mum: I'm too old for that.'

'She's seduced you, hasn't she?'

' "Seduced" me!'

'Well, you've done it together, haven't you?'

'I fucking well have, and I'm fucking glad, and it's time you minded your nosy business.'

Kik entered on cue.

'Mas! Apologize to Mum at once.'

'You speak far worse to her, and get away with it.'

'I'm not a kid, Mas.'

'You think I am?'

'I know you fancy you're not, but I'm going to show you that you bloody well still are.'

'Oh, belt up, you two. We'll leave this to Soldier to sort out when he comes in.'

'Sort what out?'

'He's been with that slut.'

'Which slut? Aphrodite?'

'No: her lady-bloody-ship.'

'Has he! You have, Mas?'

'Now, look! Why don't both of you give over? Do I ask you two what you do?'

'Mas!'

'Well, I'll be buggered! Mother's darling's growing up, and putting everyone to rights.'

'You're jealous, Kik!'

'Of *you*?'

'You know Mum doesn't mind what *you* do, because she likes you less.'

'Don't say that, Mas! I've always been fair to both of you, and you know it.'

'Then be fair to me now. You're jealous too, and you won't admit it.'

'Listen to him! Everyone's jealous except saintly sodding Mas.'

'That's enough of that. I'll have to tell your father.'

'Tell him, then! And tell him that you're jealous of a woman half your age.'

'Mas!'

'Oh, fuck *off*, little brother, and go and boast some-where else. Leave him alone, Mum, till he simmers down.'

'He's been polluted.'

'Now, Mum—really! I've fancied her myself.'

'Shut up, Kik, you've no right to say that.'

'Who says I haven't? You, or amorous Aspen?'

'Leave her out of it!'

'Leave you out of her, would be better. Look, Mum, I'm making tracks. And don't quarrel with him any more. I expect the lad's just growing up.'

*   *   *

Evie brooded after Mas went out, sat awaiting Soldier and, when he thwarted her by failing to appear, had the inspiration of phoning through to Rattler.

'I'm not disturbing you, Captain?'

'No—not one whit; I've just concluded my siesta.'

'It's that I have a minor worry on my hands, that may be major.'

'Indeed! Well! We must see what can be done to put your mind at rest. Would you care to step across for a chat among the tea cups?'

'I'd really rather see you alone. Perhaps I should tell you Aspen is involved.'

'Dear me! Well, why don't I come over and see you? Would that be acceptable to you and Soldier?'

'Everyone's out, but I'd like to see you all the same.'

'Consider me practically there, my dear. And whatever it is, suspend your worrying till we see what we can do. All problems have a solution, I believe, of one kind or another.'

The Captain pondered also as he strode across the park,

midsummer falling. A tactful knock brought Evie to the door; she seemed abashed.

'Do come on in, then, Mr Rattler, while I unload my cares. I hope you'll bear with me when I tell you what's on my mind.'

'Please do so, Evie. You wish, I take it, that the matter of our conversation should be revealed to none?'

'Well, not yet, though I suppose it's all bound to come out, and might make things awkward here. What's happened is, that Aspen's raped my boy.'

'Aspen? *Raped?* Which boy?'

'Mas: she forced her attentions on him.'

'Did she now! Are you sure of this? Has she avowed it to you?'

'No—he has.'

'Ah, yes. But dear Evie: it wouldn't be a boast or fantasy on his part?'

'Certainly not: I've evidence.'

'Evidence?'

'It's something I'd rather not mention, but I'm certain.'

'I see, I see. Well now, if Aspen *did* do this, it would be most remiss of her.'

'I'm glad you think so.'

'Oh, yes—remiss indeed. Not, need I say, because of any difference of status or even age, but because there's really not much that she can offer the boy; unless, of course, what's called "experience".'

'He should go with his own sort when he's ready for it.'

'Ah, yes. Well, on that, of course, I really can't quite agree so fully with you—apart, that is, from Aspen herself being the wrong sort of person for him. But youth often knows best when it is "ready for" such things. And as for "his own sort" ... well, he's a bright, attractive lad, and in these days of greater social mobility...'

'Don't give me that crap, Captain! He's a working class

231

boy, and he should find a decent, intelligent girl of the same kind.'

'I know you're upset, my dear; any mother would be. Mothers, I think, are often disturbed when their youngest male child turns his affections to another woman.'

'His "affections"! He's just a randy little immature goat, I'm sorry to say.'

'Oh, I think you're a bit hard on him, despite my own displeasure at his conduct. But for this, I would principally blame Aspen.'

'Me too.'

'Well, well—we'll have to see. I shall certainly raise the matter with her instantly. Perhaps you'll suspend judgement a bit till you hear what she has to say for herself?'

'I don't think there's much she can say, except to admit she's used my boy.'

'Yes, yes. Well, cheer up, my dear—it's not the end of the world, after all. Perhaps this little episode will soon blow over.'

'It can't be an "episode"; anyone's always marked forever by their first love affair.'

'You think so? It may be so if it *is* a love affair... You found this ... forgive the question ... you found it so yourself with Soldier?'

'As a matter of fact, Captain, I've never made love with anyone else. Not yet, at any rate...'

'Indeed! Well, that's a fine record, to be sure, and a tribute as much to him as to yourself.'

'He takes it for granted though, as all men do. In fact, he takes me altogether too much for granted. He's not as loving as he used to be.'

'Alas! But Evie! Couldn't that just seem so because you're both growing rather older? We all do, you know...'

'You don't think I'm an old woman, do you, Captain?'

'Now—Evie! As if I did! No, no—you're at the flower

of your age; at least to a man of my sadly mature years ...'

'You don't find me a worn-out bag, then?'

'My dear! Do you wish me positively to declare my passion to you?'

'Well, it might brighten me up, mightn't it?'

'It might? Well, then! Would you like me to proceed from words to deeds?'

'I don't know.'

'Don't you? I think you do. Get undressed, Evie.'

'But look ... here and now ...'

'Here and now are perfectly appropriate. Strip off, and stop messing me about. It's what you want, isn't it?'

'Now, Rattler ...'

'Do you prefer it rough, Evie? If not, I want you naked quick.'

'Well ...'

'Shut up! Hurry!'

'You are a tyrant, aren't you!'

'Yes. Come on—everything.'

'Well, here I am. Do I look like what you expected?'

'Yes, you cock-teasing little whore. Lie down!'

'What did you call me? Now—don't be so rough!'

'I think we'll have you on your belly. Over we go! Ah: as nice a piece of arse as I ever saw.'

'Now, watch it, Rattler—get your hands off me!'

'Quiet. You'll like this.'

'Get off, fuck you! Stop it, you sadistic pervert!'

Evie, though inexperienced, recalled one of Soldier's stories—or confessions. She swivelled round, kneed Rattler hard and, reaching up, seized and bit it.

'You foul bitch!'

'You've met your match, haven't you! You've met one of your own bandit kind.'

'You think so? Then see how we dish out this!'

Rattler lashed at her with his buckled belt. She screamed.

'It won't kill you, dear. Just teach you what is and isn't, foolish Evie...'

*   *   *

Mas came running back when he heard the cries and found his mother in shock, and bleeding.

'What's happened, Mum? What is it?'

'It's all right, Mas. I'm all right, dear. Get me a whisky, will you?'

'What happened?'

'An accident ... don't look at me, Mas, stop looking. Just get that Scotch.'

He came back trembling.

'Don't spill it, dear. That's better. Yes, yes, an accident —I'll be all right. Just let me recover, will you.'

'Who was it, Mum?'

'No one: it's nothing.'

'Mum!'

'Hold me, dear—I'll soon be better. Please don't say anything to anyone—you hear? I'll have a wash and tidy up, and we'll say nothing—promise?'

'Mum! You won't tell me?'

'Please, Mas! Do as I ask you. Here: wipe that blood off yourself, and I'll get straightened out.'

'Oh, Mum!'

'Quiet. Don't cry, Mas. You'll make it worse for me. Just help me by staying steady.'

In came Kik.

'What the fuck's going on? What you done, Mas?'

'He's done nothing—quiet Kik!'

'You foul little shit!'

'Kik! Stop it! It's not your brother!'

'Who, then?'

'No one: not your brother.'

'Let me hear *him* say so. What did you do? What happened?'

'Nothing.'

'Nothing! Just look at her! Come on! What did you do to her, you little bastard?'

'Get your hands off me!'

'Kik! Stop, will you! Leave him alone!'

'Not till he tells me! Come on, now—give!'

'Mas, son—get out! Don't touch him, Kik!'

'Touch him? I'll slaughter him! Come back, you little coward!'

'Leave him go, Kik! Calm down and listen!'

'Will I fuck! I'm going to get the truth out of that rotten rat of a brother!'

Kik ran out after him: Mas was pounding up the lane. Kik swerved, and headed for the Capri: it had its keys. He jumped in and accelerated: Mas dodged towards the ditch. Kik swerved the car, and that was it.

Kik got out, walked back, bent down, and handled him; then slowly rose up staring.

'Mas, oh Mas! Oh dear, what have I fucking done? Help me, someone, for God's sake! Mas—you hear? Help me!'

* * *

Soldier, returning from the factory estate and a solitary soak, absorbed the shocks as best he could, rallied and asked questions, reacted to urgent tasks, then went back over to get Rattler.

'What do you know about all this?'

'What, Adams?'

'My son.'

'What? Adams, will you tell me what you're talking about?'

'Mas is dead.'

235

'No!'

'Who did it?'

'Dead? How? Where is he?'

'In hospital, but it's useless. Evie's with him there, or what's left of him. I found him by the track down to our cottage.'

'When?'

'Less than an hour ago. Quite dead. A car hit him, I think. Where's yours?'

'My Capri? Isn't it out there?'

'No. You haven't driven it—or anyone?'

'I certainly have not ... Adams, I can't tell you how horrified and shocked I am to hear this! You're sure there's no chance at all?'

'I can tell a stiff when I see one, can't I? Even when it's my son? Now, leave that, Rattler! Who drove that car? You left the keys in it?'

'Yes, I believe I did.'

'And you know nothing.'

'Adams, before God, I know nothing at all about this.'

'But about anything else? Evie says Kik and Mas had a row. And Evie was marked. I know she's been fighting too. So what went on?'

'Adams! I do hate to have to say this! But doesn't it seem your elder son's responsible? He had the car out this morning...'

'Why?'

'He wanted a drive. Under supervision in the park. I let him.'

'Did you! And why should Kik kill his brother?'

'An accident, surely! Where is Kik?'

'We don't know. Still in your car, possibly. But why should he take it? Why run down Mas? Why not stop and *do* something? And why won't Evie tell me why they quarrelled? And why is she marked, Rattler?'

'One minute! You've informed the police?'

' "Informed the police"! As if I care a fuck about the police. I expect the hospital will, and they'll soon be here. So you'd better have some answers for them, Rattler. But first of all, for me.'

'Adams! Will you drop that tone, if you please? I have no responsibility whatever for your son's death, which I deeply deplore. Instead of accusing me, you'd do better to think of what we must do to get Kik out of danger.'

'But I am accusing you.'

'Of what?'

'What went on between you and Evie? What was it sparked all this off?'

'Nothing "went on".'

'Rattler, this is it. You or me. What happened?'

'I don't answer to threats.'

'Just tell me, then. Tell me as a man.'

'Sit down, Adams.'

'Rattler! Now!'

'There was a slight flirtation.'

'A *what*? Look! Did you screw her? Or did you try to?'

'I tried to, but did not.'

'Did not, or could not? Answer! You couldn't, so you bashed her about—is that it?'

'Yes.'

'You're a slimy shit, Rattler.'

'I understand how you feel.'

'Yes, yes ... And she led you on, I suppose? Why haven't you told me that as well?'

'My dear fellow ...'

'Your "dear fellow"! A gentleman doesn't rat on a lady, even when she's not one—is that how you see it?'

'Adams! Where is this getting us? Isn't there a more pressing problem? What of Kik?'

'Kik can look after himself. And I'm going to look after you. I'm going to kill you, Rattler.'

'No, you're not.'

'You've raped my wife and murdered my dearest son.'

'Have I? I failed in the first, and have nothing to do with the second.'

'You tried one, and caused both. I'm getting that gun.'

'Then for fuck's sake get it, Adams! Or pick up any handy lethal weapon you see, and get started on me now —if you want to. I shall defend myself, of course. Do what you feel you must, but do stop threatening. I'm taking no more of it, I tell you.'

'You'll take it ...'

'I will? And you? You're going to join your son for years on the Isle of Wight? Do start to *think*, Soldier, just a bit. Or if you can't think, act, but don't waffle at me with all this melodrama.'

'But there's Mas.'

'Yes. Well—what can I say?'

'He's gone.'

'Yes, it's hard to take it in.'

'Hard ...'

'Adams, the decision's yours. If it's war, let's have it. If it's a truce, let's both think of the future. The immediate future of us all, especially Kik's.'

'Well, if he's done it, he'll have to take what's coming to him.'

'My God, what sort of a father are you? You really believe he should "pay his debt to society", and all that crap? You don't think we should try to get him out of the country *now*?'

'The law will catch up with him; they always do. And it'll only be manslaughter, at the most ...'

'*Only?* My God, you are a noble Roman! For fuck's sake, Soldier: you wouldn't have covered up for a pal in the forces? You've not done it for far worse than this, most probably? But not for your son? And "man-slaughter"—oh yes! But won't it be a rather juicy case, once they start probing a bit?'

'You thinking of your own part in it?'

'What do you *take* me for, Adams, for God's sake? Oh, yes—sure: myself, myself, a hundred inconveniences—but no danger. Kik is in *danger*, Soldier.'

'So are you.'

'Yes, yes. So why don't we save Kik first, and then you can dispose of me afterwards—or try to?'

'How can we save him?'

'If you stop wasting time, I can have him out of the country by tonight.'

'Where?'

'Look, I've got resources. Don't fuss about where and how, but help me find him, and let's get things moving fast.'

'If he faced up to it, he might get acquitted. If he runs, he'll be a marked man forever.'

'That's about it, except that he might *not* get acquitted, and there's no such thing as a "marked man" when the world has five continents and you have contacts and money.'

'I'll have to ask Evie.'

'Ask her, then. But can I start some action? To find Kik? To make arrangements?'

'How do you think you can do all that?'

'I know I can, Soldier.'

'All right, then. And what of me and Evie?'

'You stay here till the inquest, if there is an inquest. And for the questioning, if there is any questioning. And you say you don't *know*, because you don't, you're only guessing, although I'm sorry to say you're probably guessing right. If there's a warrant out for Kik, which there

239

may not be, then you still don't know anything, because you won't, till I tell you later where he is. And after things calm down a bit, as they usually do, we'll get you and Evie out of the country too for a while … I can find work for you to do, in fact I have the very thing in mind…'

'Perhaps I should tell them I did it: I was drinking, and it was an accident.'

'Adams—really! The idea does you credit, but, well— just think of the complications! No. Either you help the law to track down Kik and wreak its vengeance, or you help him out of a nasty mess that was certainly unintentional.'

'Evie may be too upset to agree to anything. She doted on Mas.'

'Soldier, I know, I know. But think of Kik a bit, if you love him too.'

'I do.'

'All right, then.'

'But there's one I don't love.'

'Me? I know. You feel that I caused all these disasters, don't you?'

'I feel that you brought me here to destroy me. I knew it from the first.'

'Then why did you come?'

'And that you're still out to ruin me, and not help me.'

'Soldier, this is too much! You're a mature man. We've been through a lot together. We've coped with crises many a time before. You've trusted me—or not mistrusted me. Now, you're not sure. Well, here's the acutest crisis of them all, and the time has come at last for you to really make up your mind.'

* * *

Rattler sought out Aspen, coldly, angrily, told his story, and asked hers.

'All right, weep, my dear, for that poor little fornicator! And congratulate yourself on the chain-reaction that you've started.'

'*I've* started? Enough, Rattler, enough!'

'You must know best! You must display your devotion to me by knowing more, and wrecking all my plans.'

'That sweet little kid.'

'And his sweet little brother? Well, what now? Are you prepared to listen, or have you further brilliant initiatives to perform?'

'You want me to find him?'

'You think you can?'

'Oh, yes. I know where he'll be . . .'

'And you'll tell him? I can rely on you? I've phoned to the coast, and my Flemish adjutant's expecting him. You think you can get him down there all in one piece?'

'I'll see him, Rattler. I'll take the Marina—it's nice and anonymous.'

'Be off, then. Don't fuck this up, please, dearest Aspen.'

'Rattler: you don't feel anything for that boy?'

'Which one? The late Mas? Well no, bugger it, I don't. Aspen: I'm used to sudden death and corpses. The only person in the world I feel anything for, is you.'

'Or what I am for you. Oh, well . . . You're sure that, from your own point of view, not mine, you're not over-complicating all this as you've done so often?'

'Aspen, my dear, there's a vital time element involved! Do you wish for a probing philosophical recap on our unusual relationship? Or will you master your doubts and help out when I ask you urgently?'

'All right, Rattler. I'll do what's best.'

'And quickest. I have other phone calls to make, so do you mind?'

Aspen, possessed by a certainty, set out for the discothèque at the factory estate. Yes, they said, Kik had been seen around: with a sharp car, and a bird. Further enquiry, and touring unlovely concrete drives, located the 'murder vehicle', but not its occupants. Aspen examined the Capri for signs of earlier disaster, and found none. The keys were left dangling, and she removed them, returned to the Marina, smoked a cigarette or two, and waited. Kik emerged at last from a decorous semi-detached.

'Hi—you! Come over here!'

'Why, hullo, Asp! Where you spring from?'

'Hop in, lad. I want a word with you.'

'I've got my own car.'

'And I've got its keys. Hop in.'

'What is this, beautiful? You tracking me down, or something?'

'Kik: just how stoned are you? I mean: can you take in much of what I'm saying?'

'High, but not stoned. I've had a lovely smoke and a gorgeous grind. With Aphrodite, in there, whose ancestors are up in London for the day. She'll be out in a minute, and we're going places.'

'You're going places with me, just now. Sit tight.'

'Hey—what's the idea? A hi-jack?'

'Sit still. I've got to talk to you, and stoned or otherwise, you're going to listen.'

'Say on! I like a drive with a gorgeous girl. Old Aph's a bit arm-pitty, anyway—you know what I mean? She goes greasy on you, after a while.'

'Does she?'

'I'm afraid so. Suggests that I've knocked her up, too—can you believe it? In these days of the pill, and all? The birds are getting irresponsible.'

'Really?'

'Oh, yes. If I *have* done, I'll recognize my son, and if she doesn't abort, we'll call it Enoch-up.'

'This will do nicely here, Kik. Now, then. Do you know what you've done, you foul little slob?'

'Hey! Easy, now!'

'Kik—Mas is dead.'

'No!'

'Oh, yes.'

'I didn't just knock him over?'

'You did, and that was the end of him. You didn't go back and have a look at your handiwork?'

'No! I thought I'd just...'

'Kik! You did, and you knew, and you ran away, and indulged in these delights.'

'I was upset, Aspen.'

'Poor boy. And Mas was dead.'

'I didn't mean to.'

'I hope not. So what now? You're waiting around to get arrested in circumstances that will make a possible accident look deliberate? Or at any rate, callous, and cruel, and stupid?'

'Now, just a moment! Who are you ...?'

'Shut up. Shut up, you foul-mouthed nit, you heartless little coward. And listen to me.'

'To what?'

'You've three choices. Do nothing, and wait on events —of which there will be plenty. Or give yourself up at once. Or make a run for it, if you want to and think you can. Now—which?'

'I don't know.'

'That means, do nothing.'

'What should I do, Aspen?'

'Kik, before I tell you what I think of that, there *is* something I would like to hear from you. Are you sorry you did this?'

'Of course, but there were reasons.'

243

'There are always "reasons". Are you *sorry*?'

'Yes. I liked Mas.'

'Sorry for him, or for yourself?'

'Don't push me, Aspen. For myself most, I suppose. So what am I going to do?'

'Rattler thinks you should skip, and he can fix it. But you'll have to decide quick.'

'Rattler! Well, I wouldn't trust his advice.'

'Oh, no?'

'Oh, no! Smoke makes you think, you know, and I've been thinking. I was wild with Mas because I thought he'd beaten Mum. But come to think of it, he couldn't have. He's not that tough. And besides, she'd have said something when I came in.'

'You found her alone with Mas, and beaten? Is that it?'

'Yes. And who do you think did that, if I was wrong about Mas? It couldn't have been, Dad—I don't believe it. So who does that leave us with?'

'I might have guessed.'

'Yes, and I'll bet he didn't tell you. So you see who the real murderer is.'

'All right. But that's not what the Law will say, is it?'

'I've fucked things up so much I might as well go back and finish him off too. Don't think I couldn't.'

'I don't, but you're not going to. Now, then: skip or stay?'

'This skip thing: it would work?'

'Oh yes, I think so. Small boat, money, papers, travel to foreign parts—all that can be arranged, I'm sure. But you must look beyond that. It would be a fugitive, vagabond life, even with protection. So: decide.'

'I can't trust myself.'

'Do you trust anyone?'

'Yes. My Grandad. I'll shoot up and ask him.'

'Sure that's what you want to do?'

'Yes. You'll give me those keys?'

'Of course not. Take the Marina—we're back beside it now. I'll take the Capri.'

'You think I'm right, Aspen?'

'I think it's your first sane action of the day. Get cracking, then, and try to arrive there intact.'

'Thanks, Aspen.'

'So long.'

*　　　*　　　*

Aspen avoided Rattler till the late evening: she had things to think about, and calls to make, that needed a head clear of the turmoil he was apt to cause there. Her bedroom, by custom, was inviolate, so she stayed there; yet was not surprised when at last he knocked upon her door.

'I may come in?'

'Do, dear old fellow.'

'Not too exhausted for a chat?'

'Exhausted, but ready. What news are you bursting with?'

'Not much, really—there's a strange tranquillity: the calm after the storm, as one might say. Peace reigns in the bereaved cottage, it would appear; and no minions have arrived from anywhere.'

'It's Saturday: the English lethargy.'

'You got that lad off as I suggested?'

'Off, but not as you suggested. I've sent him to his grandfather in London.'

'Then that ancient Bolshevik will ensure his ruin, by excess of worthy guile. Why not the swift migration I proposed, and made arrangements for?'

'The lad trusts his grandfather.'

'And not me, of course. He hasn't his father's loyal faith.'

'I think that will be shaken too, henceforward, Rattler. Considerably so.'

'Ah! The boy Kik mentioned the episode with his mother? Or what he'd guessed of it? Don't look so reproachful, Aspen! We've both had congress with the family, and it was you who first broke the barrier between us and them.'

'My motives were rather different, I believe.'

'Doubtless ... yours were yours, and mine were mine. But however generous your intention, if it was so, the upset originated with you.'

'In fact, but not in deeper intention towards them. That was yours, and still is so.'

'I concede that. Yet I would venture to say you have not been entirely true to the terms of our alliance.'

'That I'm sometimes not, is in the very nature of our union, Rattler. Ideally, for your sake, you should be able to operate without me; but since you can't, apparently, you must expect the unforeseen from me occasionally.'

'Not the unforeseen, really ... I know your nature, and that our disagreement is as profound as our attachment. I have long accepted this, of course, as you have. So for now, then: we must try to mend fences. Soldier, I think, will steady; Evie fall into line. Adams because he is what he is—a follower; Evie, because she is a woman, and one of great, and as yet unaroused, curiosity. Nor would I say that our personal encounter, much as it shocked and displeased her, utterly repelled her. I may flatter myself, of course; but I fancy her lust for experience will overcome her pride.'

'Possibly, Rattler, but I don't think in the way that you predict.'

'Can you elaborate?'

'I don't think even Soldier will be so docile; or that you'll be able to persuade him, by fear for his son or years of habit, into your Irish schemes. As for Evie ... I think she *has* learned something from you; but as much as she'll ever need to.'

'Oh, really? Why so?'

'You have aroused her, certainly, and done so ever since your two paths crossed; but now I would guess she knows what she wants, will use it elsewhere, and need nothing more from you.'

'You seem very certain of this, Aspen. And if it were true, it would be fatal to my intentions for this family, whom I wish to be utterly dependent on me.'

'I think you've lost them, Rattler. Mas is beyond your reach. I don't think you'll see Kik again ... Soldier has seen the light at last; Evie the darkness, and understood it.'

'What are you saying to me, Aspen? Are you telling me that all my efforts for Adams and his family should be abandoned? It can't really be *that*?'

'Your Ruin too, I fear.'

'Oh? Why?'

'Warsaw will not support you. Not in the way you hoped, at any rate.'

'How do you know this, Aspen?'

'We've had a long conversation on the telephone; all the more cordial for being disembodied. I told him I was entirely yours, and though honoured and flattered by his proposals, could do nothing for him.'

'So "entirely mine", Aspen, that you have betrayed me.'

'Yes.'

'Not for the first time.'

'No. Nor for the last, possibly ...'

'Aspen!'

'Rattler! And, my dear, *was* it really a betrayal? For wouldn't Warsaw have been a bit too much for you? I don't mean just his lucre, but his soul: it's a rather empty one, I think, while you still have vestiges of yours.'

'Such profundities can be apprehended over the telephone?'

'By memory and reflection, also: I met Warsaw, dearest, in my escort days.'

'And said nothing at all of this to me! Nor did the slavonic traitor either!'

'To fathom such a person, Rattler, you needed a personal encounter, I believed.'

'I consider you have doubly betrayed me!'

'Oh no ... Warsaw's loss is the greater, is it not? For if you lose the Ruin, it need not be he who wins it; nor has he you, my dear, or any part of you at all. I might mention, in passing, that he has even less of me ... We have triumphed over him because, however much we thwart each other, we are two spirits to his one.'

'But the whole adventure of the garden falls apart! And that wretched family will have learned some of my secrets, and yet yielded nothing positive to me! Oh, if I had been absolute enough to operate alone!'

'Sorry, my dear old Rattler. But if your nature is such that you cannot function without one so different from yourself, you must accept disappointments from time to time.'

'You are not different—you are part of me! And you can never exist without me, either. All the initiative comes from me, all that invents and moulds and dares—yet what do you offer, though so dependent on me? To deny, and thwart and hinder! To wreck the most cherished wishes of my being!'

'Please, Rattler dearest. You can start again, and will ... It's just, I suppose, the way we are, or what we each

248

embody: you the incessant plots and plans, and me the instinct to ask whys and wherefores...'

*   *   *

Evie came back from the hospital at night exhausted to calm, and though wretched, resilient. It was rather Soldier who needed consolation.

'They've done all they can for the present, and that's that. Funeral arrangements are on hand, and they'll let us know about any inquest. So there it is, Soldier: we've got to get used to the idea there's no more Mas.'

'I'll never get used to it: nor to what Kik did. It's his not stopping I can't forgive. Still, we've got to save him: keep him out of the way, in case they go after him. Rattler's got plans, and it's all in hand.'

'Fuck Rattler—he's got nothing in hand! Kik's up with Dad.'

'With your father? How do you know?'

'I phoned him from the hospital about Mas. He called back a bit later to say Kik was on the doorstep up in London. He'll be down himself soon when he's fixed up Kik.'

'And how will he fix up Kik?'

'I don't know, but I trust Dad's judgement. He'll get him away, or hide him while we wait and see, or he'll make him own up. Whatever he does, will be for Kik's sake, and ours. Whatever Rattler wants, is for his own. I do hope we've both got wise to that.'

'I told him I'd stay around, but that I'd have to consult you first.'

'Well, you've consulted me, and we're leaving here.'

'You're leaving me, Evie?'

'No. Why? And isn't it you who's got the right to leave me?'

'I'm not speaking of "rights" ... But why did you do it with **him**?'

'Why? Oh, Soldier! If you want the truth, I didn't "do it", because he started belting me before we got down to anything. But if you want the real truth, I did want to, yes, and I made it clear to him. What I mean is, he could say with a clear conscience, if he's got one, that I led him on.'

'I know "why" is a silly question, but could you tell me? Or is it just that you weren't satisfied with me?'

'I can go the whole way on this, Soldier?'

'We'd better have this out, if we're going to mean anything to each other from now on.'

'Right, then. I was *not* satisfied with you, as you put it, because you didn't give me much occasion to be. It was clear to me you'd gone off me for some reason, or were sick or something—I don't know. But it was more than that, and I think you know it, and always have. I've missed out on so much in our life together, if you can call it "together". You were always out there doing your soldier bit, killing and fucking around and fulfilling yourself, I suppose. But I, neither ugly nor stupid, hadn't much of a time except waiting and hoping and raising the kids. It's a life I chose, and I'm not complaining, or blaming you, but it grew harder and more horrible each year I was losing. And then, along comes Rattler—your great friend, whom you trust and admire, and I come into all this with you. You know I was doubtful, because perhaps I guessed what would happen, but I came. And what I saw here made me even more dissatisfied, and I still am, and I think always will be, you might as well know. Not that I mean I ever want to see your dear Captain again, if you should be supposing I do.'

'I should have killed him, like I meant to ...'

'Hit him anyway, as he did me ... Oh, yes! But in your mind he's still your officer, isn't he, Soldier?'

'Leave it, Evie ... So what do we do now?'

'I'm not sure what we *do*, but I can tell you one thing we don't, or I don't, anyway, which is to have anything more to do with this fucking Ruin and its complexities.'

'Yes, but what do I do?'

'I dunno, Soldier! You want to stick it out with me and see what happens? Go back to the dear old army? Emigrate? Any ideas?'

'I've got one—I'd like to fuck you, here and now.'

'Would you though! On the day of your son's death?'

'All the more reason. Let's strip off and make another.'

'You know, you encourage me, Soldier! I was beginning to think that deep down, you're really a bit of a coward.'

'Maybe I am, but I can react against it. You want to try?'

'Yes, but not now. Dad'll be here any minute, and it might look peculiar, don't you think? Later on, then— and there we'll go again! You getting me pregnant, and going back to honest toil.'

'It's a man's lot—sorrow and labour.'

'Labour! You've never done a stroke in your life. No soldier has.'

'You've got a point, perhaps.'

'We'll call it Seth.'

'Call what?'

'The boy. It's Dad's name—did you know? He's a marxist from a strictly Baptist family. The two often go together—I mean love of dogma.'

'So we're going to have one.'

'Oh yes, I think so. But not here in this spooky place— not any more. Somewhere sweet, where we can roll around as the good Lord made us, all relaxed: before the autumn comes, and all those heavy clothes.'

'We've saved quite a bit—we could take a holiday.'

'My God, what would anyone think of this conversation, if they knew we'd had it on a day like this? The thought makes you want to hide your head.'

'Mas wouldn't mind.'

'I dare say not. He was a forgiving boy. He had a lot to offer.'

'And Kik?'

'A lot to take, he always will, I think. It's his strength, in a way, his selfishness. But he hasn't much to offer, the poor boy.'

'But Mas had.'

'Yes, he had a lot: and no time to give or receive much, though perhaps he did a bit before the end ... Soldier, he went with Aspen.'

'He made it with her?'

'Let's hope it was a joy. Oh, dear ...'

'Oh, fuck it all: let's have a drink.'

'No, I can hear a car. Old Dad would blow his top.'

'Yes, it is him. I'll open up. Hullo, father. Thanks for coming down.'

'Good evening, lad. Evening, Evie. I grieve for you two, from the bottom of my heart.'

'Thanks, Dad.'

'Where is he?'

'He's at the hospital.'

'I'll go and see him later. Are you all packed?'

'Packed, Dad?'

'You're leaving tonight, you two. We've got the cars, and we can take what you want for now. I'll come down and collect the rest later, after the funeral.'

'What's the rush, father?'

'Soldier! You want to stay a minute longer than you need to in this place? Don't you know that it's corrupted, and it's brought you nothing but disaster? Come on, now! Get some things together!'

'I'll do it, Soldier.'

'No, Evie—you chat with your Dad. I won't be long.'

'He's blind, Evie—he doesn't see, he never did.'

'Don't be unjust, Dad ... He's learned a lot here, and I'm sorry to say I have too. But it's just as well we're going, before we learn too much.'

'I'd like to liquidate that bastard Rattler for bringing you down here! He'll suffer for it, mark my words!'

'He's not the only one who'll suffer.'

'I know, I'm sorry, Evie. He was your favourite, wasn't he?'

'Yes. But I still love Kik.'

'Don't worry about Kik. From what I could make out, he behaved like you'd expect, but we'll sort him out.'

'Sort him out how?'

'Leave that to us—we have our justice, girl.'

'Don't be too hard on him, will you?'

'You're too easy-going, Evie: it's always been your fault. You've put up with too much, and let yourself be exploited.'

'I think you'll find I've changed too. Whether for the better or not, I don't know, but my life's going to alter quite a bit.'

'High time. Are you ready, Soldier?'

'Coming. We'll just take this lot for now ...'

'Take what you need: there's plenty of room at the buildings.'

The grandfather saw them off ahead for, despite attempted dissuasion, he was determined to see the body of his daughter's child. His car was beneath the ash, and he tripped over a stream in the darkness reaching it. Cursing, once aboard the car, he turned the headlights to a blaze that lit the Ruin. Then revving the engine to a high pitch of defiance, he swung in an arc of light and noise, and jerked off down the road towards the gate.

253

Dearest Great Great Aunt Clarissa,

This comes to you, as you'll see by the pretty stamp, from County Donegal, of all places. For here Rattler and I have journeyed, in a great deal of fuss and flurry, since things became rather tense and troublesome at the Ruins. Rattler himself, and his Mr Watson, will be writing you and your excellent Mr Macpherson about the financial details, which I fear are involved and intricate to a degree! And you'll also, I think, be hearing from a charming Mr Warsaw, a most affluent Pole who has plans for making your fortune out of what's left of the Ruins. Do lend an attentive ear to his proposals, dearest, for then you'd be able to abandon that craggy dower-house, and come south if you wished, or even settle somewhere grotesque like the Bahamas.

For I'm sorry to say Rattler's plans for the Ruins themselves lie in like condition. It wasn't for want of trying, I do assure you: indeed, since I've known and loved Rattler, I've never seen him throw himself into any enterprise so fervently. But fortune refused him her favours, and perhaps he made a mistake or two, as he so often does, through over-confidence or eagerness. A good fault, or, at any rate, an attractive one, in its way.

Yet he is not one whit downhearted, nor willing to admit defeat: of that, as you know, he's quite incapable, so long as he endures. Over here, he's as busy as a bee with other projects—major ones, in fact, that he'd already set on foot from England. He darts across the frontier, which we can see from our friendly farm here, as if the dream of United Ireland were a reality; a common custom in these parts, where the most peculiar persons flit to and fro, most, if not all of them, maniacal in one aspect or another; which makes appropriate company for Rattler, though I do hope he'll take care. However: to coin an optimistic phrase, let's hope 'the devil looks after his own'.

I sadly miss the Ruins, and dear England, and can't tell you how ravishing both looked on the pure June day when we left forever. That exquisite toughness of the English countryside—its delicate, enduring brilliance! I do hope some of it survives the march of concrete!

Nor, would it seem, are our travels yet at an end! For Rattler, even in the midst of his Celtic preoccupations, is beginning to drop the name 'Mozambique' around with an increasing note of obsession. So could it be that romantic-sounding Lourenço Marques is our ultimate port of call? How I look forward to the game parks, and all the other activities in that area!

You remember our steward I told you of—a chap called Adams, and his friendly family? Well, there was a sad occurrence there: his son, the younger, died in a car accident, and was a darling. I know one writes 'I shall always remember him' without quite believing it oneself; yet in this boy's case, I think I shall. For apart from Rattler, for whom I feel something deep but different from love—more like devotion, really—I've not felt that for anyone, yet, besides this boy. And perhaps I never will; for as Rattler rarely fails to remind me, being too 'wise' may not be the best way of opening one's heart entirely.

Write to me soon, dearest, c/o the British Embassy in Dublin, if it's not burned down again. Meanwhile, I am, as always,

Your devoted and admiring
Aspen